SECRETS IN THE WOODS

Susan D. Levitte

HISTORIUM PRESS U.S.A.

SECRETS IN THE WOODS

HARDCOVER ISBN: 978-1-964700-46-5
PAPERBACK ISBN: 978-1-964700-47-2
EBOOK ISBN: 978-1-964700-48-9

First Edition
Historium Press, a subsidiary publishing house of
The Historical Fiction Company
New York, NY / Macon, GA USA
www.historiumpress.com

To the ones who left too soon and would have wholly cheered on this project. Especially Angela Phillips, Frank Stegmaier, Jenny Vanden Heuvel, and James Bachman, I think of each of you always.

Prologue 1871

I don't know if the small form strapped to my chest is still breathing.

Prologue 1941

The box arrived at Gaspard's farm on what should have been the beginning of spring 1941. Instead, there were large puffy balls of crystal-white snow swirling around one of the prettiest cars in the county, a 1940 DeSoto Coupe. The car belonged to Atlantique Gaspard's son-in-law, who had stopped in town to pick up the parcel at the post office along with a few items his in-laws might need if the weather turned into a messy April Wisconsin snowstorm.

Shortly after the beginning of the year, a letter from a Mr. Anders Nilson in Minot, North Dakota, brought news to the Kewaunee County Gaspard farm telling them that his sister, Edna Mae, had died just before Christmas in the San Haven Tuberculosis Sanatorium in a town called Dunseith, also in North Dakota. They knew that Edna Mae was ill from her letters but by 1940 it was less common to die from the dreaded consumption, and they had believed she would recover. In fact, they had hoped that Edna Mae would be well enough to make the journey to Wisconsin for the fall *Kermiss* celebration in the community at the bottom of the hill.

The blue, nearly black rectangular box had a beautiful pattern of flowers and scrolls painted on the front celebrating Edna Mae's Swedish ancestry through the artform of *dalmålning*. The inside of the hinged lid had been left it's honey-colored natural wood. When opened, it revealed more of the painted flowers and included the date 1841. According to a small scrap of paper stuck to the inner corner of the box lid, it had come to America with '*Morfar* C.O. Svensen.'

The contents were bound in different piles, some with vivid red satin ribbon and some with plain brown kitchen twine. Each of the bundles contained the history of the bond between Edna Mae and Emilie Gaspard. On top of the papers was a brown, nearly brimless hat that had been in style several years before. All the notes from the article that Edna Mae had written for the Green Bay newspaper, as well as Emilie Gaspard's story of the fire were bound together with the elegant ribbon. The wooden cask contained a stack of envelopes containing the letters Emilie had written to Edna Mae nearly weekly. There was a marked-up copy of the book they wrote together. The paper cover still looked new even with the paper slips and bookmarks hanging between the ecru pages. The packet of papers labeled in Edna Mae's crisp hand: *Women of the Fire*, had weathered to a silky-smooth finish on the paper.

There was a group of sketches and even some block prints that Edna Mae had created to help illustrate the story. Several years before the farm had celebrated with Edna Mae when one of her etchings was chosen for an art award in the state of Minnesota. At the very bottom of the box was a thick, roan-brown, leather-bound book whose edges were rubbed darker than its center from years of handling. When the book fell open along its cracked spine, it was crammed with Edna Mae's writing and dates marking the events of her life starting shortly after the Great War.

The box's arrival cast a melancholy over the farm for several days. Edna Mae had become a friend to the entire family back in 1931. After they had discovered the personal diary among the papers, they sent Edna Mae's brother a letter asking whether the leather book was meant to be included. His reply was that all contents were to go to the Gaspard farm.

Chapter 1

(August 1931 Wisconsin, Emilie's Story)

It's strange the things you noticed when you were waiting to experience something new. My Elgin clock had roosted on its oak-wood shelf for years beyond my memory, but I didn't remember its gold pendulum clicking the time away so loudly. When I glanced up at it, it still looked like an old friend, but now it shouted at me that things could be changing by the minute.

The newspaper in Green Bay, Wisconsin, had combed the country looking for people who would talk to them about the coming anniversary. There was some unseen compulsion that thrust me into replying to the request. So many of the people who were adults after the fire have since passed away, and they likely wouldn't have wanted to talk about those days anyway. For just about sixty years, I had watched the entire neighborhood stifle their dark anger and sadness at what was lost. The collected written narrative about an event that shaped the lives of thousands would scarcely make up a slim pamphlet. But I knew. I knew what had been taken and what had been put in its place. I knew that the wounds were deeper than the glossy puckered scars exposed through thinning hair, and arms covered to the wrist with sleeves, no matter the temperature. I knew the shared trauma was just under the surface.

In the sigh of a breeze in early spring 1931, I wrote a reply to the newspaper and posted the letter that day. When the response came asking if I would be able to meet with their writer this week, none of us expected that it would be a woman. Single women in rural

Wisconsin worked as teachers or nurses, sometimes an office clerk —usually until they married—not as a newspaper writer.

I had never been interviewed, and I had no idea what was going to happen. My brother Leopold had said that it would be like having a visit with a friend. He had also explained to the newspaper that there might be some interpretation issues with language, since I had not started speaking English until I was in my teens.

A green Ford Model A chugged up the dirt path, scattering my mottled hens to the front of my house. Years later, my nephew would explain that the green used on the Model A by Henry Ford was called Kewaunee green. That day, the dust cloud continued drifting after the machine stopped, and Edna Mae stepped out of the car.

The modern woman in front of me explained that she was a traveling writer for newspapers. She had written for newspapers as far west as Montana and as far east as Michigan. She told me she grew up in North Dakota and that both her father and mother had traveled from Sweden to farm in Dakota Territory. As she talked, I got the sense that she was more worried about my reaction to her being Swedish than her being a woman traveling-newspaper writer. The settlement where my house was located was dominated by generations of Walloon immigrants. Starting in the 1850s, we brought our customs and culture here to make a new life. Many of those things stayed for years and often gave outside visitors the impression that we were clannish and uninviting. It wasn't that we didn't welcome new people—we simply preferred, in those early years, to speak the same language and follow the traditions of our homeland.

While Edna Mae began pulling the items of her trade out of a saddle-brown leather bag, I took the time to observe her appearance. Her hair was the color of sun-ripened hard wheat and shorn to the length of her chin. I wouldn't call it curly, but rather it was frizzy where it stuck out beneath the straight sides of her brown brimless hat. She wore a nearly shapeless dress in a shade of green I could not name. The hem of the dress sat below her knees, where legs clad in brownish stockings met small feet in leather shoes that laced in the front with a short heel in the back. I had seen women in Algoma wearing their hair this way and clothing of this style, but my own brown and blue gingham work dress was easily eight years old, and my fine white hair was pinned back from my face, falling just below my shoulders.

I was intrigued by Edna Mae and the voyage she traveled in 1931.

Edna Mae pulled out a sheaf of papers, bound at the top, and placed them on the linen covered kitchen table. Aligned next to the papers, she placed three sharp pencils and a small knife with a pearly handle, to sharpen them further if needed. As she stopped shifting in her chair, I met her frost-blue eyes and realized she might be older than I originally thought. I wanted to ask if she had a husband who traveled with her to these states when she wrote for newspapers. Instead, I tucked the idea away, hoping that she would reveal more as the conversation continued.

The woman across the table squared her narrow shoulders beneath the unnamed shade of green dress and said, "Miss Gaspard, tell me about why and how you came to America."

I blinked and let my eyes drift to the window, looking out the side yard. I squinted at the cotton floss clouds. The clock kept at its loud clacking while I studied the four-pane window, no longer looking out of it but beyond it.

No one had ever asked why I came to America.

Chapter 2

(Spring 1870 Wallonia, Emilie's Story)

The voices coming from the decades old floor below the bed started discussing moving away again. *Mi pére* was the one who started the talking each night. His voice also carried the clearest through the well-worn boards. *Pére* wanted to move to America and *Mame* did whatever he wanted. She never said much during those evening discussions, and I suspected it was because she was fearful of what could happen so far away from what we knew.

The talk of moving had been happening for at least the last two years and escalated a year ago when *Pére* announced that he had the money to purchase passage for him and Leopold to travel to America. The plan was for them to go to Wisconsin where *Pére's* oldest *fré* had been farming more than ten years. They would find land and prepare for Mame and me to join them.

Mi mame was not *mi Pére's* first *feume*. His first *feume* died while giving birth to *mi fré* Antoine. *Pére* married *mi mame* quickly after because he had *efant* Antoine and my oldest *fré* Joseph who needed a *mame*. I once heard *Grand-mére* tell her *cuzén* in her hushed voice that he was no longer the *fi* she raised after his first *feume* died. I felt angry when I heard her say that. It seemed impossible that the strict, stern man I knew as *mi pére* had once been the exact opposite. As long as I could remember the entire Gaspard family collectively avoided making *mi pére* angry.

The voices tonight crept louder than usual. *Pére* wanted to leave very soon and *Grand-pére* asked him again why he was rushing to leave. The tension slipping through the cracks in the attic floor was palpable, engulfing the room under the eaves with a thickness like running your hand through turned soil.

Twenty years ago, many people started leaving Wallonia for a better life. Food shortages and the lack of work plus a series of illnesses had visited the country. The many gravestones in the churchyards and graveyards heralded how thinly life was balanced in *Grez-Doiceau* and throughout much of Europe at that time. There were people who made it their living to be an agent for the new country. They actively sought people to expand into the west of a giant landmass that seemed to have endless opportunities for personal success. Success that felt unattainable in Europe due to wars, primogeniture, cholera and typhoid epidemics, and other health issues that caused a high child mortality rate.

After the first group landed in America, letters began to arrive in the villages of Wallonia and across the continent. They contained stories of inexpensive land that would be high quality farmland if you were willing to do some hard work. *Pére's fré* François—*Nonke* Frank—left for America in 1853 and had a large area of land in a place called GrandLez, Wisconsin. *Nonke* Frank had sent a letter around the new year that said there were two started farms adjacent to his land that were available for sale. He didn't include an explanation of why these desirable farms were suddenly available. *Nonke* Frank wanted *Pére* or one of his *fis* to come to Wisconsin and buy them. *Pére* had already made up his mind before the letter arrived, but having a ready-made solution to obtaining land in Wisconsin brought the discussion to a solid boil.

"François was offering an opportunity that I would never be able to offer *mes fez*. If we stay here, there would be even less for each when Leopold marries."

Pére stopped, but I could tell he was on his feet and pacing the back of the room below. "It was not that we want to leave you," he continued, "but I want *mes fez* to be successful." Antoine and Joseph have been trained as shoemakers. In 1870 there were nearly 3,000 people who lived in the village. In addition to the Gaspards there was another family of shoemakers. *Grez-Doiceau* wasn't big enough for four shoemakers from one *famile*—plus the Pirards. Our small plot of land had scarcely been able to feed the seventeen people the *famile* had grown to be.

I laid as still as I could, holding my breath. I started letting out the air in small wisps. This was always the same point in the discussion where *Grand-pére's* voice grew its loudest, which wasn't nearly as loud as *Pére*. I strained a bit to hear, but I already knew what he was going to say.

"I have given you a trade and we have some land. There is no need to leave."

Out of reflex, I rolled from my back to my side as lithe as possible and glanced at the empty space in the bed next to me.

My older *soû* Eugénie was married just two weeks ago. I had hoped having one less body in the house would ease the burden and quiet the talk of leaving, once she had moved to her new *ome's* house. We had shared this bed nearly my entire life and the habit of rolling over to see if Eugénie was listening would take time to break. I shifted further to stare into the darkness across the long room to see if *mi fré* Leopold was also listening. All the Gaspard children slept in the room under the eaves. *Fiyes* on the end furthest from the stairs, *djouvas* on the other. Not so many years ago, the room under the eaves housed Joseph, Antoine, Eugénie, the twins Thérèse and Ament, me, and Leopold the youngest. Joseph, Antoine, and Eugénie all left the *famile* house with the fanfare of wedding parties.

The long, narrow room was the length of the house, probably twenty-five feet by ten feet, with full standing height only in the middle and at the two dormer windows overlooking the street. The wood-beamed sloped roof came to within a foot of the floor. There were four narrow beds tucked up to the slopes that had been shared by all the *efants*. Now only two of them had occupants.

When I was three, one of those terrible illnesses came to our village. Everyone in the *famile* got sick and *Mame* and *Grand-mére* could barely care for themselves, as well as all the sick *efants*. They were very worried about Antoine, whose birth had resulted in the death of his *mame* and seemed to have laid a path for childhood illnesses and the inability for him to recover quickly. As he was seeming to improve, the twins Thérèse and Ament became so sick that they sent for the priest and doctor. I couldn't think of a time that the doctor had been called to the house since. *Grand-mére* had learned from the women in her family which herbs and plants could restore health to the ill. She would make a tea or poultice with her simples that brought comfort. Her skills were known in the community, and many would seek her skills when someone was ailing in their home.

Grand-mére told me that after three days of worrying fits and fevers, the seven-year-old twins seemed to be getting better. Thérèse had even asked for water. On the night of the fourth day, *Grand-mére* stayed awake looking after the *fis* so *Mame* could rest. She was pleased to see that I was no longer burning with fever, and that Antoine, Joseph and Eugénie had eaten some broth before falling back to sleep. She sat in the wooden chair that had been placed in the moonless dormer and dozed. As the only clock in the house rang three times in the room below, a hollow thud brought *Grand-mére* to her feet. She was drawn to the twins' sick bed and found them both dead with their hands clasped between them the same way they had slept as *efants*. I have very subtle memories of the twins: Ament with dark hair, lifting me to see things or to keep me out of the way, and Thérèse with her lighter hair and freckle spots on her nose, wiping my hands and face after eating.

We were not the only *famile* to lose loved ones to this brutal illness. The churchyards had many stones with the year 1857 stamped into eternity, but as a rule we did not speak of the twins' death aside from praying for their souls in church. I knew *Mame* thought of the twins daily. Once when I was cleaning her room, I noticed that the small dark wood box that *Mame* normally kept on the lamp shelf was open and lying on the bed. I slowed my cleaning so I could get a better look at the inside. Tied with small pieces of cream ribbon were a stick straight lock of dark hair and a slightly curled lock of lighter hair. These were the only items *Mame* had to remember two of her *efants*.

Straining to see through the distance of the dark room, there was only Leopold for me to seek in the deep-water black of the rafter room. As my eyes found the mound on his bed, I tried to focus in on potential movements indicating sleep when my search was interrupted by the next words.

Pére announced that he would be leaving with Leopold in the autumn. "Rosilia and Emilie would come in the early spring." *Pére's* voice was so firm and final that the others went silent. There was still no movement from Leopold.

I was a few months away from being fifteen and considered an *efant* in *mi famile* until I married. *Efants* obeyed *leus pareints* and elders. We were to complete the chores that were assigned to us without question. I had witnessed *mes fréres* fighting with *Pére* to build their own lives, but they were *omes*, not a *feme* or *ene fiye*. The expected paths were to marry or to become involved in the church. I did not feel called to be a sister in the Catholic faith and hoped to find an *ome* instead. Some local *familes* placed a heavy weight on their *efants* to consider entering a Catholic profession, but the Gaspard household didn't weigh it as high as being a contributing citizen to your community. This likely surprised our neighbors due to *Grand-mére* being a Lateau. Two years ago, she had received word from her *cuzén* Vosine Lateau that they had all survived the cholera epidemic that had ripped through Wallonia and that they had been visited by a miracle. Vosine's 33-year-old *feye*, Anne Louise, had been held in the ecstasy of the Lord and had been marked with stigmata. *Grand-mére* had explained to me and Leopold that stigmata were extremely rare and holy. Anne Louise had been touched by God, and the proof was in her bleeding hands, feet, and side. Many of the strongest believers in the village thought that surely the entire *famile* was blessed by this extraordinary occurrence, and one of the old crones would ask to check my hands and side after mass.

I rolled to my back and pressed my hand under the starchy lace hem of the pillowcase. The quilt that covered me felt like a heavy clothing iron heated to red-hot, but I couldn't bring myself to toss its bulk away. I didn't want to leave Wallonia. I loved my neighborhood and never saw a life outside of it, much less on the other side of the world. The only person I dared to speak to about this was Eugénie and being recently married, I knew I must wait the proper amount of time for the newlyweds to build their home together before speaking to her.

My chance to speak to Eugénie came two weeks later when she and her new *ome* visited for a meal. Standing elbow to elbow, we worked at washing dishes and spoke nearly silently. *Pére* had very little tolerance for what he thought was gossip or idle talk when you should be completing chores. As we reached our former tempo with the clean up, I mouthed that I did not want to leave for America. Eugénie paused her work for the slightest of moments. When she turned to look at me with her orange-brown eyes widening, she nodded slightly and mouthed the word 'later.' Relief and hope rushed into me. Eugénie moved ever so slightly next to me and our upper arms touched. I hoped the warmth I felt between the fabric of our sleeves was a good omen. I didn't dare ask what she was thinking because anyone could have come closer and heard the conversation.

I hadn't expected a response from Eugénie so quickly, but two days later I found a note from her tucked into our childhood secret hole in the stone fence behind the house. The gray stone fence had been there as long as anyone could remember, and it was Eugénie who had discovered the space behind one of the smooth rocks that was just the right size for a small treasure or wisp of paper. Eugénie had asked her new *ome* if I could live with them, making it possible for me to stay in Wallonia, until I married, but he had refused because he was afraid of what *Pére* would say. Eugénie's note ended suggesting I speak to *Grand-mére* privately. Hope was not completely lost. I loved *Grand-mére* on my own, not because I was told to love or respect her as an elder. We spent many hours together during the day doing the cooking and gardening. She would surely understand and knew that I wasn't asking to stay on a whim.

The next day, *Grand-mére* and I pulled the weeds next to the rows of soft green shoots that would become food for the rest of the year, and I quietly asked if I would have to go to America. *Couldn't I stay and live with her and Grand-pére until I married?* She stopped pulling weeds in her row and looked directly into my eyes. She was a small woman, round in the middle with sloping shoulders. Her black hair was feathered on each side of her temple with a shocking white stripe, and she still wore it pulled back the same way she did when she first married. Her plain work dress was washed to a hazy light blue and was covered by what she called her garden apron. I tried to fix my face into an expression that didn't look desperate. I couldn't hold it very long. I dropped my gaze to her impossibly tiny feet clad in two pairs of thick gray wool stockings and wooden shoes, hoping she didn't notice.

If I was honest with myself at this point, I knew I was going to have to go to America.

What I should have anticipated was *Pére's* reaction when *Grandmére* inquired about me staying.

The next afternoon, when *Pére* returned from a day of making shoes, he ordered me to the sitting room. Leaving the door open behind him, he revealed the ebony-brown leather strap in his hand. This type of punishment was nothing new in this house, but being nearly fifteen, it had been several years since I had been at the end of that strap. It felt foreign, like something from a different life. When *Pére* delivered punishment, his five-foot six-inch slight body seemed to gain mass. His dark brown hair and eyes appeared black, and his expression was always blank.

Without saying anything he twisted my arm and spun me around, so I was no longer facing him. He was not much taller than I was, but years of working his trade had given him a sinewy upper body strength and since I was cornered in the room with nowhere to go, there was no use in prolonging the punishment. The first blow was always the worst. It was shocking, loud, and the seconds before the pain registered were filled with an odd bliss before breaking way to reality. He continued raising the strap and brought it down around the backs of my legs. I heard fabric tearing on my long skirts and could feel the whoosh of air with each blow. The movement of air however wasn't accurate enough to predict where the next blow would fall, not that there was much you could do but prepare yourself for the hit.

He hadn't said a word since ordering me into the room. The silence fueled my anger, and the plaster covered wall in front of me that was normally whitewashed, flooded crimson with my rage. There were no tears, there were no words coming from my mouth, not even a whimper. I would not give him the satisfaction. As I floated outside my body in a cloud of red, I didn't hear my *fré* Antoine enter the room.

"*Pére!*" Antoine's voice was so loud that I slipped out of the rage-charged cloud and back into myself. I heard the strap slide to the floor with a hollow thwap. Without a word, *Pére* turned, and I risked turning my head to glance behind me. Antoine had *Pére* locked in a stare. I took the opportunity to slide my entire body along the wall past *Pére* without turning around or touching any part of him. Before I turned away from the wall, I adjusted my face to what I thought was a perfectly neutral expression.

The back of my skirt was ripped, and my legs felt sticky. They stung, but my anger stung more. I walked to the kitchen and started gathering items to set the table. *Grand-mére* didn't look up from the cupboard that she was grasping. Her fingers turned white from the grip. As I turned to set the table, I saw *Mame* standing in the doorway. She was very pale, and her shoulders were slightly shaking. When Antoine came through, he paused in front of *Mame*, and I could tell from the back of his head how disappointed he was in the entire scene. He then took three steps around the table to where I stood and touched my arm lightly. When I looked up his expression looked like kindness and contempt for the scenario. His kindness nearly brought tears to my eyes, but I didn't cry. Instead, I took my place at the table for a silent supper.

After eating and cleaning the kitchen, I joined the *famile* in the sitting room for our usual evening. The pain in my legs had settled into a throbbing buzz, but I sat in my torn skirt and pulled out my lace-making project. My project was ragged since there was still the haze of red hanging around me. I wasn't very good at lace making anyway. There was no conversation. At one point, I met Leopold's eyes for a moment and saw a mix of rage and helplessness.

When it was time to retire to bed, I returned my lace project to the corner cupboard and took the stairs to the room under the eaves.

Each stair creaked with welcoming distance from the day. Away from the rest I took off my skirt. I peeled it away from the backs of my legs and started bathing my welts with water from the pitcher by my bed. The light was too dim to see if I was bleeding yet, so I pulled on a *chemise de nuit* and slipped face down into the bed, carefully pulling the hem up as high as I thought the hits landed.

A while later, I heard Leopold ascend the stairs and a nearly un-hearable three-knock rap on the wood floor. Three usually meant there was something to see. I rotated my head from facing the wall to facing the stairs, I tried for the minimal amount of movement. I could just make out a parcel in a white towel placed right at the top of the stairs. I knew that Leopold didn't want to cross the floor for fear of being heard by *Pére* and I didn't blame him. Instead, I slid my legs over the side of the bed, still faced down to avoid rubbing the bruised backs on the bed. Slowly and silently, I walked to the parcel in bare feet.

It was a small pot of salve that *Grand-mére* kept on the simple's shelf.

I would be traveling to America.

But I did not want to leave Wallonia.

Chapter 3

(August 1931 Wisconsin, Emilie's Story)

The ping of a pencil nib breaking dragged me back sixty years to my kitchen table.

Edna Mae didn't immediately lift her eyes to meet mine. I could see she was collecting herself and her thoughts, which abruptly stopped when the lead broke.

I had said too much. She was going to leave, and I was going to have to explain to Leopold and the others that I didn't do the interview correctly.

Edna Mae still hadn't lifted her head. I wanted her to unfreeze but didn't know what to say. I was about to clear my throat when a spot of water dripped off her straight, thin nose and landed on the paper instantly thinning the parchment and changing the color. At first, I thought it was sweat from her brow, but it was not overly warm that day. The door was open, and a light breeze kissed the air in the room and exited through the open window near the stove, confirmed by the slight movement of the white lace-trimmed curtains.

Another tear skimmed along the well where her nose met her cheek. Before it made its exit, she became unstuck and quickly lifted her head. She dragged her red tipped fingers across her nose to remove the tear, and she finally looked up.

"Your father beat you for talking to your grandmother?" Her words exited her mouth in short puffs, and she rubbed her thumb and fingers together as if she could erase the tear.

I watched the ruby-nailed fingers rub harder together. "I was a child who had disrespected my father. He was not a man who would tolerate disrespect in his house."

Anger, sadness, and fear slid across her face like clouds blowing across the sky. "Couldn't your mother or grandmother have stopped it? Or explained that it was simply that you would like to stay in the home you knew?" The previous emotion clouds moved past, and her expression of curiosity and professionalism came back.

"No." I stopped because answering the question felt disrespectful even though they had all long ago passed away. *Mame* and *Grand-mére* had no power to stop *Pére's* authority over anyone, even themselves. It was shocking that he had stopped when Antoine shouted.

Edna Mae looked down at the injured pencil in her right hand as if she had never seen it before. The clouds edged to the corners of her eyes again. "Miss Gaspard, were you comfortable with continuing? I would like to come back tomorrow if that was okay."

"Yes."

I couldn't tell who was more surprised at my answer.

After Edna Mae gathered her writing tools and drove away, I found that I couldn't get myself to move from the kitchen table. The light outside the kitchen door turned plum-colored and blurred the scenery. The breeze that was welcoming just thirty minutes ago had turned its back on me, and I felt the stale air stick to my skin. I was just not ready to stand up.

The punishment replayed. I could almost smell the whitewash on the sitting room wall. There was a paint brush stroke dancing in front of my eyes and the smell of *Grand-mére's* cooked chicken took over the room. Immediately, I felt ready to cry. I didn't allow myself to think of *Grand-mére* for too long or too often.

Grand-mére had lived nearly her entire life on the same block in *Grez-Doiceau*. She was born Marie Thérèse Lateau in 1776.

Sometimes she would tell stories about what it was like growing up with her *fré* Jean. When I was a child, I could clearly imagine the colors and sharp sounds as if I was there. Today, I couldn't remember those details. Instead, I could only remember the essence of her. She seemed to have had the ability to know things that were going to happen and see things others couldn't.

She was a soft place in the house. *Grand-mére* could excuse missteps with a kind look if *Pére* was not around. When I thought of her life, I knew she had been sad. *Mi Pére* had changed after the death of his *feume* and had become angry and fierce. Her *fi Nonke* Frank had left for America, and she knew she would never see him again or meet his *famile*. Her *pareints* had died when she was in her teens when she married *Grand-pére*. The marriage was necessary. If she didn't wed *Grand-pére* her only other options were to join a convent or spend a year in an orphan home. The orphan home would have ultimately encouraged her to join a convent or become a servant. Being married to *Grand-pére* meant she had food and shelter, and she could rebuild a family of her own.

I remember their relationship as silent. Neither of them was known to talk much and the evening conversations about moving to America were the most words *Grand-pére* spoke all day. Then, we left for America and her *famile* shrunk again, and she knew she would never see us again. I was ashamed that I added to her trials by requesting to stay in Wallonia. I believed she wanted me to stay; she wanted all of us to stay, but that's not how we honored her.

It had gotten so dim in the kitchen and I was uncomfortable to the point that I started shaking from the lack of movement. My knees creaked as I stood up, supporting myself on the table edge. I paused in front of the open door for a few moments. The teacup on the table chimed a second too long in the breeze from the closing door.

Chapter 4

(August 1931 Wisconsin, Edna Mae's Journal)

August 11, 1931

Conducted first interview with Miss Gaspard in her home which was built after the fire. She's taller than I thought she would be and speaks English as well as those who learned it from birth. I was happy that the interview was flowing easily, and she was willing to share details beyond just the tragedy of the fire. The corporal punishment meted by her father had unfortunately brought me back to those years with Peter in Minneapolis and had sent me down the path of wondering where William and Catherine were today and if they knew about me.

Edna Mae pulled over to the side of the thin dirt road to try to collect herself before she got to the hotel. The view next to the road was a late summer green studded with barns and black and white bovines. She had been on assignments all over the Midwest covering whatever story the paper sought. Like many other times, this assignment came when she most needed the work or the change of scenery. Her last assignment had been in the town of Langdon, North Dakota—a berg tucked close to the Manitoba, Canada border. Her assignment at the community paper, *The Cavalier County Republican,* had been typesetting for a woman who was taking an extended visit to California. Once the woman returned, the newspaper editor had asked Edna Mae to stay as a reporter.

The editor was a painfully thin man who appeared to be any age, between twenty-five and forty-five. His hands were always darkened with ink and often it was smudged to his elbows. Even with his sleeves bunched to the middle of his upper arm, you knew he brought home a stained shirt to his long-suffering wife each night. Edna Mae had promised she would think about staying but when she walked back to her room at the UTC Hotel on Main Street, there was an envelope from the paper in Green Bay.

The Green Bay Press Gazette had obtained her information from her former editor in Minneapolis. They hoped she would be interested in working between typesetting and etching for several people who were going on vacation during August. Edna Mae had done some work in the past for Wisconsin newspapers and almost immediately decided that it was time to go back. She wrote to *The Press Gazette* and then explained to *The Republican* editor that she had an opportunity in Wisconsin that paid more. He understood and said he would keep her in mind for the future. A week later, she was on her way to the city of Green Bay.

The Press Gazette offices were located in a newer building. Its modern exterior, with taupe stone and large windows, was impressive. Upon entering, the batwing staircases seemed to gather what she thought were the homey smells of paper, ink, and machine oil. As she toured the typesetting department, she heard a familiar voice.

"Edna Mae Leighton? Is that you?" Loping toward her on a knee that was damaged at the Battle of Saint-Mihiel, was Walter Raymond.

"Walter! What are you doing here?" Her tour guide gave her a quick nod that it was all right to slow the tour to greet him.

"I'm on staff here now. What are you doing in Wisconsin? I thought you were in Montana or Idaho or somewhere."

"I was in North Dakota last. What happened to *The Daily Gazette*?"

Edna Mae and Walter had met at *The Janesville Wisconsin Daily Gazette* several years ago when they were both temporary newsroom employees.

Just as Walter was about to explain, a handsome gray-haired man with a bow tie stepped out of his office and shouted Walter's name. They both knew that tone of voice, it meant more work.

Walter darted to the editor's office with a knowing nod. Two days later, she found out that Walter had spoken so highly of her writing and willingness to travel for stories that she was assigned to cover the anniversary of the fire, instead of typesetting and etching.

The assignment was going to mark the anniversary of a tragic period in the region's history. The Peshtigo Fire, or the Great Fire as those on this side of the bay often referred to it, killed at least fifteen hundred white people and countless American Indians in a few hours. Because it had happened sixty years ago, there were not many people left to tell their stories. Many of those still alive had just been small children at the time, with memories dimmed and shaded by stories they had heard in hushed tones during their lives. When Edna Mae was told she would be interviewing a woman who had been fifteen when the fire happened, she was secretly happy. At fifteen, she would likely have clearer memories that would help add more texture to the piece. Edna Mae knew that her counterpart had been sent to the city of Peshtigo to interview a woman in her early nineties. If that woman was still clear of mind, she would likely become the star of the article.

The parish priest of Peshtigo had published his eyewitness account of surviving the fire, leaving behind a legacy that this side of the bay didn't seem to have. Father Peter Pernin's vivid account was published after the fire as a way to make money to replace the nearly completed church that had been destroyed that night while he bobbed in the Peshtigo River fighting for survival. His was one of the very few written accounts of October 8th. That night fires had raged across Wisconsin, Michigan and tore through the city of Chicago. On October 9th word traveled faster from the metropolis than the rural burnt areas around the Bay of Green Bay.

Edna Mae had started combing through old issues of the 1871 and 1872 newspapers but found that much of the coverage was lists of property lost or damaged. In Kewaunee County, where the Gaspard family survived, the slim coverage often stated that they didn't know the full loss of life. As she worked through the weeks and months after the fire, a complete list never appeared in newsprint for the Wisconsin burned areas.

When she had walked into *The Green Bay Press Gazette* offices last week, there was talk that the special anniversary section could become a printed memorial book. While she had been published nearly weekly during her career, she had never been published in a book. It was a strange twist that she was now in a position that it could happen. The idea of a book helped push the tears out of her immediate vision on the roadside.

The ten-mile drive to Algoma seemed simple based on the directions they gave at the paper, but Edna Mae knew Wisconsin was different from her home state of North Dakota. In North Dakota, square-mile roads were the norm and were not often broken by natural landmarks that caused roads to curve and in most of the state you could see for miles undisturbed. Here the roads went around swamps, groves of trees and diverted to the narrowest part of a creek for bridges. If she stayed on this dusty trail and was mindful of ruts, she would be able to get to the Hotel Stebbins in time for supper.

The hotel had been a part of this town since 1858 and had likely housed individuals after the fire. In the early 1900's the brick front was added including a rounded corner with dome and curved first floor picture windows. Her second-floor room faced Second Street and the lakeshore. The room had two beds covered with matching woven blush pink bedspreads. The headboards, dresser, chair and desk were all a warm maple wood. Between the chair rail and the picture rail the walls were papered in an Art Nouveau style paper that featured bouquets of pink flowers tied in green ribbon on a blush background. It was clean and tidy, and the lace curtains shifted with the breeze off the lake.

When she reached the hotel, she would have time to type her notes from the day and review past issues of the Kewaunee County papers. The desk in the room looked out at the people conducting business in Algoma. Being just a block from an expansive bank of sand belonging to Lake Michigan, the birds swooped, and boats bobbed, but she wasn't ready to explore the lake yet. It was too soon.

She instead focused on how the interview went. Miss Gaspard was refreshing to interview. There had been many times that Edna Mae had sat in front of a person and asked for details on a subject only to have them suddenly become shy and start answering her with as few words as possible. Miss Gaspard had started talking and didn't stop. Her brother Leopold had warned the newspaper office that she may have language issues, but Edna Mae understood every word and each emotion that went with them.

Edna Mae knew firsthand the terror and sadness that Miss Gaspard went through to tell that part of her story. The physical punishment would not go into the article—she only had so many words to work with for the newspaper special section and wanted to make sure the most compelling details made the cut. As a writer she also knew there would be a way to include it using veiled language that the general reader might skim over, but which the careful reader would recognize. This type of interview made her entire body tingle.

Flipping words around in her head and phrasing statements in practice to get the most out of each word in the short allotment of space was the best part of being a writer.

After finishing New Rockford Public High School, in North Dakota, Edna Mae hadn't found a husband—nor was she interested in being married. Her parents weren't concerned. She grew up with a legendary mother who had homesteaded even before she was married. She was one of the few women who owned land of their own in what was now North Dakota. Edna Mae's older sister had married a successful businessman from nearby Grand Forks and had four children. Her brother Paul had been a foreman at an automaker in Detroit, Michigan before passing away at thirty-seven the previous year, and brother Anders was a railroad engineer with a wife and two small daughters. The pioneering genes from her mother were passed down to her, along with the belief that she could forge a path in the world that fit her own vision. She could make her own future.

She graduated from the Phillips Academy's English department in New Rockford, being one of just a few women attending. As an avid reader, she had learned about female writers and thought it was something she could enjoy. Without a topic to write a book about and lack of interest in composing poetry, the idea of writing for a newspaper seemed like the best start. It may have been the best way to get started but it wasn't any easier than the other avenues. Her first job at a newspaper had happened only because the newspaper's writer was fighting in a trench on the Somme River basin in France. It wasn't a great piece, that first one, but the act of researching and interviewing to obtain details that later became a narrative was exciting.

She met Peter in 1918. He was eating at a café table in Minneapolis, Minnesota. Edna Mae often came to this café and that day she was reading through her notes from an interview she had just done with a bank teller who had been robbed days earlier. He was still in uniform and desperately needed a haircut and shave. His coffee cup was being continuously filled by a young woman working at the café and that was what caught Edna Mae's attention. He must have had four cups of coffee in the last half an hour. She didn't realize she was staring at the white ironstone cup in his hand until he set it on the table with a clink.

Her eyes lifted to meet his. They were an unusual shade of brown. The closest she could think of was the color of brown butcher paper. His dark brown lashes and eyebrows made his expression seem stern. If his hair wasn't nearly the color of sarsaparilla, he may have appeared to be downright angry. She smiled, but it wasn't matched. With the same serious expression, he got up from his table and walked over to hers with his coffee cup in hand. She could still hear the scrape of the chair on the tile floor as he sat down across the table. His thin fingers clasped the white cup and tremored slightly in the motion of setting it on the café table.

The men and women who had fought or provided aid in this recent war all came back different. Some wore their scars outwardly; others smiled without it reaching their eyes. It felt strange to hope that it was a tremor from war and not the illness that papers out east were reporting was killing at an alarming rate.

It was hard to remember how things moved so quickly after that meeting. By the end of the week, they had slept together. That day she had taken her usual table next to the wall facing the large windows looking out at the street front. It was warm, but not humid like many late-summer days in Minneapolis. The bell above the door jangled when he entered, and she quickly moved her notes aside, gesturing for him to join her. They hadn't talked about what would happen next. They walked toward his apartment, enveloped in the smell of rain, but the drops didn't start until they reached the block of his apartment.

Edna Mae had no experience with courting or dating. There were no boys back home who had interested her in that way. Peter was fascinating. He didn't talk much; instead, he always seemed to be listening to her. When he spoke, it was about how he was going to go to California and get work that was good enough that he could buy some land. That afternoon was so foreign to her.

Lying on his narrow, springy bed, listening to the rumble of impending thunder she wondered how she had let this happen. Shouldn't they be married? When they were together, his tall frame could shade her eyes from the sun and dim her judgment at the same time. By the end of the next two weeks, she had spent the night at his apartment.

When she returned to the house where she boarded, the following day the Norwegian proprietress, Mrs. Marta Svenson, likely assumed Edna Mae had been working on an important story for the newspaper. Marta knew that Edna Mae had returned very early that morning. The cellar door at the rear of the house had an intricate pull-lock that only three people knew how to manage, the coal delivery man, Mrs. Svenson and Edna Mae.

The widowed owner was somewhat sympathetic to the schedule she needed to keep for her job. Edna Mae suspected that the older woman needed the weekly money more than the value of decorum. The light in the room was still a dark liquid when Marta heard the bedroom door above her softly close that morning. The women would at times share details over meals if Edna Mae could, about stories she was working to craft. Marta didn't push for information. She knew it wasn't easy for women in jobs that weren't considered feminine and assumed that if it was shareable she would hear from Edna Mae eventually.

There was no newspaper story to share, but Edna Mae would have welcomed telling someone what had happened that night. In the middle of that night, she felt the narrow bed start shaking and the brass headboard began scraping the wall. Before she could fully open her eyes, the screaming and thrashing started. Peter was shouting for unseen people to keep their heads down and to run. The neighbor was rapping on the thin shared wall, and it sounded like he was saying "Pete, it's a dream" but it was beyond garbled.

By the time she was able to get him to wake up, the sheets were in a tangle on the floor, and he was covered in sweat. Her head had started pounding, and like cornered prey she began scampering around the room gathering clothing and planning her escape. Peter said nothing to her after the nightmare—he just sat on the end of the bed in his gray striped boxer shorts, staring at his hands that were trembling more than usual. She had finished dressing and ran out of the building into the 3 a.m. darkness without even turning her head to look at the distressed man. Maneuvering the tricky cellar lock was complicated at that hour, but there was nothing that would bring her back into that apartment. Keeping up the canter, she cleared the five blocks to the three-story slim, red-brick Victorian structure that was her home in record time. This was the first man she had ever dated and while she was inexperienced, she knew that what had happened that night was not normal.

She didn't see Peter for the next six weeks, but she knew she was going to have to talk to him. She hadn't had her period and had been sick each morning. One day one of the secretaries at the newspaper walked into the bathroom as she was being sick. The secretary was a few years older than Edna Mae and seemed to always be dating a new man. She took one look at Edna Mae and asked her if she was pregnant.

Edna Mae was stunned. The ashy-colored walls of the bathroom started swimming with the dark wood trim, and her knees nearly buckled. The secretary went with her to a doctor that she knew.

When she explained to the young doctor that she hadn't had an exam like this before, he paused, checking her heart rate and gave her a look of compassion. After the exam she could only nod at the secretary who had waited in the tiny entry hall next to the office in the doctor's home. He had confirmed she was pregnant.

The doctor's office wasn't close to the café where she first met Peter, but she welcomed the walk. None of the normal city street scenes registered as she walked. She had never thought about having children. Her life to that point had been filled with stringing together jobs in her chosen profession and meeting newspaper deadlines.

She pushed open the door and didn't feel the normal warm welcome from the tinkle of the bell. Peter was sitting at the counter with a coffee cup in his hand. He was surprised to see her and even more surprised when she asked if they could go to his apartment to discuss something.

That was the first time he hit her.

She was standing in the tiny living area that barely fit a chair, two-person table and radio. Her mouth had been slightly open when the palm of his hand met the side of her face. Immediately her jaw made a strange movement, and a tiny ping started in her ear. She could feel where his heavy gold class ring had hit her molar through the skin, and when she moved her lower jaw to close her mouth it made a sickening movement and started to ache. Stunned, she stared through Peter's chest. He didn't raise his hand again. Instead, he dropped into the chair.

"How could you have let this happen?"

She couldn't tell if he meant the pregnancy or him hitting her. Both seemed like they weren't just her fault, but how would she navigate either?

Chapter 5

(August 1931 Wisconsin, Emilie's Story)

Much of the night before, I sat by the lamp in my front room and thought about how I might have made a mistake. Edna Mae didn't care about my relationship with my father. Her question had been about why we came to America. I needed to remember that for today. I'm sure she was going to want to go back to her second question, about how we got to America.

Many years ago, one of the neighbor children had asked, with a glint of explorer in her eye, if sailing to America had been exciting. I told her that for some it was a great adventure, and that she should ask the same question to my brother, Mr. Leopold Gaspard. She scrunched her already pert nose and said, "But he's a boy. Boys do those things all the time. You're a girl." And she was right. As America became more civilized, churches, schools, sidewalks, and roads offered less adventure for young women.

This neighbor girl went to France as a nurse during the Great War. Her parents had been hugely opposed to her going, and it wasn't until many years later that we found out that the daughter had run away without their permission. After the war, she was a nurse on a ship that was wrecked in the bay that curves where Spain meets France. She was one of only thirty or thirty-five people who survived. Undeterred, she had started working as a camp nurse to a group who had discovered tombs and artifacts in Egypt, Africa. I would never tell anyone, but I was terribly proud of that girl and a little of myself. I could have squashed her adventurer spirit because of my experience with leaving my home; instead, I held my tongue when all the others told her she should just practice caring for the health of a family here in Wisconsin. I think I was also a bit jealous of her willingness to see change as an adventure.

Edna Mae reminded me a bit of that girl. She was plucky, willing, and appearing to be unafraid of what others would say about their path. I expected her to drive up the road at any moment, and I decided that we should take advantage of the cooler temperature on my porch. The porch had been an addition many years after the house was finished. The air was already heated, and the sun would make the house stuffy before noon. I pulled the round wooden table that I normally used to shell peas or clean other garden items to the shadiest area and placed two kitchen chairs next to it. Edna Mae should have enough room on its top for her papers. Instead of tea, I added some wild berry cordial to cold water for a more refreshing drink. The new-growth forest adjacent to my house had produced a lot of wild raspberries and grapes. In the ditches, wild strawberries could be found in the spring. The fruit syrup was usually one of the last things I put up each year, using previously canned fruit juice and whatever fruit was left before the snow. I never knew how much I would yield, so it always felt like a treat when I shared with guests. This batch was the richest shade of vermillion, and even when diluted with the water would stain your teeth if you drank too much.

My house was situated a short distance from the dirt road that led to the village of Lincoln, formerly GrandLez to the south, and Rosiere to the north. My beloved porch was only a few paces wide but ran the length of the red brick front of the house. Over the years, I had collected a mix of items for the porch; a rocking chair with a place next to it for the butter churn, and a large round cracked clay bowl that I planted flower seeds in each spring. That year, there was a wild variety of colors that smiled at me from the bowl. Looking down at the surface of the table, I remembered the cold day it was delivered to the barnyard after the fire. It had been donated and arrived in a wagon with a mix of other furniture. It was way too small for everyone that lived with us after the fire to all sit together and have a meal at the same time; we took turns back then. I ran my finger over the top of the table feeling the kitten-belly-soft finish that came from being wiped clean so many times.

After adding a starched linen cover, edged in a lilac crocheted lace to the table, I heard a vehicle coming up the hill. Anticipating the ruckus, my hens started scattering in every direction. The mottled goose I named Joséphine came toddling around the corner of the house unconcerned. She was not the smartest fowl I have ever known, but I secretly loved her as much as I did my brown dog, called Skittles. Skittles could trace his ancestry back to my cousin John's dog, 'Lake Trout.' With the children out of school, Skittles spent much of his day trotting behind them hoping for extra attention and adventures. I didn't see his dark blueberry eyes all day, and he would reluctantly come to my back door when the last child went to sleep. Once he was in, he would curl in his basket by my chair and continue his explorations in his sleep, letting out yips, and moving his paws as if he was running with the children in his sleep.

The Model A pulled close to the house, with puffs of brown-gray road dust floating around the wheels. Edna Mae lifted her hand in a short wave. When she came around the side of the car, I noticed that that day she was wearing a chocolate-brown dress in a similar style as the green one the day before. It had tiny dots all over it and yet it still worked with the hat from yesterday. I wondered if wearing the same hat was a personal preference or if it made packing easier when she was in different regions. I had my black hat, trimmed with a black ribbon, and a sprig of quail feathers tucked in for decoration. I wore it to town and church. There was also a cotton, calico bonnet —generally out of fashion in the 1930s. I wore it while working in the gardens, with the animals, or helping in the fields. Women today didn't care to wear the sight-restricting old-fashioned style, and I saw many wearing straw hats, while they worked.

Edna Mae had barely stepped on the porch when she stuttered—something I hadn't noticed before. "Miss Gaspard, I, I want to apologize. My behavior yesterday was not terribly professional. Your story was so compelling that I, I became emotional. I wanted to assure you that I would not let those emotions overcome me and make it impossible to tell the story."

I didn't bother hiding my surprise. "Mrs. Leighton, I didn't think you were in any way unprofessional. It was more my fault for sharing things that didn't answer your questions."

She looked me in the eye and fixed a wobble of a smile on her face. "On the contrary, knowing more about you would only help tell the story better." She was very curious about how the Gaspard family got from Belgium to the United States. "Will we be out here this morning?"

I barely nodded when she started taking out her writing materials and placed them on the table. "Shall we get started?"

"Yes, there will be a breeze out here." I was ready.

Chapter 6

(Autumn 1870 Wallonia, Emilie's Story)

Pére did not leave two weeks later. Instead, he and Leopold were scheduled to leave the first week of September, and Antoine and his *famile* were to leave two weeks before them in August. *Mame* and I would follow in the spring of 1871. *Nonke* Frank had warned that it would be late, and they could run into poor weather when they got to Chicago. His letter assured *Pére* that in the end it would be okay since both the farms had some trees removed and habitable buildings. *Nonke* Frank had referenced the amount of work needed to get through a Wisconsin winter and inquired with the mills for open positions for *Pére* and Antoine. This would give them the chance to earn the money needed to purchase seeds for planting in the spring and for *Pére* to send money to Wallonia for *Mame* and me to sail to America.

Mame and *Grand-mére* spent much of their spare time packing and repacking the wooden trunk that was in the corner of the kitchen. The trunk seemed so tiny, considering *Pére*, and Leopold would need to live with all its contents in a completely new country. There was a man in town who had made an entire business from crafting these trunks for villagers who were leaving for America. He bragged that since the first trunk he constructed in 1853, none of his had ever broken in transit. I had picked up the corner of the box with its edges still sharp, and I was surprised at its weight. Daily the packing decisions for this box revolved around what *Pére* and Leopold may need immediately versus what they could potentially buy. What was Antoine packing that could be shared? What would

Mame and I need when we arrived that we couldn't carry in a trunk? It seemed like each day something was removed, and two things were added.

The day that Antoine, his *feume* Sofie, four-year-old Adele, three-year-old Rosilia, and two-year-old Honoré left was a jumbled mix of scary and sad. Antoine's *feume* Sofie was in every way visually ordinary. She was average height, had plain brown hair, and equally plain brown eyes. Where she wasn't ordinary was in her mothering. She adored her *efants* to the point where *Pére* had accused her of spoiling them. That was the only time I had seen Sofie get her back up. She inched up to her full height, her brown eyes sparked and snapped, and she said to *Pére*, "Since we do not live under your roof, I would take your comment as a suggestion toward the way I parent your *petit-efants*." *Pére* was so shocked that he stood there without saying a word until she slowly backed away with Rosilia on her hip. As I watched her gather her *efants* to leave, I knew that her, the woman who stood up to my *Pére* would use that strength and love to get them across the ocean.

While the preparations for the first two groups to sail were nearly complete, we had heard several different stories about the voyage. Letters had come back from the United States talking about sickness, bad food, language confusion, uncertainty, and sometimes even bodily harm. Immigration was different for each traveler. When I heard the stories, the mass of worry in my middle flexed and rolled. When Leopold heard the same stories, he heard adventure, opportunity, and the future.

The sun was too bright the morning we sent Antoine and Sofie away. We didn't all go to the train station but said our *ă r'vèy* at our house. I squinted to see this section of my *famile* through the warm light. The three-year-old Rosilia wrapped her arms around my legs and wept a nearly incoherent string of words that Sofie explained meant she was going to miss me and wanted me to go on the big boat with her. Sofie was always free with her affection and kissed Eugénie, Joseph's *feume* Marie, and me on the cheek, and hugged us twice. At least she would be in Wisconsin when it was my turn to make the bitter voyage. Using my hand to shade my eyes, I watched them roll away. Two little faces looked back. Baby Honoré would likely never remember this scene, and it made me wonder how much Adele would carry into her future from that moment.

The scene was repeated a few weeks later when *Pére* and Leopold left for the train. This time, the weather was a misery of mist and wind, and *Mame* was the one stringing words together incoherently, tossing them toward Leopold. He kissed her on the cheek several times and assured her that he would be careful and not fall off the boat or under the train. *Pére* was at the height of anxiousness—he vibrated with it, making everything seem exaggerated. He kissed his *mame* on the cheek and then did the same with the rest of the *femes* in the party. After shaking *Grand-pére's* hand first he moved to his eldest *fi* Joseph. Joseph was holding his *efant* Jean Baptiste and his *feume* Marie was holding two-year-old *feye* Mia. *Pére* said something to Joseph in a low voice, then touched Jean and Mia's feathery heads. Joseph didn't respond, and his face didn't move, making the comment even more of a mystery. Marie looked worn. I suspect that Joseph wanted to go to America too, but Marie wasn't willing.

Marie grew up in a large local *famile*. Over the years several of her siblings had sailed to America. Two of her *frés* had traveled together five years ago and had never been heard from again. Marie's *pére* had contacted newspapers in the United States, running advertisements asking for any information on the two *omes*. The day *Pére* and Leopold set out, Marie's *famile* still didn't know what had happened to them between Wallonia and America.

When it was time to leave, *Mame* walked with them down the road and the rest of us went into the house. *Grand-mére* pulled her work-worn apron from its peg next to the stove and dabbed her eyes with its corner before putting it on. *Nonke* Frank had left for America almost twenty years ago when it was a difficult time in Wallonia. For the second eldest *fi*, leaving for America opened so many more options for Frank than he would ever have had in Wallonia. In 1854, when he left, the journey took him six months total-sailing across the ocean, then through the Great Lakes until reaching Milwaukee. He had worried about money the entire time and took a job for the winter working for a shoemaker in that city. In spring he started walking north, stopping in a community near a town called Sheboygan along the shore of a lake he referred to as an inland ocean. He learned there that nearly all the Walloon immigrants from the previous year had moved further north to Green Bay, where there were settlers who spoke French.

Green Bay was the oldest city in Wisconsin, seated at the basin of the large Bay of Green Bay on Lake Michigan. Much of the region's French-speaking heritage came from the fur trade and French missionary priests years before. He was comforted knowing that there would be some understanding of the language. When he arrived in Green Bay, he learned that most of the previous Walloons had found land in the woods of Kewaunee and Door County on the peninsula to the north. *Nonke* Frank met Honoré LaCrosse while he was in Green Bay. Honoré was from the village of Namur in Wallonia and had traveled across the ocean alone. He too hoped to find farmland and start building his future.

The men learned from a French-speaking priest that the first step was to travel to the Menasha land office, south of Green Bay, and determine what land was available. They ultimately picked land near each other, thinking that being together would lighten the workload. *Grand-mére* didn't hear from *Nonke* Frank until a letter arrived in

1857, nearly three years after he left Wallonia. When she finally received word from him, he was married to a *feume* called Odile, and they were working and sacrificing to make their own farm successful.

I had heard *Grand-mére* whisper to *Grand-pére* two weeks before that she could not see all her traveling *famile* in Wisconsin. I watched her pick up the corner of the apron again and bring it to the crinkled corner of her eye, the gesture squeezed my heart.

Chapter 7

(Spring 1871 Wallonia)

The house immediately became lighter after *Pére* left. *Mame* would sing in a quiet whisper while she worked around the house and *Grand-mére* and *Grand-pére* told stories about their youth and people who had left for America. Some might have felt grateful for the respite from the dark cloud. I didn't trust myself to feel the relief that hovered. Secretly, I felt angry that I had been cheated out of the lightness that could exist in a home. We could all work alongside each other, laugh and not be forced to behave like ghosts.

It was hard to resist this new light, and I was lulled into this different reality. Talk of our leaving hadn't started yet, and the atmosphere in the house was more pleasant by the day. While I helped *Grand-mére* with laundry on an early November day, she stopped churning the clothing in the boiling water and looked towards the west and said, "They were in America."

It wasn't unusual for *Grand-mére* to make statements about things no one else could see or knew, but it could be startling when it happened. With my clothes brush midair, I asked, "*Grand-mére*? Did Sofie send a letter?"

"No." As she said it, a small winter bird landed on the stone fence outside the window and looked directly at me; it made me wonder if the bird had told *Grand-mére* about their arrival.

Shoving her paddle back into the water, she continued, "We need to get the small trunk from under the eaves and wash those things before you leave."

I knew the trunk but had never opened it. Eugénie and I would often use it as a place to set a lamp when we cleaned the space. With only two small dormer windows, it was never fully light in the room in the eaves. The trunk was only about a foot high and two feet long and was so plain that there never seemed to be anything to be curious about. I could not remember anyone in my *famile* opening that box.

Grand-mére had already gone back to her task, leaving me to speculate on what was so important in that untouched trunk. I got the answer at the end of the day when I made my solitary way up the stairs. I wasn't fearful of being in that room by myself, but the silence at times felt smothering. For my entire life, there had been the rustle of fabric, hushed voices, and light steps in this room; now it was just me and whatever items needed to be washed in the dull wooden box.

I was no longer worried about making noise during bedtime preparations, so I pulled the wooden box near my bed and placed the lamp on the floor next to it. The box wasn't very heavy and made a low skidding sound, stopping at the hem of my quilt. The lightweight metal latch on the front swung to the side easily. When I lifted the lid, a puff of faded, dried floral scent rose to my face. Under a thin, slightly ecru-colored paper were tiny gowns, caps, and two small blankets. *Efant* clothes. I was five when Leopold was born, and I remembered the blankets. *Mame* was pregnant. The items in this box had been there for nearly ten years. After Leopold, no other *efants* came. How could we possibly go to America with an *efant*?

A few weeks later, everyone just knew that *Mame* was going to have an *efant*. It was never announced, but her clothing was already fitting differently, and she had a haggard look around her edges. I didn't remember Sofie or Marie having this look when they carried my nieces and nephews. I thought maybe it was because they didn't live in the house with us and I hadn't noticed that part of their pregnancies. As the weeks continued the weariness hung around her. It was an icy day in December when I asked her about our plans now that there was an *efant* to think of.

She stated that we would go to *Pére* in America as planned. "Many women had traveled across the ocean in this condition," she continued that she had had *efants* before. There was nothing to be concerned about. She looked at the wall next to the kitchen basin when she spoke. When she turned, she spoke again. She explained that she would need my help now more than ever. *Grand-pére* was working on finding someone who could help us with the trunk since I could not be expected to lift it myself. She said there was nothing to worry about; we would be on American soil well before she had the *efant*. Her voice said the words, but there was a tiny ring in them that didn't make me believe them. All hope of staying in Wallonia was gone. I was going to America.

Time from December through March felt both fleeting and endless. The routine of the days and the lightened workload aided in the illusion.

It was early February when money came from America with a note that Sofie had written in her unadorned script. My hands shook as I delivered the envelope to *Grand-pére*. He saw the foreign postage and handed it back to me asking that I get *Mame* and *Grand-mére* before I opened and read the missive. I found both women in the kitchen planning the weekly market list. When they saw the letter in my hand, they abandoned the list and prepared for whatever news could have come across the ocean.

Dearest Wallonia Family,

I write to you from Green Bay, Wisconsin. It took longer to get here than we expected and have wintered in this city. Antoine and Father Joseph have visited Uncle Frank and the land a few times this winter when the roads were open, and it wasn't too cold. Sister Odile, nephew John, and niece Marie Louise have been a joy to meet. Both Antoine and Father Joseph have been working at a local sawmill, which has provided the needed money. There is some extra that you should use if you run into any travel delays in America. The children were all healthy after several long weeks of illness.

Greetings to all family and if you could please share this letter with my Mama and Popa.

Good Blessings, Sofie Gaspard

My eyes tingled as I thought of Sofie writing this letter. I imagined the long hours of her caring for the *efants* while *Pére* and Antoine were at work and wondered if she had anyone to talk with who understood our language. It sounded like they hadn't seen Odile and the *efants* often.

As if she knew what I was thinking, *Grand-mére* said, "Quick, run to *Monsieur* Defaux and tell them there was news from their Sofie. I will get some *speculoos* and *café*."

I was out of breath and had nearly lost one of my *sabots* tripping up the stoop of the Defaux house. They didn't live far but it was slightly uphill, and I knew how important this message was. I knocked loudly and announced myself. *Madam* Defaux came to the door looking confused. She was all soft edges and had the same ordinary aura as her *feye*.

"*Madam* Defaux, we have a letter from your Sofie. *Grand-mére* said to come." The relief that washed over her entire body was visible, and she staggered slightly. She shocked me by shouting over her shoulder to her *ome* and was pulling her heavy plum-colored shawl from the hook near the door when he appeared. *Monsieur* Defaux was anything but ordinary. He was the tallest *ome* that I knew and likely had the thickest, shapeliest set of mustaches I would ever see. I repeated that we had news from their Sofie, and the three of us scuttled back to our house.

I am sure the neighborhood was amused watching our lopsided group rushing through the stone streets—the Defauxs were nearly running, *Madam* Defaux matching her *ome's* extra-long stride, and I felt a stitch in my side as we came to the last few paces before our door. *Madam* Defaux stopped, smoothed her hair, rearranged her shawl, brushed her hand down the front of her dress and motioned for *Monsieur* to do the same. He was smoothing his hands over his mustaches as I opened the door. *Madam* Defaux nearly knocked me over to get to *Grand-mére*.

"Marie Thérèse, tell me it's true—you have heard from our Sofie?"

"*Oyi*, come into the sitting room. You could see for yourself."

In my rush to get the Devauxs I hadn't noticed *Mame's* reaction to the news. She was in the sitting room adjusting a plate of *speculoos*. The tiredness at her edges persisted during these winter months, but this news had brightened her complexion. *Grand-mére* insisted that she sit, and she didn't argue. Even though I knew she wasn't to have the *efant* until we were in America, I worried about her being even more sick when we were traveling.

Madam Defaux explained to *Grand-mére* that she couldn't read as well as *Monsieur* Defaux, so *Grand-mére* handed the tall *ome* the letter. Almost immediately his mustaches started moving but no words were coming out of his mouth.

"Jean Baptiste, perhaps you could read it aloud to your *feume*?" *Grand-pére* had filed into the room behind our clutter and brought *Monsieur* Defaux to the present.

He read the letter three times; each time he stumbled over a different sentence, and by the third time both Defauxs had tears freely running down their flushed cheeks. This was not a house that saw many outward emotions, happy or sad, so seeing adults crying was a new experience for me. *Grand-mére* ruffled around and produced two handkerchiefs for the couple to wipe their eyes.

Monsieur Defaux collected himself and stood to his full height, and I feared he would scrape his head on the wooden-beam ceiling. "*Mèrci, mèrci, fo*r sharing. You must know how worried we were for our Sofie and her *famile*…" he trailed off.

Madam Defaux picked up the dialogue, "We heard so many terrible things about the journey—sickness, accidents, ships sinking. When we didn't hear from her…"

Grand-mére placed her hand on *Madam* Defaux's soft forearm and led the *feme* to sit in one of the chairs by the fireplace. The tears started again at the gesture. *Grand-mére* made the smallest head movement, and I saw the corner of her eyes meet *Grand-pére's*. They had been sick with worry too and because they didn't show it outwardly, I had missed the signs. The relief I felt knowing that *mi famile* had made it to Wisconsin drifted away as the reality of getting my pregnant *Mame* across the ocean and then America started building a nest of worry in my middle.

From the corner chair *Mame* fixed a hint of a smile on her face.

"I look forward to the day we will see them all. I miss seeing Antoine and Sofie's *efants* grow and learn. I am so thankful that this *efant* will have them in America." The statement surprised me since pregnancy wasn't something that was normally spoken about in front of company, but the Defauxs were extended *famile* and likely already knew that *Mame* was to have another *efant*.

The smile didn't last long and faded into the distant gaze she had started adopting in the last few weeks. When *Mame* spoke, she was neither worried nor excited about going to America. She had clearly stated it was her duty, but any hint at her actual feelings toward the move were veiled.

Just thinking about that miserable week before we left for the train made the back of my throat dry. I didn't want to leave, but I had no other choice. I had no other schemes or options. I would be on the train with my pregnant *Mame* with instructions for a Pierre to assist us with our trunk. I would never see half of *mi famile* again.

I spent several days with Eugénie to say our goodbyes. Eugénie did her very best, telling me that with the prospects in America, I could come back once everyone was established. It no longer took six months to make the journey. I wanted to believe her, but it seemed impossible. I couldn't work in the sawmill to make money for the return journey.

The final *å r'vèy* was such a pitiful sight. Both Eugénie and I had sobbed our farewells for hours in her home. It reached the point that her *ome* went to the barn as a respite from our mourning. Eugénie thought that if we did it this way we wouldn't be as much of a spectacle on the day we left. Our similar faces were so puffy from the tears, you would have thought we had both walked into a door.

The night before we left, I found it impossible to go to sleep. I rolled from side to side in the room under the eaves until before dawn. The wood knot shaped like a smiling face in the beam above the bed had been a beacon of sleep for my entire life. I tried to memorize it in case I needed a talisman for sleep in America. It didn't help me sleep that last night, so I finally got up and dressed in my childhood home for the last time. I walked slowly down the stairs and was met with *Grand-mére* sitting at the kitchen table. She was fully dressed and alone in the dark. I could make out the movement of her head when I reached the bottom.

"*Ma feye*, come and sit with *Grand-mére*."

I obeyed and sat opposite her. On the table she had laid out a small version of her simple cupboard. There were dried herbs, seeds, a piece of paper folded into a tight square and a small clay pot with a wire clamp on the lid.

"*Mi* Emilie, you need this in America. We need to find a way to get them into your trunk. I had Joseph write down all the instructions and what to use for which ailment. Your *Nonke* Frank never said if they have simples in America and I cannot send you without them." Her well-worn hand patted the top of the clay pot.

I covered *Grand-mére's* hand with mine. I promised her I would learn her recipes and that I hoped to be as gifted as she was some day.

Grand-mére brushed her free hand across her face, wiping away tears. She said, "Ah, Emilie, your heart will remain here in Wallonia, but you are needed in America." I held back the fear and anger that made my shoulders ache. I squeezed *Grand-mére's* hand harder because I wanted her to be assured that I would get *Mame* across the ocean to Wisconsin. She sighed and turned to look at me. "Emilie, this journey will make you an adult. I don't want you to be afraid. There will always be helpers if you look. When the time comes and you need help, take it."

In a voice that came out much smaller than I expected, I said, "Maybe once everyone was settled in Wisconsin, I could come back to visit you."

The tears were still gliding over the ridges of her crinkled cheeks when she pulled me close in a hug. "*Mi* Emilie, I wish this to be true."

The sun shot sparks in that way that only seems to happen in the spring as it rose that morning. *Mame* and I managed to get to the train station after the farewells. I knew that *Mame* was crying the entire way. More than once, I wanted to stop and tell her that we could just stay here, but she had set her jaw forward and marched along, acting as if she were happy to start the journey and that the tears weren't happening. At the station, a hive of people moved with confidence toward the smoking beast. I had never been on a train before. I had seen them snake through the village, but they were much bigger when you were standing next to them on the platform.

Grand-pére had hired Pierre Claes to help me get our trunk on the train. He appeared through the smoke as if he had been conjured, our trunk perched on his shoulder. His cap was askew due to the load, and he was barely taller than me. "*Madam* Gaspard?" He directed to *Mame*.

She nodded and handed him some coins. He asked us to follow him through the moving crowd to our car. The mob of bodies swallowed Pierre, and it was hard to spot him until he started shouting with authority that he was coming through. The crowd, however, started to split as he walked through with the load, and we closed the gap behind him.

When I think about the train ride, it was the loudest thing I believe I had ever heard to that point. There was a persistent smell that carried an unpleasant metallic tang. The seat was an uncomfortable plank that had been rubbed with something that made it slightly slippery while we were being bumped around the tracks.

Those of us who had never been on the train before were not sure if we were to lean into the turns or lean away from them. I'm still not exactly sure, since I tried both. Neither of them made my giddy stomach calm. If it wasn't for the beauty of the land chugging past the window I might have broken down and cried like an *efant*.

Mame spent much of the trip opening and closing her eyes and taking thin breaths. As the train swayed, she tightened her grip on the armrest until it looked like it may pop off. When we slowed to stop at another village station, *Mame* quickly got up from her seat and rushed to the door. The man in the worker's uniform did his best to get the door open, but *Mame* got sick before he could. I rushed to help her and try to clean the mess, but the man in uniform was kind and told me that I should take her out for some fresh air. As soon as we got her feet on solid earth, her color returned, and she started breathing normally.

The crowd on this platform was smaller than *Grez-Doiceau*, but you could still feel the anticipation from the passengers. As we stood at that station, puffs of mechanic-smells brushed past us, and *Mame* laid her hand on my upper arm. "Ah, Emilie, I did not imagine the movement would make me ill. I am sorry our voyage started this way. I think if I could sit by the window it would help."

I didn't want to see Mame struggle when we re-boarded the train. At our seat I took her shawl and doubled it to make a cushion for her to sit on. As she settled on the seat an older woman approached us and pressed a peppermint in my hand and then pointed at *Mame* and then at her mouth. Her last gesture was to touch her stomach.

———————————————————

I had been talking without stopping for two glasses of cordial. I had never talked this much about Wallonia and leaving. No one ever asked me about it and talking about it in the past wouldn't have made a difference. Many of our neighbors had immigration stories that were not that different than mine. If anyone did talk about their journey it was always focused on what ship you had sailed and which ports you had used to get to Wisconsin. No one had ever asked me what my first train ride was like with my pregnant *Mame*.

"Are you okay, Miss Gaspard?" Edna Mae had laid her pencil down and was stretching her fingers.

"*Oyi…* yes." I was surprised that I had slipped into Wallonian.

Edna Mae looked tired or maybe sad. "Should we have a bit to eat?"

Edna Mae flexed her writing hand. "Your *Grand-mére* —sorry, grandmother, reminds me a little of my *mor*…sorry, mother."

"Is *mor* Swedish for mother?" Edna Mae nodded. "I don't think Magdaline knows any Swedish. I will have to tell her."

"Magdaline?"

"Yes, she is the hero of this story."

Chapter 8 (August 1931 Wisconsin)

Edna Mae hadn't anticipated this assignment being so emotional. She worked hard to remain professional and to prove her place in the newsroom. The urge to sit down next to the big tree in the Gaspard front yard and cry was creeping to the surface. As she walked down the porch stairs to the car the dog called Skittles came jaunting around the corner. He escorted her to the car and after she loaded her items, she couldn't resist meeting his big round eyes. She was shocked to see that the critter was one of those who seemed to have lived and seen more than their animal life would normally allow. She lightly touched the fluff of hair that stood between his ears and then ordered him to move back from the car.

Once in the car, she thought, *how could a grandmother in Belgium she had never met make her so homesick for her own mor?*

Being on the road so much of the year, she hadn't had the luxury of seeing her parents as often as she would have liked. Her parents always seemed to understand. Edna Mae's theory was that both of her parents had left their families in Minnesota and Iowa to forge a path of their own in North Dakota. Her *far* only saw his own *far* one time after he moved. Instead, they received letters with updates about the happy and sad family events. Edna Mae had never met any of her grandparents. When her brother Anders started working for the railroad her mor started taking the train to visit her *syster* in southern Minnesota. Anders job normalized their family's ability to visit each other and move around the country, but this wasn't the case with so many of the neighbors she grew up with. Many never saw family again while they worked to create a life on the plains.

When she explained to her *mor* that she had to leave Peter, her *mor* wasn't disappointed like many women of her time might have been. Instead, her *mor* offered to contact her *syster* Lovise Olafsdotter and she arranged for her to stay with her in southern Minnesota.

A mess of vile bruises and deep aches, she arrived at her *moster* Lovise's house with her writing tools and one change of clothing. Lovise looked so much like *Mor* that she could almost imagine that she was in the warm family farmhouse tucked in the quivering pastures of North Dakota. After sleeping for nearly twenty-four hours, she joined Lovise and her husband Per in their sun-spotted kitchen. Per slid a plate of *bondkakor* cookies toward her across the wooden kitchen table that was painted in a dull red with bright flowers along the edges. Lovise filled a *Rörstrand* china cup that had come from Sweden with the family when they sailed to America. Lovise and her *mor* had split the set when their *mor* helped create their *hemgifts* for future marriages, each girl taking four cups and small plates for their small marriage chests. In her *mor's* home, the use of the *Rörstrand* china signaled the arrival of an extra special guest. The Prussian blue flowers and scrolls that decorated the cream-colored cup, thinned through her tears when she picked it up and drank the first of the hot, thick black coffee.

As the rich liquid slid through her body, the tears burst from her eyes at the kindness. The fear and anxiety of the last year couldn't be held back any longer. Shaking, she picked up the closest cookie and nibbled at the crisp golden end. The buttery almond smell enveloped her like a memory hug. Lovise and Per didn't push her to talk. Her battered face and the fact that her children hadn't escaped with her spoke more than words. *Mor* had probably explained the details of her exit after their frantic phone call.

Being the daughter to a woman who dared to tame the sod without a husband in North Dakota, Edna Mae felt like a failure. *Mor* was a pioneer in so many ways. She had worked her land and then only changed her surname on the land deed when she married. The norm at the time would have been to change it to her husband's full name. It never seemed to bother *Far* that *Mor* wasn't like the other women in the county. They worked as a team without separating chores into women's or men's work. *Mor* milked cows and plowed, *Far* made the best pancakes. When she chose to be a writer and not marry after high school, neither were surprised. Instead, they made sure she knew she could use their home as a base. It was rarely loud or angry in her childhood home. How had she gotten so out of the balance of stability her parents had created?

Her parents assumed that Edna Mae and Peter were married. They were not. When she asked Peter if they should get married since they had a baby on the way, he flatly refused. Instead, he said that she could tell people they were married, but they would not be going to a church or courthouse. She knew not to push him on the matter of marriage, but by ignoring it, she also ignored any action that might have protected her from Peter's unpredictability and abuse in the future.

After that discussion, Peter took a job at a local service station, and she continued writing under a pen name. The newspaper feared that if subscribers discovered she was a pregnant, unmarried woman, they might cancel their subscription—or worse the advertisers might pull their ads. She needed to continue working. Peter claimed he was saving his weekly pay to move to California and buy property. So, she paid for the household expenses with the money she made writing.

Peter did not hit her again while she was pregnant with William. He shouted and grew angry, but he always left the tiny apartment before things escalated. When the baby arrived, he was a purple-red color all over with a set of lungs to match, but overall, extremely healthy. Peter said nothing the first time he saw his son. She was thrilled with the boy she called William. She had picked the name for the writer and printmaker William Blake. They went back to the tiny apartment where Edna Mae learned how to mother an infant. She worked with her editor so she could continue working. She was willing to take any work, and the newspaper courier would deliver a variety of jobs from proofreading to fact-checking. These could be done with William at the local library. As they built a normal cadence, some more writing projects were added that she could manage from the apartment.

Edna Mae loved William fiercely but noticed early that while he looked more like her side of the family with light eyes and light brown hair, he had a quick temper like his father. As he was learning to walk, he would get overly frustrated when he didn't master the steps on the first try. Many toddlers would quickly stand again and try to get it right. William dissolved into anger, tugging at his clothing and pulling at his hair. He was two when she realized she was pregnant again. Peter hadn't exactly been easy to live with, but the abuse was carefully kept from their son's eyes and was mostly verbal. Peter often reminded her that she couldn't survive without him. Even though she was earning the money that was keeping them in the apartment, warm and fed. She suspected that any money Peter was making at the station wasn't being saved for a future in California. It was more likely being spent in local taverns.

It was two weeks before Catherine was born when Peter came home swinging. He had been fired from the service station and hadn't come home for five days. On the third day of his absence, she had walked to the station with her giant belly and William in the pram and found out about the job loss. The owner handed her Peter's last paycheck and said he hadn't seen him since two days before. Her *Mor's* voice popped into her head, cautioning her to save for hard times. She walked directly to the newspaper from the station and asked her boss to keep the money safe.

When Peter burst into the apartment late the fifth night, he slammed the door open so hard the upstairs neighbor banged on the floor with their cane. He reeked of hard alcohol and *Coty L'Aimant* perfume, wearing only his undershirt and trousers. He stumbled around the apartment, and alternated yanking at his ragged hair and the items from the drawers of the dresser and hangers in the closet. When she asked what he was doing, he spun faster than she thought a drunk man could and felt the back of his hand connect with her upper cheek. Her first instinct was to shove William into the closet and protect her pregnant middle. Peter stood before her, listing to one side, with his eyes blazing but unfocused. He raised his hand to hit her again but when he swung, he was too unsteady to connect with the same force. His hand grazed her temple. On reflex, she scrambled to the floor where William was watching the scene with a confused expression.

She clutched blindly at the boy, then it was as if some unseen switch had been flipped. Peter seemed to collect himself long enough to tell her that "this" was over. He had been seeing another woman for the last year and that she could stay here at the apartment, but he wasn't going to support her or the children anymore.

Stunned at how abruptly he stated what she had suspected, she shook her head, trying to force her brain to form the right comeback. She finally stuttered that she would leave and would take the children. Fury flushed his face with red, that deepened quickly to purple. He screamed and weaved and told her the only way she would leave was in a coffin. Then he slammed the door so hard the lights flickered, and the neighbor's cane banged even louder from above.

If only this had been the end.

Once sober, Peter showed up at the hospital the day she gave birth to Catherine. He acted like a normal father. He took William with him to the waiting room and visited each day during her recovery. She knew this wouldn't last and sensed the nurses suspected something wasn't right. It had been the doctor who had alerted Peter that she was in labor.

The day she was released from the hospital Peter arrived, with William in tow and made a show of paying the bill. She had no idea where he had gotten the money. She had been hiding her earnings in an account at the bank. By the time she reached the front door with Catherine in her arms, only William stood in the waiting room. The poor little boy spun around slowly, looking for his father. They waited by the door for a few minutes, but she knew he wasn't taking her home. They walked the few blocks to the apartment and settled into life with just the three of them. Using the money from Peter's last paycheck and her earnings from the newspaper, she did her best with the two children in the little apartment where it had all started. Peter stayed away.

Catherine was an easy baby, it seemed like she understood that her mother needed her to be that way. William had grown more prone to temper once he realized his mother wasn't his alone. One afternoon, after she had finally gotten both children down for a nap, she sat to work on an assignment for the paper. The door flew open, sending papers to the floor. Peter—unshaven and drunk—stormed in. He seized her by the shoulders and lifted her from the chair so that her shoes barely brushed the floor. In a flash, he bashed her against the wall. The pain didn't even register. Her only thought was how to reach the bedroom and to protect the children.

Time jumped around as he continued to bang her head against the wall. When he tired of that he decided to punch her in her middle and finally kicked her in the face while she lay next to the table, where her writing materials bounced around with each blow. A black soup slipped over her eyes that she couldn't fight.

She came to with the sound of voices in the hall. Her face was pressed to the cool linoleum floor, and she immediately felt afraid to move knowing the pain and stiffness that was to come. Opening the one eye that wasn't swollen shut, she saw that the apartment door was wide open. She pushed herself onto her side and terror hit her like a bus: her children had been left unattended, and she had no idea how long it had been. Using every bit of mental strength, she forced herself to focus on the open door while everything else swam around the room. She could feel the beginnings of her stomach lurching but gulped air to avoid being sick. Summoning some form of superhuman strength, she pushed up to her knees, then grabbed the edge of the table and she flipped one foot then the other under her, standing bent over the table. The short eight steps to the bedroom took too long. It was empty. No William, no baby Catherine, no pram. There were only the wooden blocks that William played with endlessly that told anyone there had been children there.

The volume of panic surpassed any sort of feeling of pain. She fumbled out of the apartment and started running down the block toward the police station. She had walked past the gray-stone building nearly every day but had never been inside. She knew that someone from the newspaper crime beat might be in there, but she had to find her children. Her nose wouldn't stop running no matter how many times she ran the back of her hand past it, and the side of her head that had been introduced to the wall over and over again, was swelling and making her feel unbalanced.

Pushing through the door, she nearly stumbled over her own feet on the polished travertine floor. Looking down, she noticed for the first time that she had left the apartment in her stockings, and no shoes. The stockings now had her toes poking through the ends, and there was a run that snaked up her leg to below her skirt hem.

The building had recently been completed and the art deco woodwork still smelled of varnish. She pulled her hand again to her face and wiped away a mix of blood, snot, and tears. On the left was a window with an officer. She walked to the window while trying to pull the hysteria out of her voice. She steadied herself and spoke into the metal circle, her words coming out pinched and slurred at the same time. She tried to explain that she needed help getting her children. Everything hurt and she felt like she could just slide to the floor and sleep.

The gray-haired officer on the other side of the glass shifted in his chair, his uniform gaping to reveal chest hair and a white undershirt. The sight distracted her. He started to reply to her through the metal circle that made his voice sound far away. She couldn't piece together what he was saying. Watching his lips move, he swore and motioned for the woman sitting behind the desk to help him. Bustling, she stood up and pulled the horn-rimmed glasses she wore on a chain around her neck, up to her face. Her irritation with the officer was clear as she pulled a pencil out of her tightly curled hair and used it to push the white button on the counter under the metal circle.

Now at full volume, Edna Mae jumped as the woman said, "Bob, I have shown you twenty times. You need to press the button before you talk to the visitors." She looked up at Edna Mae with a look of sadness.

Bob brushed her off, and she scuttled back to her desk, replacing the pencil in her hair. "Ma'am, your husband will probably be home for dinner. You need to go home and make sure you have something on the table."

He seemed proud of his response and puffed his barrel chest, which stretched the shirt to its limit. She reached up and rubbed the eye that was less swollen, trying hard to pull her focus from the buttons ready to flee the blue cloth. She had heard about other women in this situation from the newsroom's crime writers, but for some reason, she didn't think it could happen to her. After several minutes of begging the officer for help, she turned to the opposite wall to decide what she could do next. The wall had a framed lithograph of a gray-haired man in round spectacles. She searched the gray face for guidance, but he only offered a silent, thin-lipped smile.

With his hand still on the talk button, she heard Bob say "Doris, I need to hit the head. Watch the window."

Fighting to think clearly, she realized that the cold from the floor had seeped into her stockinged feet. Her head throbbed with her heartbeat, her stomach hurt, and she wanted to double over to relieve it. There was no one she could talk to. She didn't want the paper to find out. She needed that job to support her children.

Turning from the lithograph, she hadn't noticed that Doris had come out to the hallway. She hissed, "Honey, where do you live?"

Sniffling, she replied, "The Stanford Arms."

Doris handed her a handkerchief, and said in a low voice, "Go home. I'll come to your apartment in thirty minutes. If you want to meet me downstairs, we could get you to a phone to call someone."

This was her only option. The police didn't consider her children being taken by their abusive father a problem, never mind that she looked like she had been pushed in front of an oncoming train. Spousal abuse was considered a private matter, between husband and wife. The wife likely deserved it, even if she wasn't legally the wife. No one was going to step between that unit. Except Doris.

And Doris did.

As promised, Doris came down the block toward The Stanford Arms apartments exactly thirty-five minutes after Edna Mae had left the police station. When she returned to the apartment, she put on her shoes, grabbed her purse, and did her best to avoid looking at the stack of toy blocks left by William. She didn't dare look at her face in the bathroom mirror. Peter had left a pack of cigarettes on the kitchen table, and she decided that she needed something to calm her nerves and ease the throbbing, while she waited for Doris on the front stoop.

The nicotine had hit about the same time that Doris reached her building. Doris was a bottle-blond with an elaborate curling hairdo. She wore a beige dress that featured what looked like a handmade lace collar pinned with a sizable cameo pin. She smelled like powdery perfume, but not a fragrance that was currently popular.

Doris plopped down on the stoop next to Edna Mae and pointed at the cigarette. "You got another one of those?"

Her hand shook as she unfurled the packet and let Doris take one. The older woman placed the cylinder between her dark, nearly orange lipstick-laced lips, and struck the match on the step. After a deep drag, she let out a weighted sigh.

"He come back?"

"No."

"Do you know where he is?"

"No."

"Do either of you have family in the area?"

"No."

An even heavier sigh pushed discarded smoke from her mouth. "Well, we need to get you cleaned up and somewhere safe. You may not want to hear this, but he may not come back. It happens. And the law wasn't going to be on your side. Bastards like the man who did this to you rarely get their due."

Edna Mae knew this was true. There were whispered stories of the fates of abused women. Even if people knew about the abuse, there were very few options that helped the woman. If she was to get away, she would likely need to relocate for any hope of avoiding judgement from the community. Finding employment would have been extremely hard, leaving many stranded, and many women stayed in abusive situations. Some of these women died at the hands of their abuser. Edna Mae had read the snips of stories in papers hinting at the real cause of a woman's death. More often, she knew they left no trace.

Doris took charge. She stood up and pulled Edna Mae to her feet. "Let's get some of your things. You can come to my house to get cleaned up. We have a phone so you can call someone, maybe your parents?"

This time, Edna Mae sighed. Her parents didn't have a phone yet, but their neighbor Mr. Severson did, and her mother had written to her with the number in case she ever needed it. She explained this to Doris as they walked down the block, the small, packed bag in between the women.

"Well, when you get to my place, you can call Mr. Severson and have him fetch your mother or father. That will give you time to get cleaned up while you wait."

This was the calm thinking that Edna Mae had craved since the first blow.

Doris lived on the top floor of a chocolate-brown two-family house. She lived there with her husband. When she swung the door open, they were met with an eclectic mix of old furniture mixed with the current trendy Art Deco décor. Doris had tossed her pocketbook and Edna Mae's bag on the table and made a sleek black panther vase jump on the quarter-sawn oak table. In the corner, an elaborate birdcage held two small blue and snow-white Budgies. The birds were thrilled to see Doris. She had picked up the black phone receiver and cradled it by her neck while she waited for the operator. With her free hands, she fed the birds to reduce their chirping.

Edna Mae had time to wash, change her clothes, and throw away the ruined stockings before the black phone rang.

Doris answered, "Yes, she is here. Yes, right here."

Edna Mae sat down at the telephone table and pulled the receiver to her ear. Doris had busied herself wetting a towel in cool water to place on Edna Mae's swollen face.

Edna Mae started sobbing and was all but blubbering what had happened into the handset. On the other end, *Mor* was quiet through the entire story. When Edna Mae had nothing more to tell, her *Mor* said, "*Min dotter, försök att sluta gråta. Vi kommer att lösa det här problemet.*" '*My daughter, try to stop crying. We would solve this issue.*' No one had spoken Swedish to her for so long. It felt like the tiny coos that baby Catherine would deliver once she was fed.

She needed to get to William and Catherine.

Within a few hours *Mor* had arranged for her to stay with her *moster* Lovise and *farbror* Per just south of Minneapolis. Edna Mae's brother, Anders, worked for the railroad and would come to her next week. It was *Mor* who told her she should get the paperwork for a divorce. She didn't tell her that it wasn't necessary.

Back in 1931, Edna Mae sat by the window in her hotel room watching the foot traffic below as it whirred in the background. She needed to write to Doris. They had kept in touch, with Doris calling Lovise and Per's house each week. The conversations were extremely short and sometimes she only spoke to whoever answered the phone.

"Was Edna Mae doing okay?"

When she got the answer, the expensive long-distance call would end. Doris had been her eyes in Minneapolis. Unfortunately, Peter seemed to have disappeared.

She blinked the whir out the window into focus.

Chapter 9 (Spring 1871 At Sea)

We made it to the pier in Antwerp, and *Mame* hadn't been sick again. There was a *gamin* named Jules Peeters whom we were to meet on our sailing day, and he would help us with the trunk. Before that, we needed to go to a market and get supplies. We were to sail from Antwerp to England where we would board a larger vessel that would take us to America. Each passenger was expected to provide their own provisions including plates, cups, flatware, and linens for the journey. We had been advised to purchase familiar food items if we could, since the food served on the ships would not be our usual diet.

Grand-pére had spoken to a local man who had made the trip and returned to Belgium after three years. He provided many instructions on where to buy things and what was going to be needed. *Grand-pére* had tested me daily on the names of the men who would help us with our trunk and items that I was going to need to buy for both sailing legs. I could see *Grand-pére* was pleased when I recited back what he had asked me to learn.

Antwerp was an enormous city compared to *Grez-Doiceau*. In 1871, more than 15,000 people lived in Antwerp. From the 1850s through the 1930s, more than three million people would have boarded vessels in that city and traveled to America. Antwerp was a highly traveled port for German, Swiss, and Belgian emigrants. The crowd at the pier held the same anxious energy. I was relieved that there were people in this swarm who spoke Walloon. Compared to the next port in England where there was no guarantee that someone would understand us, Antwerp felt easier.

It rained while we boarded the ship, intensifying the briny smell of unfamiliar water. Relentless sea birds flew overhead, swooping occasionally for bits of fish. An *ome* who looked to be as tall as he was wide pushed his way through the crowd calling for "*Madam Gaspard.*" Jules would be helping us with our trunk and had somehow found us in the waves of people. He was surprisingly quick, and darted back and forth between groups of passengers, as his *sabots* knocked on the wooden plank as he went. He spoke both Dutch and Walloon, which I assume was to increase how much money he could make at the dock. When it was our turn, he lifted the larger trunk with our smaller provisions crate on top making his upper half invisible. Without hesitation he quickly moved to the area where this cargo was being loaded. I realized after he put the load down that he was wearing multiple layers of clothing making him stockier than he was. I was about to say *mèrci,* but he had already run down the pier.

Mame stood on the dock with her face turned to the south and east. She wore her best dress, which had been let out to accommodate the *efant. Grand-pére* had insisted that we both wear our leather boots and not our *sabots.* He had heard of one man who had fallen into the sea before sailing because his *sabot* had slipped on the wet boards. *Mame's* ankles were quite swollen from our train travel, but we managed to get her boots on with loosened laces. I touched her shoulder when it was our turn to board the ship. She turned slightly and her face was so incredibly sad that I gasped.

"Emilie," she stuttered. "Ah, *ma feye.* Remember this with me."

I stood with her for a moment. This town and pier were not my home. I had left my home before, on a train ride. This was the first time *Mame* realized it was forever. I touched her shoulder again and we walked toward the next leg of the journey.

Compared to what lay ahead, this first sailing leg was uneventful. The different languages spoken slipped together in my head and created one foreign tongue. We were surrounded by people from all of Europe all transferring in England for America. You didn't need to speak all their languages to understand the underlying hope and fear. Aside from the people working on the ships, there couldn't have been many people who had made the journey before because you could feel the anxiety as it rippled through the crowd with each lap of the water against the dock and each shout from someone who seemed to be in authority.

I was grateful for the lessons with *Grand-pére*. The picture he had painted of our accommodations was so grim that, when we finally arrived below deck, I was relieved to find anything other than a bed of needles to sleep on. The ceilings were low, and the smells were assaulting, but it wasn't the prison I had created in my head. We would be on this boat for about two days—we would manage.

I noticed Magdaline on the docks in England, waiting for the ship that would take us to America. She stood by herself, with her eyes scanning the landscape. Her hair was neither red nor yellow, but something in between and was twisted into plaits and wrapped around the back of her head. Fixed to the back of this braided head was the largest red bow I had ever seen in my life. The ends of the bow stuck out from her face like wings. I couldn't study her for long because we needed to find a man named Charles Smythe who was going to assist with our trunks.

This port was even larger than Antwerp, with several ships waiting to sail. The sheer number of people all speaking their native languages made my mind race. We stood on the pier looking around and I hoped to latch on to someone who could help me make sense of what we needed to do next. By chance we found Charles. He spoke in what I assumed was English, and it didn't seem to bother him that I neither understood nor could reply. He had quickly secured our items and completed the transaction of getting us on the ship with hand gestures. His signal for paperwork was to point his finger into the palm of his other hand, and it took him gesturing toward other passenger's documents for me to understand. I wondered if Charles was what *Grand-mére* had meant when she spoke of helpers.

This ship felt newer—or at least it smelled newer—than the ship from Antwerp. Our berths were wooden beds stacked upon each other, with a board rail on the edge to keep us in place at night when the ship rocked. In each alcove there were four of these beds, with a basin between and a walkway large enough to fit one woman at a time. There was a small box on the wall above the foot of each berth that provided space for personal items. There were no doors on the alcoves, so you could see across the main hall into the alcove opposite. Once the items we needed daily were unpacked, the large trunk was moved to the storage area. The next task was determining where our plates, cups, and cutlery were to be stored. One of the ship's employees spoke French and had explained that we would need to wait until all the third-class passengers were boarded.

I was shocked to see *Mame* seated on the floor next to the basin. She looked exhausted. Ladies didn't sit on the floor of their own home. *Mame* sitting on the floor of a boat was as unusual as seeing a flying pig with a group of wild geese. As worried as I was about *Mame* sitting on the floor, I was curious about the woman with the red bow. The more women that filtered in the space, the louder it became. Women and young children were housed together, while men and boys were in separate berths. Women buzzed around the tight spaces, tucking linens into beds and scolding small children when they strayed. The women were so busy preparing their tiny temporary homes, that I worried we might miss our next set of instructions. Hovering over everyone's heads was a fog of anticipation mixed with uneasiness. I don't remember seeing any of the women smiling with delight or excitement. I guessed that was because the adult women knew that while it may be stated that men were building America, women were equally responsible for creating a livable society, and the volume of work that was ahead did nothing to quiet the nerves of those crossing a vast ocean.

The women who claimed the beds in our alcove appeared that they knew each other. One was tall and rail-thin with sunken cheeks and black hair that shone even in the dim light. The other was so short she might have been mistaken for a child if her hair hadn't been streaked with gray and her face telling a different tale. They both wore scarves tied around their heads and thick black woolen dresses that looked so stiff I wondered how they managed to sit. They spoke to each other rapidly in their native language that I couldn't place. Occasionally, they paused and looked my way and smiled.

The woman with the large bow had removed it, replacing it with a day cap. Stepping into the hall between alcoves, she called out to both groups, "*Sprichst du Deutsch? Parles-tu français?* Speak English, you?"

I recognized the question in French. While Walloon was its own language, it was quite like French and, at times, would seem to be the formal equivalent of Walloon.

"*Oyi on m'lome* Emilie." I replied, pointing at myself, hoping she would understand. I knew, I wanted to know this young woman with the bow.

"Ehhh, *es m'lome, um, mon nom est* Magdaline." She paused to see if I understood. I nodded and she continued, *"ich heiße* Magdaline."

One of the women in her alcove nodded in recognition of the third language. This woman was very wrinkled and seemed fragile yet stout at the same time. She was clutching a piece of lace with a string of wooden beads that I assumed was a rosary. Magdaline turned to the women in our alcove, and then the other women in theirs, to see if there was any understanding. The five women just smiled, seeming not to understand.

Mame roused herself from the floor and said, *"M'lome Madame Gaspard."*

It was hard to follow, but it seemed that Magdaline knew French and German, was learning English, and, at one point, *Mame* noted she spoke some Latin to a timid-looking woman with a small baby in her arms. The baby had the most beautiful lace bonnet on its head. I had never seen another one like it and sometimes wondered if that baby still kept the tiny hat tucked in a memory chest.

Our first evening meal on the ship was a lesson in patience. We had gone to the deck to watch the ship leave the port, and by the time we returned each woman needed to get in line to cook for her family. With the many different languages, it was hard to manage how and where to wait in the line. After we stood for nearly an hour, *Mame* and I decided to dine on bread and get to the line earlier in the morning. It was nearly impossible to be calm enough to sleep that first night. There was maybe one woman who slept that night. You heard her heavy breathing—not quite snoring—coming from down the row. I stared into the dark ceiling while the boat swayed. Occasionally someone would rise and become ill from the motion, but then everyone would fall back into the sleepless din.

The next morning, Magdaline's gift with languages was recognized. People often stopped her to ask for help in understanding what was happening. After gesturing and pointing, she determined that the tall, thin woman in our berth was Beata, and the short woman was Dorota, and she believed they were sisters from Poland. Magdaline had learned that the woman who spoke German was *Madam* or *Frau* Schweister, and she was traveling with her family of all nearly grown boys. The three women who didn't seem to understand French, Walloon, German, or English were probably Bohemian. At the time, Magdaline tried to just learn their names, and we hadn't guessed that they were from that part of the world. Later, after meeting Bohemian neighbors in Wisconsin, we realized their language and dress were similar. Each of the women at the time caught on to the pointing, and through thick accents we learned that their names were Adela, Dominika and Eliska. I repeated all these women's names over and over in my head while I lay awake that next night… Magdaline, *Frau* Schweister, Beata, Dorota, Adela, Dominika, Eliska… over and over, but still, I didn't sleep.

As soon as the first woman rose from bed, nearly all the others followed each morning. Likely they felt as tired as me, but you could feel the determination in their movements. We were going to make sense of this new day and its schedule, when I noticed that *Mame* hadn't gotten dressed yet.

"Emilie, I think the rolling of the boat was making me ill again. Could you help me? Perhaps walking and sitting at the table would help."

She struggled a bit to get out of the berth and made an unusual peep sound when she stood up. She immediately grabbed her back and leaned more heavily on my arm with her other hand.

"*Mame*! Are you okay? What was it?"

"Oh, just my age showing—and all of the travel."

While the women still ate on one side of the room and the men on the other, families were able to connect and plan for the day. We were permitted to go above deck if the weather was fair. I felt my skin tingling at the thought of getting out of the stuffy interior and seeing a horizon line. I had not been outside since the day we set sail. I hadn't felt seasick, but even during breakfast there were many people who had to run from the wooden benches in the dining room multiple times to relieve their rolling stomachs.

We took turns and cleaned our items and then retreated to the alcove. With Magdaline leading the way, we gathered shawls and head coverings with the goal of fresh air on the upper deck. The wind gusted and set the carefully placed garments askew the minute we stepped out into the morning sun. The air wasn't exactly fresh but was a welcomed change from the mix of clothing and bodies in various states of cleanliness below deck. The birds that had swirled around the boat when we left the pier were gone, and I wasn't exactly sure which way to look for land. It seemed amazing to me that we had been on the boat for only a short period of time and already were so far away from firm soil. The water met the sky with no telltale brown or green break.

Family groups quickly formed in the pockets of space on the deck. That morning the children seemed eager to play with each other, but shy at the same time. Some clung to their parents with wide eyes, some even stood motionless next to their families, openly staring at the youngsters in their viewing area. I wondered how my nieces Adele and Rosilia had reacted. They were not normally shy, but perhaps the experience that brought us to this point caused all of us to react out of our norm.

I cannot tell you the exact times we fulfilled our duties of cleaning, washing, and eating, but I could recall the image of those children on deck with clarity down to the red color of the buttons on their clothing. Our lives were dictated by the sun, stars, and the ship's hands.

By the third day at sea everyone had settled into a pattern of activity. *Mame* did not feel well much of the day, and by the fourth she had chosen to stay in our berth during our deck visit. I was concerned, but her color seemed better than it had in the past weeks, and she had assured me it was likely due to the constant motion of the floor beneath her feet. When *Frau* Schweister, Magdaline, and I returned to the berth to get ready for the midday meal that day, we heard shouting before we realized it was Beata kneeling next to *Mame* on the floor of our berth.

Tipping her dark red face up to mine, *Mame* said ever so calmly, "Emilie, the baby was coming now."

Beata was gesturing frantically, trying to get someone to understand her rapid speech, but I didn't understand a word she said. When *Frau* Schweister saw the dark stain on *Mame's* skirt and the small puddle on the floor next to her, she understood. She immediately began shouting orders to Magdaline in German. Magdaline launched into a flurry of translation to French.

Frau Schweister needed hot water, linens, and someone needed to alert the captain that a baby was going to be born. She kept injecting orders to Magdaline, and had jostled Beata to the side, and then helped *Mame* to her feet. In her staccato accent, *Frau* Schweister smoothed the edges as much as she could in her German language and said softly *"jetzt gehen wir,"* (*now we go*). *Mame* nodded as if she understood perfectly. Magdaline translated *"Maintenant nous marchons"* (*now we walk*), which I knew meant they were going to walk.

This seemed completely wrong to me. Why when a woman was to have a baby, would you make her walk around? Shouldn't she be tucked into her berth where she might be more comfortable? I whispered my worry to Magdaline while we gathered extra linens, but she assured me that her own mother had also walked when her younger siblings were born. She also told me that it could take a long time before the baby arrived.

I would never forget how that entire wing of females came together for this birth. *Frau* Schweister assigned other German speaking women to take turns walking with *Mame*. One of these women calmly gave instructions to a lovely young girl who had blond curls tied together around the back of her head. The girl quickly gathered up all the small children and took them to the far end to entertain them. Her high, crystalline voice could be heard carrying laughter and song as she entertained the children who didn't seem bothered that they didn't understand the words. Beata and a group of women quickly worked together to gather a large pile of linens, and a woman from England alerted the ship's crew.

Mame was as calm as I supposed one could be in this situation. After walking for a few lengths, she would then sit on a box and breathe heavily. *Frau* Schweister talked to her as if she could understand and, at times, I think she really did. Years later, Magdaline and I both thought that perhaps the act of childbirth was a language of its own and these two women knew that language from past births.

For those of us assisting in the labor, there were minutes of frantic passing of cool linens, followed by abrupt pauses where *Mame* would stop walking, or talking, which felt like eons. Very late into the evening, she rested on her bed. *Frau* Schweister moved the box so I could sit next to her. The other women busied themselves with getting ready for the next few hours. *Mame* was resting her eyes and reached for my hand.

"*Mi* Emilie, very soon this baby will be here. It's a bit early, but there shouldn't be anything to worry about. I feel strong and this baby feels strong. When we get to New York we may need to stay a bit longer so I can rest for the next leg of the journey. We will be fine together." I just nodded. *Mame* knew best about *efants*, and we had the extra money that was to help get us to Wisconsin if we had delays.

I had fallen asleep with my head resting on the lower ridge of the top berth when *Mame* nudged me and told me that it was time. *Frau* Schweister had also taken the time to nap propped on the second box at the end of *Mame's* bed. I quickly got to my feet and shuffled to the very back of the alcove. *Frau* Schweister called for Magdaline, who joined us.

Frau Schweister was ready and explained to Magdaline that she needed to tell *Mame* that *drücken* meant 'push' and *stoppen* meant 'stop.' *Mame* reached out her hands to both Magdaline and *Frau* Schweister and repeated, "Mèrci, *ine camarådes*," 'Thank you, my friends.' As soon as she released their hands, her face changed to the most determined look I have ever seen on anyone. She locked eyes with *Frau* Schweister, and they both nodded at the same time.

From my vantage point at the top of *Mame's* head I watched her entire face turn crimson. As she expelled the breath she was holding, she grabbed the sides of the berth and pushed. *Frau* Schweister was at her feet and ordered her to *drücken* again. Once again, with her chin on her chest she released the breath with a giant push and *Frau* Schweister shouted *"Er ist hier."* 'He's here.' Magdaline had also been holding her breath, and it came out in a whoosh as she explained that the baby was here.

Frau Schweister held up an impossibly small form that was bluish with a white film. She hooked her finger in his mouth and scooped it out. She then flipped the *efant* over and held his lower face in her one hand and body on her forearm and gave his back a solid thump. On cue, a squall sounded from the tiny mouth to which *Frau* Schweister easily flipped him back over and cleaned his nostrils. One of the other German women stood ready with a linen she had been sitting on to keep warm. Her gnarled hands folded the now angry *efant* into the linen so quickly it was like watching her knead bread. She brought the bundle to the head of the bed so *Mame* could see him. *Mame* touched her fingers to her lips, kissed them and then touched his forehead. He scrunched his brow at this motion and the German woman bustled off with my new *fré*. I didn't have time to wonder where he was going. *Frau* Schweister gave *Mame* instructions in German again and they clutched each other's hands and allowed tears to stream down their faces.

I had no idea there was another part to having a baby and was shocked when *Frau* Schweister asked for a basin or bucket. Magdaline quickly grabbed the metal basin that one of the women helpers had ready. It was at least a quarter of an hour later, when what *Frau* Schweister called the *mutterkuchen* was unceremoniously dropped into the waiting basin. The helper shuttled away the mass as the German woman with gnarled fingers reappeared, holding my now cleaned *fré* wrapped tightly. She handed him to me, and it felt like he weighed less than a woolen sock. If he hadn't squirmed, I would have thought he wasn't real. When she handed him to me, she started speaking German. I shook my head but refused to take my eyes off the tiny face in the blanket.

Magdaline was shuffled back into our small area to help translate.

"*Frau* Schweister wants to know when your mother was due to have the baby. She says he is very small, and she is worried about keeping him warm." Magdaline looked at the triangle formed by me, *Frau* Schweister, and the baby.

"*Mame* wasn't supposed to have the *efant* until we were in America."

After translating, to *Frau* Schweister she quickly translated back: "We must be very diligent about keeping him very warm and feeding him as much as he would take. Babies born early could have problems with these things. She said not to worry, she would help. And Helga had two babies born early, so she knows." Helga was the woman with the gnarled fingers who had helped clean my brother.

I welcomed her knowledge. By the minute I realized that I knew nothing about caring for an *efant* or a *famile*. I nodded my thanks and turned my attention to *Mame* whose color had returned to a more normal shade and whose eyelids drooped. *Frau* Schweister helped her clean herself and the berth, piling all the linen outside our alcove where others snatched them as quickly as she set them down. My gratitude for these women became unmanageable and slipped to the surface. I remember swaying on my feet slightly, as my chin shook. Magdaline placed her arm around my shoulder to stop the unnatural sway and snuck a look at the baby in my arms.

Mame named him Atlantique Guillaume. For two days, and one night, I and the group of helpers kept him warm and fed and cared for *Mame*. On the second night, I had fallen asleep seated on the floor next to *Mame's* berth with my forehead resting on my fist. I dreamed of *Grand-mére*. We were in the kitchen, and she was trying to tell me something, but I couldn't understand. The dream was jerked away when a hand shook my shoulder.

Coming out from the veil of sleep I tried to focus on the words coming out of Helga's mouth, but they were too fast, too foreign. A half-asleep Magdaline burst into the area. She shouted for someone to get the ship's medic. *Mame* had developed a fever at some point in the night without any of us noticing. When Helga woke me, *Mame* could no longer respond or fully wake. It took the ship medic forever to reach the berth, and when he did, he announced that she needed rest and broth. A few short hours later she stopped breathing.

After the moments of shock ebbed, I could hear crying all around us. Magdaline, who cried freely, managed to get the box for me to sit on. *Mame* lay there in her berth with a clear expression, and I remember thinking she looked young and carefree, not the stressed and slightly ill *Mame* of the last two weeks.

Because of where we were along the voyage, there was no choice but to bury her at sea. I had been to funerals before, but there was nothing in my short life compared to standing on a wind-breached ship deck and watching unknown ship hands add weight to the white-wrapped form that was my dead mother. The gale bit into the side of my head and immediately made my earache. A group of women stood on the deck behind me, swatting at bonnet ribbons and openly crying as she was slowly tipped over the railing. It was too loud to hear the body hit the water, but after a few minutes we could see the white form as it bobbed and slowly slipped below the choppy surface.

Chapter 10 (August 1931 Wisconsin
Edna Mae's Journal)

Today Emilie Gaspard told me the story of her mother passing on the ship to America. I could feel my own losses slamming at my heart, threatening to send me reeling into a black hole. Emilie noticed and tried to console me by saying that she was not the first person to lose someone on the ship crossing to America or to childbirth. When she didn't meet my eyes, I knew it was a mechanism she had allowed herself to continue moving forward in the world.

Edna Mae placed her pencil on the table and started massaging her fingers. Staring into the space behind Emilie's head, she tried to make sense of a teenage girl burying her mother at sea and having a premature baby to care for when there were still thousands of miles of travel. She remembered those first few weeks with her own babies, and a wave of tenderness fell over her for Emilie. Her brother Anders's youngest daughter had been born early, and her *Mor* and his mother-in-law had taken turns for months after her arrival helping the family while he was away for work.

"It's getting late, do you want to stay for supper?"

She was startled back from the ship and the young girl Emilie. "Thank you, but I need to go to the hotel and do some more work."

Emilie nodded and started picking at an invisible lint on the tablecloth. "Perhaps another time."

Edna Mae nodded and carried her glass into the kitchen. The stifling heat of the room made her feel grateful to get into the car and drive with the windows down. The dust was preferred to the damp August heat.

When she pulled her car to the curb next to the hotel in Algoma, the lake was taut, and its color was so like the sky you had to squint to determine the horizon line. When she arrived, it was easily a welcomed five degrees cooler in Algoma. She had no problem looking at the lake, but the thought of ever setting foot in a boat on a body of water made her clench her teeth.

The mess of Peter taking the children had played out for months and ended in the loneliest way. It was difficult to function normally knowing that her children were being cared for by people who would now be their parents. She had found out through Doris, who had somehow learned that her children had been adopted to two different families. Doris thought one of the families was in South Dakota and one in Minnesota, but she wasn't sure. Since Edna Mae and Peter weren't married, there were no court records, and there were even less questions asked by the families who now had her babies. Doris promised that she would share any additional information she ever received, but Peter hadn't left a paper trail that made it easy. Of course, the few people who knew what had happened to her would try to fill the silence that ate the air from the room in giant gulps with platitudes like, "it's maybe for the best, if he was that bad," or "they were young, they won't know any difference as they grow up." There were other versions of these vile expressions, and she learned to completely close her ears to them and wait for the visual cues that the well-wisher's statement was done.

She took a role as a traveling newspaper employee days after learning of their adoptions. Sometimes the newspaper needed her to write, sometimes they needed her to set type or sell advertising. Grateful for the income, she took the train to her first assignment in western North Dakota, a few hours away from her parents. For weeks she kept to herself, taking the train to visit her parents or go to the city of Minot during her free time. On one of these free days, she was having lunch in her hometown café with a high school acquaintance when a dark-haired man with round horn-rimmed glasses came into the restaurant. Her friend jumped up from the table, and flagged him down, and had invited him to join their table. The conversation at that lunch was easy and ended with him inviting both girls to a dance taking place the following weekend. These dances were common and would take place at church meeting halls, schools, or people's homes.

Her lunch partner had found out that his name was Jasper. He was divorced from his first wife and had a daughter, but he didn't get to see her because the mother had moved to California. Edna Mae knew she felt differently about this man, but she didn't trust herself to make decisions about any new people in her life. North Dakota felt safer, but was there really any place that could protect her from what Peter had done?

Ultimately, after she talked to Jasper outside the dance hall for hours that first dusky weekend night, they began seeing each other every day they could and were married within three months. She felt lighter than ever. Jasper and the way they interacted was so different from Peter that she doubted any of it was real.

They talked about getting her children back. Since he had lived through the divorce and custody settlement of his own daughter, he knew more about how the courts worked. They even visited an attorney in Minot. It would have been the happiest five years of her life if she could have been reunited with her babies.

With one last glance at her glassine image in the window she opened the door to Hotel Stebbins.

She had been surprised at how close she felt to Emilie. Knowing that it was a story of such tragedy, Edna Mae had assumed that she was going to have to do a lot more work to get the essence of the people in the story. It reminded her of when she asked her own mother about homesteading alone on the grassy wilderness of North Dakota. The most her mother ever said was that those first years were hard, but hard work built character, and it was worth it so that her children could be successful.

To her mother, she had met her goal in her eyes and didn't care to dwell on or talk about the struggle to get them to that point. Edna Mae wondered sometimes if it was a self-protection tactic of people her mother's age who had gone through difficult times. Maybe if they stopped and thought about what they had endured, they wouldn't be able to function normally in society. The tears, the screams, the howls would come—and they wouldn't be able to stop.

Chapter 11 (Spring 1871 At Sea)

W hen Edna Mae arrived at the farm the next day, it was one of those strangely cool days for summer in Wisconsin. She had added a smart jacket to her outfit and seemed to wait just a little longer than usual to get out of the car. When she approached the door, I could see that she was glum. I got her set up on the worn dining table and added two fresh cups of coffee and some waffles I had made that morning.

I didn't wait for her to ask to start. "I needed to keep Atlantique alive for *Pére*, but I didn't know how to care for an infant so small." Edna Mae inhaled deeply and started her note taking.

The women on the ship's ward had done everything they could to keep him alive. They bundled my brother in every blanket and shawl they could find, and each took turns holding him in front of the stove. Magdaline explained to me that she was worried that the baby would turn yellow, so once a day, when the sun was at its warmest, she would take him to the deck and expose him to sunshine for a few minutes. Everyone took turns feeding him with the glass bottle and tubing that a kind woman sold to me. She didn't want to take my money, but when I saw her five daughters and found out that she had four sons also on the boat, I knew I had to insist. She would need the money to buy another bottle for the child she was currently carrying. Magdaline conversed with her in German and learned how important it was to keep this snake of tube, glass bottle, and nipple clean so the baby wouldn't get sick. So, between feedings, we would boil all the pieces in water and then dry them carefully.

At night, I felt this weird hollow feeling almost like I was hungry, but when I tried to eat during the day everything tasted like dust, and nothing filled the gap. When I did slip into sleep, I would see a white sheet on the waves that I knew was *Mame* being snatched by a sea beast. She could not hear me or escape. In contrast, Magdaline could not stop crying. She tried to hide it from me, but her already round face was red and puffy. She had said that she wouldn't leave me, and that she would help me and Atlantique get to Wisconsin. She said it was not a trouble because she was going to Milwaukee, Wisconsin, to live with her brother. Going a short distance north was nothing compared to crossing an ocean. All their kindness made my eyes sting, but I could not seem to bring the tears.

On what we were told was the last night of the sail, I dozed with Atlantique in front of the fire when *Grand-mére's* voice sounded so loudly in my head that I nearly dropped the bundle. She told me to stay with the guardian angel Magdaline—she was a helper. I scrambled my thoughts and silently begged her to keep talking or to emerge from the dim corner, but she didn't say anything else. And then I cried. I cried so much that I woke Beata who came and joined me by the stove. Her thin arms gathered Atlantique and me in an embrace, and she patted my back when a stronger wave of sadness appeared. She whispered words in her language near my ear that felt reassuring, even though I couldn't understand what they meant. She sat with me like that the rest of the night, even when I stopped crying. Atlantique started squirming which broke the trio. Beata smoothed down my hair and straightened my skirt. She squared my shoulders and looked directly into my eyes. It felt like she was trying to build my strength silently, just by looking into my soul. If I could have, I would have started crying again, but I was too tired and now nervous about getting off the boat.

To get into America you needed to be healthy and have the correct paperwork. When we got off the boat there were several lines of people waiting to be told what they needed to do next. Magdaline had stopped a man she thought was an authority and asked where we needed to go next. She had been practicing her English on the boat with the woman from England. I had tried to learn along with her but found myself distracted by the worry over Atlantique. On the ship we had been told stories about people who were sent back to Europe and not allowed to come to America. The details about why they were turned away ranged from illness to vague problems with paperwork. I was scared that I would say something incorrect when I was in front of these unknown people. *Grand-pére* had warned us to be certain we spoke to the authorities and not to other people who would take our money or do worse.

I wasn't alone in my worry about getting off the boat. The last day on board many families huddled mapping out how they would navigate if something happened that prevented them from the next leg of their journey. Magdaline felt confident that we would get into America without any issues. When the morning came to disembark, we followed the crowd into a building. Atlan must not have felt my nervous energy. The infant slept the entire time we stood in the line. When it was my turn at the desk a young man lifted his extremely thin face and looked me over with his too-close set eyes. He spoke French slowly and threw in a few words in Wallonian. I answered in Wallonian. Without a change in expression, he stamped my paper and gestured for me to walk through. I was relieved, not that I was in America, but that I had passed the inspection. The respite didn't last long. In the swarm I had lost Magdaline. I stood on my toes and scanned for the large red bow. I spotted her standing with a group of women who also wore these large bows. When Magdaline saw me, she quickly pulled me to the group. One of the men from this group explained in French that we had all passed and were free to go on to the next part of our travels.

Magdaline had hired two boys from the boat to carry our trunks. She must have paid them well, because they carried all our belongings the entire way to a boarding house where we stayed until the next portion of our trip was sorted. At first, the city didn't feel different from the others I had been through on this journey, but as we walked farther from the port, I spotted a sign in the window of a store that was in English, and it dawned on me that I was in a completely different country. My new country.

Mame and I were scheduled and ticketed through a different organization than Magdaline. Now that we planned to travel as a pair, she was going to try and find our guide so she could use *Mame's* passes to Wisconsin. On the ship we had heard terrible stories about people waiting in these new cities to rob you of your last bit of money, so my nerves sizzled at the thought of this negotiation. If we could manage the switch, we would also be able to stay with her brother Leo in Milwaukee and rest from the journey. She wanted a land doctor to look over Atlantique and to make sure we had the correct supplies for the trip north to my family. She did all of this as a matter of fact. This was what we were going to do and frankly, I couldn't think beyond making sure the baby was fed, dry, and warm.

Magdaline sent her brother something called a telegraph, telling him that we were in America. I noticed that she kept it very simple and said she had a traveling companion who would be coming with her to Milwaukee. She paid the office worker a bit extra to send it in German which he understood. She said she wasn't confident enough in her English to convey a message to her brother. She hadn't seen Leo in many years, but she held every confidence that he would help me and the baby gain strength before we went north in Wisconsin.

I felt so fortunate that I hadn't felt sick on the boat like many others, that I was shocked when, on land I still felt like I was swaying. The boarding house was not far from the docks, and I was again thankful to the two boys who conveyed our items to the front door. The house was sandwiched between two identical buildings. I shifted Atlan and knocked on the door while Magdaline double checked the address. The woman who answered the door had copper red hair and a lilt to the way she spoke English. Magdaline managed to explain who we were, and the woman told us her name was Mrs. Sheen. She led us up a steep set of stairs to the second-floor room we had rented. The dark stairs and lack of windows made my head swim. Mrs. Sheen, the owner of the boarding house, noticed and grabbed my elbow.

"Girl, you need to get your land legs back," she said, scuttling up the stairs with me in tow.

Mrs. Sheen was nearly as wide as the narrow staircase and dressed head to toe in stripes, but none of the striped fabric matched making them swim with my land legs. She spoke English with an accent that Magdaline told me later was probably Irish. I found it pleasant to listen to, with its soft edges and words sometimes running together. At the top of the stairs, she pulled a long iron key from her chatelaine and opened a dark wood door. Inside was a small iron bed with white and blue striped linens, a wooden chair, and chamber pot. She told Magdaline the wash tub was down the hall, and Magdaline seemed to fully understand. She told me later that if she understood every third or fourth word in English, she could get the idea of the conversation.

The next morning, we walked to the agent's office that was part of my ticket to Wisconsin. The agents were responsible for planning and ticketing the entire trip from Wallonia to Kewaunee County. My agent was a different company than Magdaline's, who specialized in people immigrating from Alsace and Lorraine. Magdaline stopped us along the dusty roads, several times and would pull someone from the mass to ask if we were going the correct direction. I clutched Atlan to my chest and did my best to see over the top of his little head. I didn't want to trip into the roadways that were littered with animal feces and other unnamed liquids.

The office was in the subterranean level of a multi-story building that was blackened either by paint or soot, it was hard to tell. The agent was about my height and had snow-white curls that popped out of the side of his head in stark contrast to the shiny bald top. He wore metal framed eyeglasses toward the middle of the bridge of his nose that caused him to tilt his head up whenever he spoke. Magdaline started in French, explaining our situation. He insisted that he would not give us a refund for *Mame's* ticket, that it was not his fault that she died on the ship. Magdaline tried again and again before he understood that we were not looking for a refund, we wanted to get to Milwaukee together. Immediately he stated he wanted to charge us a fee to change the ticket. I felt exhausted and Atlan was fussing. This combination made me open my mouth and I refused to give him any money. Magdaline was shocked at my fervor. He insisted and I stood up with the fussing baby to leave. Magdaline slowly stood up and was trying to determine how we would still get to Milwaukee when the agent relented. The tickets were changed, my money from home was changed to American currency and he did not charge us extra for changing the names on the ticket.

To be safe, we also visited Magdaline's agent, and she explained what happened and how we would be traveling together now. Her agent was in no way bothered, since he had already collected his fees before we even arrived. She exchanged her currency, and we were officially set to board the train west in a few hours. While I fed Atlantique, Magdaline hired two more boys to help with our trunks. These two were so small and so filthy I would have thought they lived underground in dirt tunnels. They spoke English with a German accent and didn't walk anywhere. They ran and darted between people. Even with our trunks balanced on their heads you still couldn't see them among the adults in the crowd, until they zigged in a new direction. I was worried at one point they may run away with our things, but Magdaline had been assured by their fathers that they were the best porters you could hire. They delivered our trunks to the station and even waited to ensure they made it on the train. When I think about it now, I don't think those boys were more than six or seven years of age, and they were being hired out by their fathers to carry heavy trunks.

After we got settled on our uncomfortable train bench, Atlantique made it clear that he was not enjoying this portion of the trip. He was normally quiet, but after the first whistle it was nearly impossible to get him to stop his tiny howl. Magdaline and I passed him back and forth, back and forth but nothing made him settle. We were well outside of the city when a man in a worn black suit approached Magdaline. He asked in German if he could hold the baby and for whatever reason Atlantique immediately stopped crying. Magdaline thought it was perhaps the man's mustaches that were entertaining to the baby, but I think it was his voice. He had a voice so low that it rumbled when he spoke. He held Atlantique high on his chest and spoke or sang very quietly to him and it worked. Magdaline was so relieved she slid back on the bench and let out a sigh. About thirty minutes later the man, the baby, and Magdaline were all asleep, which gave me time to gather my wits. Things felt like they were happening to me, even though I was there while decisions were being made. I felt incredibly thankful for the people who had helped me make this journey without *Mame*.

When we said our goodbyes to the women on the boat it was the most bittersweet farewell. Magdaline carefully wrote down names and locations we all hoped to be, and we promised to write to each other. *Frau* Schweister helped Magdaline fix her large bow to the back of her head and then she combed out my hair and rolled it into a tight bun fixed with pins. All the women took turns imparting wisdom to baby Atlantique, each one feeling like they had helped get him to this point. A young girl who had been so fond of Atlantique gave me a small pebble from her tiny collection, which also included a pearl button and a blue bead. I promised I would tell him about her when he grew up. In a few short weeks we had become a family. Now our new train family included the baritone baby pacifier.

The movement of the train did nothing to help me get my land legs back. Any time I got up to stretch or use the necessary if we were stopped, the wave would come down sloshing my head.

On and on, the train portion of the trip continued. Spring greens and yellows whirred past the windows. Sometimes there were stops with groups of people waiting; other times there was only a fresh wooden platform to greet those that exited the train. I still hadn't fully imagined what was ahead of me in Wisconsin. We had received only one letter from Sofie when they were in Green Bay. America felt crisp and new. Nothing like the centuries worn roads and buildings back home. There were stretches where we cut through valleys that were so lush with green that your eyes almost interpreted the sky as green as well. Then there were the lengths where the train's path was cut through trees for so long that you wondered if they covered the land endlessly. As we approached Milwaukee, there were glimpses of a blue sea that could have fooled anyone into thinking we had taken a wrong turn and were back to the ocean.

As we got off the train at the Milwaukee stop, it became clear we were in a city with its eyes toward the future. I absorbed the energy of the twenty-five-year-old city, and was refreshed. It made me feel like anything that was to happen to me next was possible and maybe even positive.

Out of the slightly hazy air, a handsome man walked through the crowd easily, looking over the heads of those around him. Magdaline leapt up when she saw him and somehow ran with me, Atlan, and our hand luggage through the other train passengers and embraced his torso. Speaking in rapid-fire French she gushed her relief at seeing her brother Leo after all these years. She tugged me toward their reunion, and she presented Atlan to him and to my surprise, he reached out to hold him. The tiny baby in the large man's hands made us all laugh. Just like with Magdaline, I immediately felt as if we had always known each other. It was nice to speak Wallonian and have them basically understand me. I hadn't realized it, but my neck was stiff from leaning in and attempting to listen or understand all the languages we had heard on the trip.

We walked to a wagon, loaded our items and headed to Leo's store. It was a three-story building on the corner of two streets. The bricks on the outside were so new that they still had sharp edges. The ground floor had a door in the center and two large glass panes on either side. The face of the building had a decorative outcropping of trim and cornices. The inside smelled like a mix of new wood, linseed oil and ground coffee. Shelves lined the walls, and two long counters stood in front of the shelves. In the middle, a giant black and silver stove had a few wooden chairs around it. Leo had a doctor and an attorney who rented the second floor of the building, and he lived on the top floor with a young German lad who was learning how to be a shopkeeper like him. The back of the shop was a storeroom with barrels and bags of items to be sold in the shop when there was room. A set of stairs at the very back led us up to the second and then third floor.

It was surprising the amount of space in that third-floor apartment. We entered Leo's home in the back through the kitchen.

The next space was a dining room that held a table that sat six people and included a case on the wall with porcelain dishes. A hallway led to the front of the building that had a bedroom on either side. Both rooms felt bigger than my childhood attic and were furnished with two beds, a chest of drawers and a chair. At the front of the apartment was a large sitting area with a stove on one end and windows on two sides. There were rugs on the floor and some soft chairs mixed with smaller wooden tables and chairs. It felt like spending time with Magdaline. Comfortable, easy.

It was so easy, in fact, that we spent nearly three weeks with Leo in Milwaukee. I had sent a letter to my family in Kewaunee County, but I had no idea if they had received it or if I would get a letter back from them. I could feel the bitterness in the back of my throat to this day, seeing it written that *Mame* had died on the boat. *Grand-mére* had said that *Pére* was not the same after his first wife had died and I had no idea what he would be like with the news of a second wife gone.

———————————————

Edna Mae put her pencil down and picked up the porcelain cup. She drank back what was probably cold coffee at this point.

"Emilie, you have said that you didn't want to come to America. What were you thinking at this time? Did you want to stay?"

I stood up and felt the familiar twinge in my knees. It took the full five steps to the coffee pot before they eased into a happier disposition.

"I liked Milwaukee. I felt comfortable there. I warmed up to the idea of living in Wisconsin, but I think that I may have tricked myself into thinking that I would be living in Milwaukee, but one that was further north." I poured the last of the coffee into her cup. "I knew I had to get Atlan to my father, but secretly I wanted to come back to the city with Magdaline."

Edna Mae stopped and looked past my shoulder, her lower lip pulled into a half frown. I could see her working out the timeline. She knew about devastation and how it had changed her own hopes for her life as plain as she was sitting in my kitchen.

Chapter 12 (May 1871 Kewaunee County WI)

That day we left the Milwaukee harbor, the memory that was the clearest was of the German man dressed in a wool coat and fur-trimmed hat. Both were far too warm for the current weather. Leo explained that he had likely just arrived from his homeland, and the coat and hat would be needed in the cold Wisconsin winters. The German man spoke loudly to his travel companion who was also wearing a warm coat. Magdaline explained that he was complaining about how terrible the smoke was and how it made his eyes and throat hurt. There were fires in the woods to the north, and the smoke caused everyone to feel like their sight wasn't sharp and their throats went dry after they spoke a few sentences. The attitude from most was that it was a completely normal part of the progress needed to make Wisconsin a great state. Railroad lines brought the natural resources to cities and ports that would feed progress. Telegraph poles made communication to these far-flung areas easy. But both came at a price. Trees needed to be cleared, and brush needed to be burned in order for the railroad and telegraph poles to march their way into the big woods. New and old Wisconsin inhabitants were willing to put up with some stinging eyes and dusty throats for progress.

We sailed up the coast of Lake Michigan to Ahnepee, where the smoke hung in ropey string clouds giving the impression of fog, but the smell was unmistakable—burning wood mixed with the soapy smell of pine. The smoke here made our eyes even less adjusted, and you could almost feel the sun struggling to get through. What you could see of the town was a cluster of two- and three-story buildings, mostly made of wood, fanned from the lakeshore. While the port was busy, the rest of the town felt dull compared to Milwaukee.

Magdaline paid a young man to help us unload our belongings when I felt a tap on my shoulder. It was Sofie and Antoine! Sofie grabbed me into a hug, and I nearly dropped Atlan with the joy of seeing them. Sofie snatched Atlan in one arm, and immediately started crooning little words to him, and then spotted Magdaline. She declared that Magdaline had the loveliest hair she had ever seen and gave her a hug. I was so thankful that Sofie was there. I hadn't prepared myself to tell Antoine, face-to-face, that *Mame* was dead. Having Sofie there would help me get the words out.

I had braced myself for a lecture, or for him to be very angry with me about *Mame*. When he came back with our trunks, instead he touched my shoulder and just looked at me as if he knew the trial of the last few weeks. Antoine looked exhausted and hungry. He always had slight shadows under his eyes, but they were nearly black, and his face was both wrinkled and tight from sun exposure. Sofie, too, looked exhausted, and a bit faded. When she smiled, it was almost as if she was so tired that it couldn't fully reach her eyes. They made me feel uneasy.

As we rode out of the town on the wagon, I noticed that the road ahead was made of logs side-by-side, rattling our teeth and making it nearly impossible to speak. The further away from the houses, the closer to the road the monstrous trees came. I had never seen trees so large or green in my life. The invasive smell of pine nearly erased the odor of smoke. It was dim and the trunks played tricks on my eyes, making me think I was seeing people or animals walking through the woods while we rode past. When I would look again more carefully there was no one there. It felt like someone was pushing with their palm on my chest. I noticed that Magdaline was very quiet, in fact everyone on the wagon was quiet by the time we were fully swallowed into the green cathedral. Bumping along the rhythm lulled Atlan to sleep and I wished I could close my eyes too.

Here and there, a swath was cut through the trees and led down paths where you might see a log house or signs of life in a larger clearing. At different times on the ride, a metallic squeal would be louder than others. Antoine explained that it was a logging camp and mill. The squeal was the big trees being tamed into planks by giant saws.

We arrived at the clearing that was *Pére's* as the sun started to slip to the ground. It was such a relief to be in the clearing. The trees were pushed back and allowed me to take in more air even though it was smoke-laden. Leopold came flying out of the door of a short brown-gray log cabin with a stone chimney on the right side. Antoine barely got the wagon stopped when Leopold grabbed my hand. He no longer had any baby fat around his cheeks, his hair was long past needing to be cut, and he had run out of the house shoeless. He started talking and didn't stop while we moved out of the wagon. I knew he wasn't totally grown when he told Magdaline that he thought her hair was beautiful. He carried things while he talked toward the house, which was the first time I noticed *Pére* standing in the low door.

Sofie told me that they had gotten my letter but hadn't said how *Pére* reacted to the news about *Mame*. I lagged behind the group, not wanting to start the conversation. I didn't want to be beaten in front of Magdaline.

At the doorway, Sofie presented the bundle that was Atlan to *Pére*. He raised his eyes above Sofie's head and looked past me. In a voice that I hadn't missed for months he stated, "Emilie killed its mother. This is not my child. Emilie can deal with it." He then turned and walked into the cabin. Sofie stood there, opening and closing her mouth, not sure how to proceed. Leopold had stopped talking but otherwise appeared unfazed and carried our items into the cabin.

Inside, it was even darker and more oppressive than the surrounding woods. One wall was nearly covered with the gray stones that formed a fireplace that had a stove sitting inside. Next to the stove, a set of rough shelves lined the walls with the cooking items. Iron tools of various types hung from the wall above a work counter with a basin. A wood table with two chairs and two crates was pushed against the back wall of the cabin. There were only two small windows on the front of the cabin—their tiny square eyes did little to help illuminate the dark interior. A ladder attached to the wall led to a cutout in the ceiling that was a loft sleeping area. Below it was a small bed with a dark quilt. Here and there were items that I recognized from home. I stood just inside the door, trying to process what this meant. I was responsible for Atlan. *Pére* wanted nothing to do with us. Yet we were supposed to live here together.

Antoine brought the last of our things into the house and Sofie started to unpack the closest trunk. She didn't look up from her work, and Antoine stood near the stove, ready to say something to *Pére*, but the words never came out of his mouth. Leopold had started his chatting again. He filled the silence from the dark corner where *Pére* had taken one of the wooden chairs. Eventually, Sofie and Antoine needed to leave to get their children from the neighbors. Sofie hugged Magdaline and me once more and stopped short.

"Oh! I should have brought the cradle. Cédonie said that you could use her cradle for Atlantique until her baby arrived this winter." She paused and threw a glance at *Pére* who hadn't moved once in his corner. "Can you manage tonight without it? You will love Cédonie. Tomorrow, we would introduce you to the Baudots and you will meet Uncle Frank, Odile, John and Marie Louise."

We agreed that Atlan would be comfortable for that night, and Magdaline offered to walk over and get the cradle if it would be easier tomorrow morning. When they left, the only sound that remained was Leopold talking about his life in Wisconsin. He had a favorite tree that he hoped they could keep. He had learned how to make shingles and even got paid for his work. There might be a new teacher for school this winter. He chatted away until, suddenly, he looked up at me and his chin shook. "I miss *Mame*."

Despite *Pére* glowering in the corner, I grabbed my brother and hugged him. Magdaline touched his shoulder and whispered something in German. It might have been a prayer. I didn't dare ask about sleeping arrangements, but once Leopold had gathered himself, he announced that we were to sleep in the loft with him. I didn't need to turn to look at Magdaline already knowing what she was thinking. The entire house would be disrupted that evening as we took an infant up and down the ladder. She didn't say anything and later, when we had created a sling to lift the baby to the attic, she whispered that my *Pére* would learn quickly. He heard the whisper and threw arrows at her with his eyes.

That night we took turns like usual with Atlan, feeding and walking the floor when he didn't want to sleep. With such a small cabin, *Pére* participated from the bed in the corner, though he never turned from facing the wall. During the early morning shift, I could feel his anger clouding the corner of the cabin like the smoke that was growing in the early dim. The only thing that kept it from overtaking the building was a sweet boy and a single candle flame.

That first morning, *Pére* was darker than ever, having not had much sleep. I wavered between wanting to get whatever scene was going to happen out of the way and fearing what would happen to me and Atlan. The best I could hope for would be that Magdaline and Leo, or Antoine and Sofie, would take me in and let me work for my keep. The worst option was living in this house, trying to raise Atlan with so much anger and contempt. I tried to think about what *Grand-mére* or *Mame* would have done in this situation, but my mind was blank.

———————————————

Edna Mae had laid down her pencil and rubbed her eyes. I thought maybe she hadn't slept well, but when she removed her fists, I saw pure frustration.

"Emilie, I'm sorry that your father was so terrible to you. You didn't kill your mother. So many women have died during and after childbirth. He must have known that from his first wife." She wavered, and the frustration rose again. "To refuse your own baby…" She trailed off, and I knew she was thinking about her own babies. The babies she didn't want to give away. The babies that were stolen by a mean man named Peter and given away like they didn't matter.

"Edna Mae, we could stop for today."

"Would you work with me on a book?"

She had blurted it out so fast that my mind needed a minute to reform the words. "A book, about what?"

"About your life. I have a friend who works for a publisher who is working with a woman and her daughter to publish a book about her life in Wisconsin. The mother was born after the Civil War, west of here. People are interested in hearing about the past—about the people who formed the middle of the country and if they were interested in one woman's story, they would be interested in yours."

A book. "I don't think people want to read about the ravings of a woman who had some hard times. Everyone had hard times."

"I think we have nearly everything we would need to create a book. Please consider it. I could write it with your help. It would be your story."

I wasn't sure what to say.

I faltered at this being my story. Without Uncle Frank, Aunt Odile, and the Baudot's, I'm not sure any of us would have survived carving out these farms, much less the fire. We weren't farmers or woodsmen when we came to Wisconsin. *Pére* was there for the land and to have a place to pass along to the next generation. Back home, we had taken care of a very small number of animals and a food plot. We were people who lived in town. *Pére* made shoes.

Those first few weeks in Wisconsin, the volume of work needed to accomplish a small level of comfort was astonishing. There was a shift in duties for men and women in America. None of us women chopped wood for the fires at *Grand-mére's* house in Wallonia. In Wisconsin, Magdaline, Leopold, and I were tasked with ensuring there was a giant pile of wood by the front door so it could be jammed into the stove. The stove wasn't even half the size of *Grand-mére's*, and it took many days before we figured out how to regulate the temperature properly to make bread or cook on its top.

Pére's farm had a well with a crank handle that ran a bucket up and down on a rope. There was a pieced-together barn of logs, an outhouse, and the cabin. The cabin felt oppressive and dark all the time. It was rustic at best in 1871, but it wasn't much different than all the neighbors.

If you walked along the path to the main road, there was a fork. A left turn on the path took you to Uncle Frank's place. He and Odile had worked for more than twenty years to clear just over eight acres of trees. There were still stumps here and there, but he had been able to plant crops between them. Their cabin had been enlarged over the years and now comprised three rooms, four windows, and two doors. Odile had whitewashed the logs in the low-ceiling room that had been added on the back of the cabin, that created an ell. In the corner was Uncle Frank and Odile's bed, which she had dressed in a spread that had been pieced together with scraps of fabric creating a celebration of color and pattern. If you dropped in you could often find Odile working on various tasks in this room, sitting next to the window.

To get to Antoine and Sofie's, you would take the right fork. The first owner of their farm had been a single man who had devoted more of his time clearing trees than building structures. Their cabin was attached to the barn, Uncle Frank explained that many of the German neighbors brought that custom from their home country. Sofie wasted no time in switching the cabin and the barn around, making a more comfortable space for her larger family. Antoine had a plan for a larger barn when they were able to add to their livestock. The barn-home had been scrubbed to shining by Sofie and Cédonie Baudot that spring.

The Baudots lived through the woods behind Antoine and Sofie. Pierre Baudot had moved to this farm with his parents in 1853 and grew up in the big woods. Their farm was a model of progress, it had doubled its original size and had several fenced areas for animals, multiple barns, and a cabin that was two stories. Pierre's father had hired immigrants new to Green Bay to help clear the land after he had arrived. Sofie once told me that Pierre Baudot's father had been a wealthy man in Belgium. There were items in the house that spoke to that wealth: porcelain dishes, a silver teapot, and patterned rugs that were not made from strips of cloth. The Baudots had added an entire two-story section to the original cabin. The walls in the new area were all covered in a sand and lime mixture that made the home feel fresh and bright. I had hoped someone would show me how to make the mixture so we could cover the walls in *Pére's* cabin.

The circle of close neighbors was completed with Jacques LaRocque. Jacques was a *Métis*. His father was a Frenchman from Canada, and his mother was a Cree Indian from the Red River that ran through Manitoba, Canada, Dakota Territory, and Minnesota. Jacques grew up following his father through the wilds gathering furs to be traded and transported to the far reaches of the Hudson Bay and New Orleans. He wasn't a tall man but had a large presence with his black eyes hooded with thick dark brows and a thicket of wild hair. He wore trousers and a shirt like all the other men, but instead of suspenders he had a red woven scarf tied around his waist as a belt and his feet were covered in butter soft leather. Uncle Frank described Jacques's farm as a fur trader's lodge. Jacques wasn't as concerned with removing trees and instead trapped in the woods, fished, and planted a small garden. To get to his farm you cut through a narrow path to the north of *Pére's* farm. He knew so many things about living in the woods that I think we were all a bit in awe.

Pére's farmyard was not square. Instead, the trees that were easier to remove had been cut first. Next, the giant pines were tackled with saws and axes. The final step was doing something to clear the stumps. Many of the trees had been attached to their current spot for more than 150 years, developing a thick root system. Immigrants tried various ways of removing these stumps. Some tried grubbing the stump out using hand tools. If you had a team of oxen and chains, you could use the animal power to remove the stumps that were decayed or small. There was a stump remover tool that was almost like a corkscrew, but most farmers couldn't afford to purchase one when they arrived in Wisconsin. Most farmers resorted to burning the stumps to reduce their size. Then if they had oxen, they could pull the rotted smaller stump later. They needed to get crops into the ground to feed their families and planted the seeds around the stumps until they could manage their removal.

Pére's land was unique. Running in almost the middle of the yard was a solid rock section of ground. Some of it was covered in soil, but a large flat portion was exposed and a bit raised. Uncle Frank told *Pére* that he was worried they would find more rock like this under the trees on this patch of land making farming impossible, but *Pére* felt he could still make it work.

Because Uncle Frank had been there longer, his yard was starting to become more linear. In fact, he was planning on building a new house for his family and making the current cabin a building for pigs. It had taken Uncle Frank and Odile almost twenty years to have a three-room cabin with the hope of building a larger home at an unnamed future date.

Edna Mae pulled me back from my thoughts. "I think we should write a book."

I fiddled with the corner of the tablecloth. "We could work on a book, but I don't think anyone would read it." I couldn't believe I had said it. I wanted to work on a book, I did. I didn't want to stop talking about the past with Edna Mae. I think I wanted to feel like coming to Wisconsin was a good thing. That even though the decision wasn't mine, it had turned out the way it should. I had been blessed with Atlan and Magdaline, and I had escaped an early death in the fire. Selfishly, I thought maybe if I helped Edna Mae write a book it would give other people hope. People who felt out of control in their circumstances. Or maybe I just wanted to be heard.

Edna Mae was equally surprised by my answer. I watched the shock roll over her and slip into hope, then excitement. "Oh Emmee, thank you so much for agreeing." She paused, like she was waiting for me to take it back. I noticed she called me by my pet name again today and smiled.

"You may change your mind when you hear about the fires. There were plenty of people who had far more harrowing experiences than I did. It may be too dull for a book."

"We will work through the story, and I promise if I don't think it will work then we won't proceed. But Emmee, your story to this point was book-worthy."

Edna Mae left for the day, and I sat thinking about how tomorrow I would be talking about the fires. There were people who talked about their experiences during those horrors with family or friends, but mostly I recall distraught faces when the fires were mentioned. The older generation would rather have eaten crow than discussed those terrifying times. When I got older, I realized that the reluctance was from guilt. They had brought children and elderly parents to this nearly uninhabitable land. They had ripped trees from the ground, burning their stumps and refuse. Men left for months to work away from the house while women and children were hungry and scared of the animals in the thick trees. All these decisions had fueled the monsters their family ran from in terror that 1871 fall. There was nothing they could say, there was no true comfort that would make up for the fear, injuries and deaths and there was no money to go back. There was no time for being vulnerable; only forward propulsion would keep food on the table and keep the land in the family name.

Chapter 13: The September Fires (September 22, 1871)

When Edna Mae arrived the next day, I was ready. Magdaline and I had walked together around the farmyard, and we pieced together what we remembered from the timeline of those weeks. Here and there, we would remember a person who had played a role at that stop on the timeline. We cried and there were even a few chuckles, but mostly we felt a bone-deep sadness. 1871 was the definitive end of girlhood.

I sat across from Edna Mae and took a long sip of my coffee and fiddled with the thin porcelain handle of the flowered cup. Edna Mae held her pencil just above the paper as if she were going into battle.

"Are you ready?" I nodded.

We learned quickly that running a cabin in the woods was different than back in Wallonia or Alsace. Odile and Cédonie were endlessly patient with Magdaline and me when we had questions on how to accomplish something when the process was different than what we were taught. Neither of us had ever canned a year of garden produce by ourselves. We had both worked in our grandparents' kitchen with hands that were more skilled than ours. We learned to spin wool, a job that Mame had loved and hadn't taught either myself or my sister Eugénie fully. I didn't have my lace-making tools because they didn't fit into the trunk, but I also didn't have time to work on lace between learning how to be a woman on a farm and caring for Atlan. I was surprised at how much I learned from Jacques. After he saw my small simples supply, he took me to the woods and pointed out plants and roots that would be helpful for food or for healing. He said his mother had taught him and when he and his father moved through the country with their furs, they relied on being able to source items from the land for survival. Jacques taught us to fish in the streams and promised to show us how to snare small game with traps in the winter.

Day after day, and week after week, the smoke ebbed and flowed through the countryside that September. If the wind blew in a certain direction, people would blame Manitowoc County to the south for the pall. If it blew from the west, it was surely the fault of Minnesota. It was so prevalent that after a while you didn't notice unless it was thick enough to obstruct your field of vision.

I remember one day as I rushed through the woods to get to Sofie's when the clear smell of the pine trees overtook any of the sooty smoke. It was so strong that I stopped scuttling and looked up at the emerald pavilion. It was the first time I had noticed the spicy smell that came behind that of the pine and the skittering of critters. They had been there the entire time, but the oppression I felt from the darkness of those trees hadn't allowed me to stop and really see what it was. It was a city of trees and plants. I still felt uneasy being in the woods and constantly felt like I was being watched, but I saw it differently that day.

That evening, the smell of the forest was overtaken again by smoke. The work to keep three farms moving toward prosperity started at first light and went until the sun set. Most nights the moon hung low in the sky and presented itself as an uncomfortable orangish-pink color through the haze. That night its rust glare struggled to show through the smog.

Nearly everyone complained about their eyes stinging, and so many had started coughing a dry rasp that only became more pronounced when they increased their physical labor. I often felt like there was a stone laid across the top of my chest, making it just slightly harder to breathe. Daily I told myself that it was just the worry of keeping Atlan alive and growing that caused the tightness.

The summer was dry, maybe not the driest it had ever been in the history of Wisconsin, but dry enough that those who had come in the 1850s regularly remarked on the swamps being nearly empty and the wells struggled to keep up with demand. The dust only added a layer of misery to those that suffered from the smoke. Uncle Frank said the only good thing he could say about this dry spell was that the mosquitoes weren't as bad as usual. I couldn't imagine the mosquitoes being worse. They were a constant buzzing plague. There was no way to keep them off Atlan without a net of cheesecloth over the cradle. The bites itched and just added to the ever-present discomfort.

People tried a variety of different ways to make the smoke sting more tolerable. They used cloth tied over noses and mouths. Women wavered between throwing open all the doors and windows or trying to seal their crude cabins against the air. Cups and dishes were placed rim down so the ash in the air wouldn't ruin your meal. Some seemed so miserable that their eyes watered and their bodies were racked with coughs. There just wasn't a lot of time to dwell on the discomfort.

By the middle of September, there were days when the smoke felt like you were slowly falling asleep. With eyes unfocused and burning throats, you had the sensation that you were being pulled under a blanket of blur. The smoked filled days made me want to put my head down on the table and close my eyes. There wasn't a time though when I felt panic. There were still normal conversations and arguments. Each night, Magdaline and I argued with *Pére* about Leopold starting school that fall. *Pére* felt he was needed on the farm and could "maybe" start once the work was finished. By now we all knew the work was never going to be finished. Leopold, however, had proven himself to be extremely bright. His English vocabulary seemed to grow daily, and Magdaline would share words and phrases in the languages she knew, and he worked diligently to carefully learn each of them. For his coming birthday, he just wanted a book. He didn't even specify which, just that he wanted a book. Magdaline, Sofie, and I were determined to get him to the classroom. Sofie rationalized that even if we only got him through eighth grade, he would be the most educated of all of us.

In the evening, I watched the window to see what kind of moon we would have while I worked on making him a new shirt and knit socks for school. *Pére* would scowl from the other corner, and Leopold would move his arm tighter around the scrap paper and pencil he was using to copy the words he was eager to learn. Magdaline, while not openly hostile to *Pére*, made it no secret that she thought he was holding his son back from his full American potential. She rebuffed *Pére* one night, stating that perhaps Leopold didn't want to be a farmer, and that all this farm work would benefit me or Atlantique. She was not one of *Pére's* children and he had no choice but to listen to her argument, and he pushed back with threats to send her to her brother in Milwaukee. I knew he would never send her back. There was far too much work to be done to lose a pair of strong hands and a good back. Magdaline had a spot here if she was willing to stay—not the other way around. In my mind I also wondered if *Pére* wasn't worried that I would take Leopold and Atlan and go with her to Milwaukee, leaving him in the woods to figure out this land himself.

We shuffled through the days like this for what felt like a minute and a millennium those first few weeks of September. At some point Antoine came back from a trip to Ahnepee extremely agitated and called a family meeting for that night. It was too hot to sit inside so we all gathered around the big flat rock near *Pére's* barn. Antoine was so flustered that he insisted even the children attend, and he had invited along the Baudots and Jacques. It felt large like a complete village.

There was a constant insect buzz in the background as Antoine raised his hand. I remember he paused for a few seconds after we had quieted as a group. Poor Marie Louise did her very best to halt her coughing, but little wisps escaped. Antoine laid his hand on her shoulder, giving her permission to cough as needed. His face was fixed in a mix of concern and determination. I would never forget how his voice was quieter than I expected, as he began to speak.

"The fires are getting worse. In Ahnepee, I heard about several families south of here who lost everything when they couldn't keep the fire away from their farms. They lost everything, and one of the children was burned and was in the hospital."

It hung there for a minute while most of us squinted in the blurry late-day sunshine. Antoine wanted us to be prepared. Everyone had worked so hard; it would be devastating to lose any of the nine current and future children in our newfound community. He wanted this little group to be safe from preventable harm.

Uncle Frank was the first to speak up. He swallowed hard and rubbed his throat, trying to clear the scratch. He too had heard in Dyckesville that the fires seemed to be getting worse instead of better. There were areas that had already burned that were burning again, something that was nearly as unbelievable as ghosts.

The plan started to take shape. We were all going to stop burning any brush from the felled trees. After the normal work was finished each day, they would start plowing up the soil around the woods at each farm to build a barrier around the buildings. Uncle Frank and Jacques would go to the cooper and have more barrels made that would be placed at the corner of each building. We would take turns in teams collecting water from the creek at the bottom of the hill. All available linens were to be collected and placed by the doors so they could be soaked and placed on roofs. Each house would make more ladders to have them available if needed. At the time, the plan felt overly cautious. If the fire came or you couldn't put out a fire, you needed to go to the well. If that wasn't an option, then you needed to run to the nearly dry creek at the bottom of the hill. Your last resort options were to go into a cellar or bury yourself in the dirt. The children were told that they should not wait for an adult or for others; just go. The youngest of the group kept looking up at the adults, shocked that they were given permission to run for safety without them.

A few days later, our plan no longer felt like enough. Word came that school wasn't going to start this week because too many students were needed to help protect their homes from fire. We heard about people suffering from "smoke pneumonia," and that a small baby had died in Kewaunee because it couldn't breathe through the smoke. It was September 22nd. I remember it because Uncle Frank planned to take me into Ahnepee to buy a book for Leopold's birthday on the 23rd.

The first explosion happened early in the afternoon on the 22nd.

Bang.

It was so loud that it echoed through the woods, and a flock of birds fled the trees and fluttered over the farmyard. Leopold was seated at the kitchen table that day waiting for me to wrap some bread and cheese for him and John. Every day a pair was assigned to go and fill the barrels, and the couple would need to go further to find enough water for the task. That day, it was their turn to take the small wagon to the creek to fill the water barrels.

Seconds after the bang, Leopold's eyes met mine and he was out of the seat before I could stop him. Outside, we were met by John, who was frantically pointing at the smoke coming from the forest between us and Uncle Frank's. Even today, I don't really understand how to explain why a tree exploded into flames when there was no open fire around it. I watched the others coming toward the house and realized this was more serious than the pop-up fires we had battled the weeks before. We needed all available blankets and rugs to beat back the flames. I dunked a tablecloth in the barrel by the door and handed it to John when I heard a shout come through the woods.

"FIRE"!

I shoved the blankets out the door as fast as hands would take them. Each pair dunked their blanket and headed to the small tower of flames. Uncle Frank brought up the rear and told me to soak one of the blankets and throw it over Atlan's cradle in case the smoke got worse. Just as I draped it over the sleeping boy, a bang came from further away. Even though the sound was fainter, it was the same as the first. A tree had exploded into flames.

For weeks, fires smoldered in the woods at a low level. The fires were not necessarily notable and there were actual outbreaks of flames that took priority. We learned later that these low burning fires ate away at the inside of the tree until it found something to ignite causing the explosion. Each time one of the firefighters came back, they were dirtier and bleaker than the time before. I started pulling water from the well to replenish the barrels by the house and started redirecting the firefighters to the barrel by the barn door.

At some point, Cédonie Baudot's oldest child came racing into the yard and begged for help. A tree burned at the edge of their woods, and they were struggling to manage the fire. On one of Antoine's returns, I told him they needed help, and he took John with him down the hill, quilts trailing behind them.

My arms screamed as I switched them back and forth pumping the bucket handle of the well. The water level was so low that the bucket nearly reached the bottom before I could feel the water enter it. Each moment I scanned the house, ready to run in for Atlan. It was Sofie's oldest, Adele, and Juliette Baudot who leapt through the tree line like two tiny fawns. Adele was just five, and Juliette wasn't yet six. The girls held hands and ran as fast as they could through the clearing. Her chest heaved as Juliette explained that Cédonie had sent them to help watch Atlan. Without waiting for my answer, they ran to the house. A few minutes later, Juliette emerged, carrying Atlan under a blanket and Adele holding a full bottle in her arms. The little hens took their chick to the rock slab and set up their makeshift camp. When I think about it today those little girls were barely older than Atlan. Their heads leaned close together as they conferred on what he may need. I wondered what such young girls felt or thought during those frantic hours.

I had pulled the last bucket of water as the sun sank in the haze. There couldn't have been much water left in the well at that point and all the watertight containers currently had just inches of water remaining in them. The fear of the fire returning that night kept my heart beating lightning quick. The firefighters started emerging from the battle, each took a drink from the bucket of water and sank to the ground. Their faces and hands were filthy, and their red-rimmed eyes wore their exhaustion. The smoke radiated from them. My arms vibrated from the lack of movement, and I realized that I had been coughing for a long time, maybe as long as the young girls had been caring for Atlan.

Sofie came through the clearing, her face blackened by dirt and smoke, and there was a tear in one of her sleeves. Both Honoré and

Rosilia rode on her hips, their eyes a mix of shock and fear. The normally animated children were sullen and silent. She was bone weary like the rest of us but came with news from the others.

She told us that some fence rail had survived the battle. Ours, Antoine's, Uncle Frank, Jacques, and the Baudot's buildings were still standing. With her voice cracking and croaking from the shouting and smoke, she explained that Antoine wanted to set up watch groups with the adults. The older children would be runners so we would be ready through the night if the fires came close again. She declared that Antoine, John, and Leopold would take the first shift of three hours walking between the three Gaspard farms, the Baudot's and Jacques's place. *Pére*, Marie Louise, and Magdaline would take the second shift. Antoine had had the wherewithal, even after fighting the fire, to equally split up the households and skill levels throughout the night. Juliette and Adele would stay with me and continue caring for Atlan. When it was Sofie's turn on watch, she would bring Honoré and Rosilia to our cabin then Cédonie would bring her children when it was her turn, adding to the small girls' charges. After she had shared the plan, she turned quietly and walked back through the hazy opening in the trees.

Antoine didn't think the fires were over. All the work over the last few hours hadn't stopped the monster. I couldn't help but think that if we had all stayed in Wallonia, we wouldn't be in this danger.

That night was probably the only time in my previous memory that we did not make an evening meal. Instead, we all shuffled into the house. *Pére* cut himself a slice of bread and retreated to his bed, where he barely removed his outer layers before he curled on his side toward the wall. He had started wheezing during the fire, and it sounded like he was struggling to maintain a normal breathing pattern. Leopold followed but sat in the chair at the table. I tried to wipe his face a bit better, but he protested that he needed to get back to work. The little caregivers had changed Atlan, and both shook their heads when I asked if they wanted to eat some bread. I packed away my worry about them not wanting to eat with the fear of Leopold out in the night watching for fires and the wheezing that had started in *Pére's* chest after that afternoon's exertion. I carried the worry, and I went back out to the rock to collect the linens and blankets the firefighters had brought back. The air was heavy with more than smoke; there was now a thick layer of fear.

On the way back to the house, I noticed that everything was vibrating, and I knew I wasn't going to be able to sleep. So, I organized the young girls to help me with sorting the linens, finding more and preparing Atlan in case we needed to rush out of the house. I tasked the girls to help me remember to always have one of Atlan's bottles ready. Until the kind German woman on the boat sold me the bottle, I had only a towel soaked in milk to feed Atlan. He was bigger now and without the bottle there would be no way to keep up with his needs. He was just over four months old but still tiny compared to other infants his age. Magdaline and I did everything we could to keep him warm and fed to gain weight and grow. At night we had started placing a damp blanket over the top of his cradle to try and keep the dry smoky air from his tiny lungs.

The little girls fixed the cradle and changed him for the evening. I remember listening to their chatter as they fussed. "Good job Adele, that will help keep him safe in his bed. He's such a good boy. So brave and not crying. Here Adele, you hold him while I get his dinner." The memory of Juliette's tinkling little voice and the little wave of her small hand as she took charge still makes the corner of my mouth raise in a slight smile today.

It was as my memory drifted down the coneflower-blue ribbon in Juliette's dusty brown hair when Edna Mae shifted in her chair reminding me of our actual work.

Edna Mae cleared her throat, and she shifted in her chair again. "I didn't know the really serious fires started before October." She seemed worried about this detail and started shuffling through papers on the table. This made me second-guess myself yet again. I might have been wasting this woman's time and causing issues with her work.

Edna Mae stopped mid-shuffle and placed her pencil on the table. "I looked through the papers from that fall, and fires of this severity should have been reported. There was mention of fires, but they all seemed like individual incidents and not... trees bursting into flames and ground re-burning. Maybe you would have been better prepared for October eighth if they had reported this."

I thought about this for a minute. "I'm not sure if we would have done anything differently. Magdaline's brother, Leo, was the only person we knew in Wisconsin who might have been able to help, and he was in Milwaukee. Getting all of us there would have been impossible, with the log roads burned out and bridges destroyed by the time we fought the fires in September." Tears prickled at the corners of my eyes. Would any of those who died during or after the fires have survived if the papers had told us to leave? Where would all the forest farmers, woodsmen, Indians, and town dwellers have gone if they had escaped? There was no way of predicting where the fire would travel. Ghost faces floated past me. I whispered as I had heard Magdaline say all these years, *"Herr mein Gott."*

We sat in silence for a few minutes as I watched Edna Mae struggling with her profession and what she felt was her duty to communicate with the public. It was hard to watch, so I finally broke the silence and said, "I don't know why the newspapers didn't report on the fires to their full extent. Perhaps they didn't want to scare immigrants away. All the villages around here were young and needed people to build them into thriving communities. Maybe they couldn't get to the burned areas. The roads and bridges were made of wood. If they were gone, getting the stories firsthand would have been difficult." It all came out in a half hiccup as I fought to hold on to decorum.

Edna Mae paused. "That might be, newspapers need to sell copies and advertising. Maybe they were getting pressure from advertisers to defray any panic. If people left, they might not come back and shop in their businesses." Her expression was somewhere between disgust and deep sadness.

In September that year, there wasn't a lot of time to keep up with the news even if the papers fully covered the fires. We didn't get a daily newspaper and most of us wouldn't have been able to read and understand them anyway. They were only in English. News and updates reached our nook of the woods by word of mouth. Neighbors who had been to town would stop on their travels and share what they heard. After church on Sunday, there was time to exchange information, but fall was normally an extremely busy time on a farm, harvesting gardens and preparing for the winter.

"Jacques had been in Ahnepee two days after the September big fire and told us that the man in the general store was reading the paper and told him about the town of Alaska, south of here. The entire community spent the night on the pier in the lake." I remember hearing about how the community had huddled for hours in Lake Michigan with the belongings they could carry. During the night, they pulled up the boards at the end of the pier when the fire got too close.

She wasn't fully convinced but said, "Shall we continue?" She picked up the stray pencil and pulled out a fresh sheet of paper.

I thought I was ready. I thought after the last few days of what felt like easy conversations with this young woman who I secretly considered a friend. I was ready to give my account of the night of hell and its aftermath. I thought that telling the story in order would prepare me. I opened my mouth, but everything was stuck in my upper chest. It wasn't coming.

There was a reason why there weren't many written accounts and scant oral details shared from that October night. It was the same reason most soldiers from *The War Between the States* or *The Great War* didn't speak at length about their experiences. The cost of drawing the visuals, smells, and sounds back, stripped away a carefully built shield that made forward movement in life possible. We hadn't been shot at across a trench; we had been engulfed by a storm of fire that made up its vile plan as it went.

Edna Mae had risen from her chair and was standing next to me shouting something. My chest heaved, and I could only see black dots in my area of vision. It was my namesake Emilie Marie who bounded through the door to the kitchen. Edna Mae was fanning paper in front of my face while Emilie Marie was wetting my face with water from the glass in front of me.

"Auntie, were you okay? Please slow down your breathing." Her chocolate-flecked eyes were large and round, and beyond worried. Edna Mae had grabbed my wrist and was pressing her fingers to it while looking at the clock on the shelf. Its thudding tick was the first sound that fully came back to me. Atlan rushed into the kitchen at that point. He was shorter than Edna Mae but flew into the room like he was a giant.

"Emmee, were you okay? What's wrong? Emilie Marie, call Leopold… NOW!" He was shouting by the end of his statement, and it brought me back to myself.

I managed to sputter, "No, don't bother Leopold. I'm okay… honest." None of the characters standing around me looked like they believed me. This had never happened before. But I had never told anyone about October eighth before.

Atlan glared at Edna Mae as she laid my wrist on the table. In a sharp tone you rarely heard from him, he declared, "Ms. Leighton, I think you should leave. Emilie has been through enough. This project isn't supposed to affect her health." His hand weighed ten pounds on my shoulder as he scolded her. My words still didn't come fast enough to explain. He continued, "You can use what you have gotten so far, but I don't think it's a good idea to continue."

Edna Mae started gathering her items, but her eyes never left mine. I could feel my mouth moving, but I couldn't push the words forward. I tried to make her understand with my eyes. I wanted to tell her. I wanted what this family and area had survived to make a better life for the next generation recorded. It was too much to convey with eye contact.

"I'm so sorry, I didn't mean to make her ill." She had packed everything into her bag so quickly that items were hanging haphazardly from the open top as she moved toward the door. "Please send me a message on her health. I'm at Hotel Stebbins."

I didn't hear the rest. Atlan had escorted her out as Magdaline came in and started fussing over me. My heart had slowed to normal. I reached for her hand. "I'm okay. I don't know what happened. I just sort of froze when we started talking about the big fire."

Magdaline slumped into the chair that had been Edna Mae's. "We aren't young girls anymore." Her eyes glossed over. "It was long ago, maybe it's a mistake to drag it all back now."

At this very moment, I wasn't sure I could fully disagree with her. I didn't want to disappoint Edna Mae but maybe talking about it in detail wasn't the answer.

Atlan was firm on his opinion that I shouldn't continue. Magdaline and I were the only mothers he had known and as we aged, the roles seemed to reverse, and he behaved like a mother to us. After seeing Edna Mae off he came back into the house.

"Emmee, I don't think it's a good idea to finish." He washed his hands in the basin and reached for a cookie out of the tin on the Hoosier. It was a movement he had made his entire life.

"Atlantique, I think maybe it's up to Emilie if she wants to finish the project." She often called him by his given name. She told me it was out of respect for our mother. Naming him was one of the last things she had done. When Atlan was young, he would ask us about her and even though Magdaline had only known her a short time she openly shared her admiration of her and any details she remembered.

"I told Ms. Leighton that we would contact her after you decided." We had raised him to be sensible, and this seemed to make the best sense. I would wait to decide and try to give Edna Mae time to interview someone else so she wouldn't get in trouble with her employer.

Chapter 14: Wisconsin (1931 Edna Mae's Journal)

August 12, 1931

M
y desire to write a book had made Emilie ill.
Edna Mae was horrified at what had just happened. She was a professional writer, and she had risked her interview by pushing too hard. Over the last few days, she had felt like she had formed a friendship with Emilie, or at least something more than an interviewer. Emilie had told her things that had likely never crossed her lips to anyone, but Magdaline. She had been open and honest and had been quick to check with her to see if she was fulfilling Edna Mae's brief for the project. When Emilie lost all her color and couldn't seem to catch her breath, Edna Mae was more than a little worried about the older woman.

As they had worked through Emilie's story, she knew that she could have rushed through and forced the details from her, but Edna Mae had read several stories from past anniversaries of the fire, and none had the details that Emilie was sharing. Her story radar was up, and the information gathered could be a book or perhaps she might help pitch the story to others. The Model A knocked along the road back to Algoma. She needed to collect all her notes and determine how to best capture the rest of the story without catching more of the fury of Atlantique Gaspard.

Following her new routine, she collected the key from the front desk and went to her room to deposit her things and refresh herself with a walk along the shore. After that first panic of seeing sailboats on the giant lake, she had shared with Emilie the story of how her husband had died on a sailboat in North Dakota.

Calling 1930 in the Plains states a mess was laughable. The winter didn't provide enough moisture for this central column of North America, and the rains didn't come in the spring, again. Many of the grain farmers in this swath had enjoyed several successful years of farming and had increased production to supply food for the Great War. More production of grain crops meant the removal of more of the thick sod, and often there was no rotation of crops to give the soil a chance to replenish its nutrients. Starting in the previous year what farmers called "dust devils" were popping up on dirt roads and unplanted fields. They looked like miniature, translucent tornadoes and people often stopped and stared at the whirl of dust they brought with them as they tripped along the flat prairies. North Dakota was a windy state. In the winter, it would howl like a banshee for twenty-four hours throwing as little as an inch of snow into blinding whiteouts. In the summer months, it was a constant feature of the landscape pushing the native grasses or green seedling crops to look like waves on the ocean.

Edna Mae's family had learned to live with the wind and snow; the dust was a new addition. Her mother began complaining about having to dust the front room twice a week as early as May. Normally this formal sitting room with its thick rug, padded furniture, wallpapered walls and formal drapery, was thoroughly cleaned on Saturday so they would be prepared for any visitors on Sunday. When she and her new husband moved back to New Rockford that July her mother was soaking scraps of cloth and placing them in the gaps at the bottom edges of windows to keep the fine dust out of the house and all the dishes were placed upside down after they were washed so you wouldn't accidentally drink out of a dusty glass.

The first "duster" as the locals called the severe storms, came in late July. The wind had accelerated to a screaming pitch, and the entire sky was dimmed with a fine powder of dust. For God-fearing midwestern people accustomed to white snow blizzards the black rage was like something sent from below. The dust got into everything. Strange things happened causing a rush of static electricity in the air sending body-shaking shocks to people doing something as simple as shaking hands. People who had lived their entire lives on a farm became disoriented during a walk from the barn to the house. If they could even stand upright in the wind. Dust accumulated everywhere including layers of clothing where it not only coated the outside, but it also built up in pleats and folds.

Homesteaders in North Dakota were a hardy lot, and most took it in stride, sweeping and shoveling out homes and outbuildings. When they read in the papers that the storms had been even more ferocious in Oklahoma most of the North Dakota population felt for these farmers and assumed their southern brethren would find a way through these storms to keep producing off their land.

The summer dragged on becoming more parched with each sun filled day. While North Dakota could be -30°F for days on end in the winter it could also be 95°F or warmer for days on end in the summer. There were more dusters.

Edna Mae had been typesetting for *The New Rockford Transcript* newspaper that summer in a temporary position. She had grown up a few miles south of the town and she knew nearly everyone and wasn't exactly excited about the job, but it brought in much-needed money. Her husband Jasper worked for a company that leased refrigerated railcars to various rail companies to transport food crops from the Midwest. The crop failures along with concerns about the extent of the drought made the security of his job a daily worry. They weren't alone. Since the stock market crash and the run on the banks, finding secure employment had become increasingly difficult. Edna Mae had just typeset a story the week before stating that nearly a third of North Dakota banks had closed since 1924 leaving their customers without security or their savings. While this news shook the financial world like the steeple of the Catholic church during a dust storm, the ever-optimistic farmers were already mapping the next growing season with an eye to the sky for the holy rain.

In August, people were still watering their gardens by hand and the 1930 crop was nearly dust itself. Spindly grayish-green twig plants that would normally be round and lush with leaves as large as your palm were fighting for every breath just a few inches outside of their protective fruit-tin shelter. Normal household chores, such as drying clothing on the clothesline became a game of chance. You would place the wet clothing out in the clear blue sun only to have to race out half an hour later to rescue your hard work from dirt streaks. Neither driving nor walking was safe. Visibility could narrow to inches in front of your face when the wind started its dance and maintaining cars became complicated with dust clogging engine compartments.

When it seemed like there was going to be a clear day the young people came out in droves taking advantage of feeling normal. Jasper's younger sister Victoria, his best friend from work Warren, Warren's wife Cora and a couple they had made friends with from neighboring Carrington, Bill and Agnes, had all planned to go to Lake Evelyn for a picnic dinner and boat rides around the lake on one of these clear days. Cora's parents had moved to the area about ten years ago and owned land that bordered the lake. They had a small sailboat tied up to a wooden dock that would take four passengers at a time for a sail up and down the thin crescent-shaped lake.

Edna Mae unfurled the blankets to place on the ground when Jasper, Victoria, Bill and Cora boarded the boat. She waved as the group left the shore. As they continued to unpack blankets and picnic hampers, Warren explained that Cora had grown up on a lake in Wisconsin and when her family had moved here, she had begged for a boat like they had had in Wisconsin. Cora's entire family spent a lot of time swimming, sailing and some fishing around this lake. Edna Mae knew the lake, having grown up just five miles from it, but aside from a few class picnics, she hadn't spent a lot of time around open water.

The boat with its faded blue hull and slightly limp, white triangle sail, looked so cheerful slowly gliding away from the dock. Cora was manipulating the ropes with Jasper's help, and everyone was waving and squinting in the sunlight. You couldn't see the smiles, but they were there.

At first the screaming seemed faint, in fact the three on the picnic blanket didn't even notice until Warren held up his hand asking them to be quiet. Then they all heard the muffled cries. Warren shot up tipping the items on the blanket and Edna Mae and Agnes helped each other up to see what was happening.

Rushing along a thin dirt path, the shore trio got to the tiny fishing dock that was a few yards from their picnic site, they could see the boat tipped in the water lying on its side like a wounded animal, and the frantic splashing and shouting, while too faint to make out the words, rang alarm. Without stopping, Warren plowed into the water and started paddling with all his arm strength toward the boat. It looked too far for someone to swim comfortably at this speed, and he was doing an awkward head-above-water stroke. Edna Mae and Agnes started running along the thin shore closer to where the boat had tipped. The shore was only about ten inches wide and sloped steeply into the water. They couldn't help but step into the lake as they shuffled forward making their shoes sodden, and slippery. The dry grasses and shortened cattails sent Agnes reeling onto the shore at one point.

Victoria was the first person the rescuers brought back to the small clearing. Her milk-pale face was marred by a large gash from forehead to chin on the right side and watery blood was pumping from the head wound. Cora had brought her back, pulling her under her armpits onto the shore. She instructed Edna Mae to start pounding on her back to get the water out of her lungs. Doing as she was told she dropped to her knees, held Victoria up with one arm, and whacked at her back with her free hand. Agnes splayed the girl's legs in a more natural position. Some water escaped her lips, but it was mostly blood from the head wound that flowed freely.

When Cora caught her breath she panted, "Agnes, you must run to my parents. It's just kitty-corner that way." She gestured to the northeast. "My mom, Bertha, will be in the back in the garden. Tell her to call for help and to send Buster to the lake. He's a strong swimmer." She had picked up Victoria's wrist and placed her fingers on the soft interior. "Go! Go now!!"

Agnes kicked off her shoes and started pulling off her stockings as she began running the direction Cora had pointed. Edna Mae turned back and continued slapping Victoria's sodden back. She had just turned sixteen, old enough to come to North Dakota on the train by herself from Iowa. Cora stood up and shouted "keep doing that and try to press on her stomach, I'm going back out. When Buster gets here, tell him to dive." With that she shoved herself back into the water and started swimming with all her might back to the boat. Edna Mae pulled her head up high enough to see over the reeds and cattails to see how far Agnes had gotten. Agnes's oak-brown hair had fallen out of the combs she was wearing that day and flowed behind her. Edna Mae thought in that instant she looked like a farm girl of twelve running back to the house to avoid getting in trouble for missing chores. If only it was just missing chores.

Bill was the next person they returned to the shore, he was just as pale as Victoria, but he seemed to be making small movements on his own. The minute he saw Victoria through slitted eyes he leaned over into the reeds and got sick. Cora dragged him the best she could out of the water next to Edna Mae and shouted, "keep him awake until help gets here. He may have been hit on the head; he cannot go to sleep." Off she went again into the water.

Edna Mae felt an overwhelming wave of panic coming for her as she looked down at Victoria and over to Bill. Sliding over to be closer to Bill, she pinched his arm which got him to open his eyes again and then she went back to hitting Victoria on the back. It was at that moment Edna Mae noticed the unnatural angle at which Victoria's head slumped when she moved her and how the girl gave no response to the whacks and pushing on her stomach. She slowed her breathing and reached down to place her hand on the girl's chest. It wasn't moving. She lifted her wrist and fumbled for a pulse point. She couldn't find one. Aside from the times she had been in the hospital to deliver her children she didn't have much knowledge when it came to nursing. Bill rolled to his side and got sick again.

Sitting perched on her knees in the dry grass manipulating Victoria and pinching Bill she sat up a bit scanning the direction of the farmhouse and then back to the area where the boat was nearly completely upside down. Cora and Warren were circling and diving below the brown-green surface, then moving a few feet and going below again.

Buster slipped through the grass about three feet away from where she was on the shore. He was on the side of skinny, wearing bib overalls with a sleeveless tee shirt and no shoes. Without stopping, he dropped his overalls, plunged into the water and shot toward the boat in his boxers and tee shirt. He joined the bobbing and weaving. Warren came back to the clearing and crawled next to Bill, panting and wheezing. "I'll go back out. I just swallowed too much water… I'll go back out…"

Agnes came back from the farm, out of breath and wild-haired. She had been crying and the tears cut through dust-stained tracks down her face. "Mrs. Miller called for help; they're on the way. She's going to meet them by the road and show them the way here." Her eyes fell to Bill on the ground. "William… William James Johnson… wake up right this minute!" Her voice was shrill enough that a bird at the end of the lake took up and left. It worked. Bill opened his eyes.

It felt like a year had passed before the Carrington police and fire department appeared and it took another forty-five minutes before, they pulled the lifeless body of her husband Jasper from under the boat. His foot had been caught on an old car that had been pushed into the lake more than fifteen years ago. It took the fireman time to reach Jasper, cut some, adjust some, come up for air, then go back down. Edna Mae stood on the small strip of shore, the heels of her shoes sinking into the mud and coarse sand staring at the early evening light that brushed the water with a pinkish tinge. Then, like the sound had been turned off the entire time it all came on in a whoosh. People were shouting and screaming. Bill was being carried toward the rescuers' cars. One of the policemen was trying to get Warren to drink some water from a canteen and under the hands of one of the firemen lay a crumpled sixteen-year-old girl.

She had never told anyone but the Carrington police the full story of watching the boat sail out, then knowing they were in distress, and then watching the boat slip below the horizon. No one had ever asked her for details. It was something no one spoke about to her about directly. It was something they stopped talking about when she came into the room. She dreaded the compassionate glances from people when the accident came up the same way she dreaded the grief when people spoke about her William and Catherine.

Emilie wasn't like them. After she told Emilie, she watched the woman get up from her chair and walk over to the Hoosier cabinet. At first Edna Mae felt slighted until she saw Emilie pull a thin bottle of brown liquid from behind a few other items. Emilie took their water glasses and dumped the dregs into the potted violet then poured two fingers of the liquid into the glasses. Emilie was the first to lift the glass to her lips and take a long drink, wincing from the hot alcohol.

She then said something that would stay with Edna Mae the rest of her life. She said, "No matter how well you think you have planned out your life, or how much you wish for things to go the way you want, the universe is ultimately in charge. Magdaline and I had made a pact after the fire that we could feel all the emotions. We could talk to each other about that terrible time. We could scream and cry, but we had to do all of it while we kept moving forward." She tipped back the rest of her brandy. Emilie eyed her, glass midair, then said, "You are an intelligent woman. I suspect you already knew this was the secret to getting past these upheavals in life." She was right, it was why she went back to work weeks after Jasper died. It was why she threw herself into this project. It was her way of moving forward. It was what she needed to remember now as she worked through how she was going to get the rest of the story. It had been a year.

***

Magdaline and I walked around the farmyard before starting the evening chores. We had started these walks long ago, when we were worried about Leopold's education before the fire. As seasons changed and life moved forward, we would sneak these short walks to talk through what needed unburdening.

"I want to finish the story. I've told everything up to the fire in September. I know that she will only use portions of it for the special section, but I want to tell it. Did you know there was a woman who was born on the other side of the state who is writing her story with her daughter? Edna Mae knows someone at the company who is publishing the book. If people want to know about the old days, I want them to know that what we have today came from hard work."

Magdaline had stopped and plucked a long, dry strand of grass, and started picking at it. Like all other plant life, it was dry and brittle. They had been reading stories in the papers about dust storms in the central portion of the United States, and it seemed like there wasn't enough rain anywhere. When she turned to face me, I was surprised to see that she wasn't the girl who made sure Atlan and I made it to this spot in the woods. She was going to be eighty-one this year complete with faded strawberry-blonde hair and patches of skin from her wrist to elbows that had never lost their brighter pink hue from the burns in 1871.

"How do you want to finish it? Atlan isn't going to let you have another episode like this last one."

I sighed. He was such a good man. While many people over the years had helped us raise him, it was Magdaline and I who were his primary parents. I knew Magdaline was right, and I couldn't guarantee that I wouldn't have another spell. I turned to face the valley. "Edna Mae might have an idea. I will write to her at the hotel."

The response came two days later in the form of a large parcel. Edna Mae had sent a large sheaf of paper and several pencils along with a letter.

Dear Emilie,

I am so relieved to hear from you. I didn't want to disturb you further and wanted to honor Mr. Gaspard's wishes. Knowing that there is no lasting harm to you from our last visit is exactly the news I had hoped to hear.

I am glad that you were willing to complete the story. I have secured a small increase in my deadline for the newspaper. I will be here at Hotel Stebbins for the rest of the week writing the first half of the story. I am sending you writing materials so you can write the rest for yourself. Perhaps this way it will be less taxing and will allow you to take it at a comfortable pace.

Please send word to the hotel if you agree to this arrangement.

Your Friend,

Edna Mae

Chapter 15: In Emilie's Hand (October 1871, GrandLez, Kewaunee County, Wisconsin)

My own breathing has reached such a rapid pace that I'm not sure if I am taking in air. I do not know if the small form strapped to my chest is still breathing.

October 6, 1871

We hadn't had a normal day for so long. Every day was now filled with all available hands batting back flames, watching for flames, or preparing for the flames. Normal fall chores were neglected so we could find more water, scratch together food that could be eaten on the hoof, treat wounds and burns, and rotate chores in the hopes of being able to step back into normal when this was over. That Sunday was the same. Small fires were popping up in the woods, and the trees continued to burst into flames, sending the firefighters to protect the nearest property. Even the little girls who had cared for Atlan were put to work fighting the flames at their homes.

Coughing, gritty eyes, skin burns, and grime were the things we didn't even notice anymore.

When Antoine asked us to meet again, he had brought back news from Ahnepee that there were no bridges in all of Kewaunee or southern Door County that weren't burned, and most schools and churches were either damaged or razed. He said there was a family closer to the village of Kewaunee who had fought the fire for hours, but the farmer had lost both his daughter and wife. His daughter's hair had come loose and caught fire. Before he knew it, she was running through the woods fanning the flames. His wife ran after her, catching her long skirts on fire. When he finally got to them, they were both engulfed in flames and even though he tried to beat out the flames with his sack they died. I remember Antoine gulped after he finished the story, and his red-rimmed eyes stared off above our heads.

It was decided that all women and girls would wear trousers and Magdaline offered to tightly plait our hair around our heads pinning it carefully so it couldn't get loose. Sitting on the rock, she sang in her off-tune alto a song in German and scraped each of our hair into elaborate and skin-tight weaves. Jacques even sat to have his shoulder-length hair braided. She then did hers and had Cédonie help her with the last bit to ensure it was fully attached to her skull. The little girls hugged Magdaline and thanked her as they carefully felt their heads.

There had been several nights when I had not changed out of my work dress and stayed in the kitchen at the table with Atlan all night. When I walked back into the house to find trousers for Magdaline and me, I caught a reflection of myself in the window. My hair looked like a crown woven around my head. It was so tight it made my scalp tingle, but the story of the mother and daughter wouldn't allow me to even touch my head to ease the tingling. Magdaline slipped on *Pére's* black dress trousers, and I pushed my feet into Leopold's. I couldn't remember the last time either of the males in the house had worn something other than their work clothing. It felt strange to have fabric brush against your legs without swirling like a skirt. We cinched the waists with ribbons, and we took a long look at each other.

"Tomorrow I was going to start burying things in the yard—things we might need if something happens to the house. Could you help me fill some crates?" Magdaline said this as if she were asking for a second cup of coffee.

"Yes, I have some in the barn." I met her tone, because what else could we do?

We buried several crates in the yard. They contained flour, sugar, salt, a kettle, matches, candles, the extra tubing and nipples for Atlan's bottles, and after the careful packing, I placed my meager simples kit in the corner of one of the crates. Magdaline met my eyes when I gave the satchel of supplies a small pat.

"Good idea adding your simples. Then we will have some medicines if we need them. I'm going to mark the spots that I dig with flat stones. We don't want to forget where they are." She chuckled a little, then turned and, in the quietest voice I had ever heard from her, said, "Emmee, I'm scared." So was I.

October 8, 1871

Pére was in the barn finishing the evening chores and Magdaline and Leopold were hauling water back from wherever they could find it that day. It hadn't rained since July. Swamps had dried up, and the small creek closest to the farms was a muddy trickle. When they left in the morning, Leopold stated that they would likely have to go even further today to collect water and they each took additional bread to stave off any hunger if it meant being out past the evening meal.

The strong, dry breeze from the southwest pushed warm air around the farmyard and caused more than one pop-up fire during the day. Uncle Frank had announced that this was warm for the beginning of October in Wisconsin when he had made his fire check that afternoon. We stood together just outside the door of the cabin while he drank water from the largest cup I had. He looked like a different person. He looked like *Grand-pére*. The weeks of additional labor on firefighting had aged him eighteen years. Where his appearance diverged from the elder was the tinge of worry that hung around his edges. The worry made him move differently. It was almost feline.

Atlan had been fussy all day and wouldn't settle. Cédonie had tried everything she could think of when it was her turn to watch the smallest of the children. When my turn minding the tree line and fighting back any fire that popped up was complete, I brought him into the house. I think that was around 7 p.m. and I placed him in the rocking cradle on the top of the kitchen table. I wet the blanket and draped it over the bed. He was still fussing, but it was more like his usual overtired crying. I eased myself into the chair next to the table. I felt thirsty but was too tired from the day's effort to get back up and get a cup of water. With my left hand, I started pushing down on the rocker at the corner. After a few more fusses, he calmed even more.

I don't remember laying my head on the crook of my right elbow on top of the table.

With my heavy head rested, I kept moving the rocker. I woke slightly to the feel of the back of my *Mame's* cool fingers running down the side of my face. It had been so long since she had stroked my face, and for that second everything was going to be okay.

Then before my ghostly mother could even fade, I was scraped to my feet, and a man I knew shook me awake. It was Jacques. He was shouting so loudly and so quickly that I couldn't get my mind to accept the words. I stood there looking around the room catching the last essence of *Mame* standing behind Jacques. She mouthed '*aler*'—*Go*. Then she slipped away as my eyes came back to Jacques, and his wild expression brought me fully to the present.

He pulled Atlantique out of his crib and tied him to my front, like the reverse of the way Indian women carried their babies on their backs. He had shoved a baby bottle between my stomach and Atlan's. He grabbed my skirt and petticoat off the table, ripped the curtain from the window and scooped up the rug on the floor by the door. I managed to snatch the satchels I had packed for Atlan and me in case we needed to leave the house. As I was trying to tie them around my waist, I realized just how thick the smoke was in the house. It was hard to see across the room, and I started coughing on reflex. Pulling my arm, Jacques dunked all the gathered items in the barrel by the door and had to bend at the waist to reach the water at the bottom. Magdaline and Leopold had not returned.

The air had changed, it was prickly, and the wind kept shifting directions. The sky had taken on a sickening hue, making the thick haze a putrid yellow green.

Pulling me by my wrist he started walking quickly toward the barn. I could see who I thought was *Pére* at the edge of the trees swinging a rug toward the ground. A line of fire was ringed around the tree line. As we rounded the corner of the barn the wind kicked into a rage so strong it pushed us back and I could see the tops of the trees all around our clearing were an angry red fire. The birds were flying in strange formations and one dove headfirst into the ground just a few feet in front of me. Jacques emerged from the barn and shoved something into my hand then started pulling me by the wrist again. My mind wasn't catching up.

Whoosh, thud, whoosh, thud.

With this new wind the sky started throwing flaming chunks at us. One of these chunks landed on my shoulder near my ear. I shrugged it off not understanding what just happened. Jacques saw it and started pounding on my shoulder then tried to tug my damp skirt over my head.

Bang.

Whoosh, thud, whoosh, thud.

He pulled me to the stone base of the well. The rug was only half over my head, and I could see there was a ladder placed inside. He didn't wait for me to move. Instead, he lifted my leg over the side and placed my boot-clad foot on the first rung. My foot stuck and it registered that I was glad that Antoine had insisted we wear our leather shoes and not our sabots. When our faces were even Jacques said *"noh-tâ-w i-nan ki-se-ma-ni-to."* '*Watch over us to help us.*' I didn't hear the rest, but I learned much later that it was a Cree blessing to keep us safe. I was off balance with Atlan strapped in front of me but skittered down the ladder, missing rungs and hanging on too long to others. When I reached the bottom, I felt my feet enter water that reached to about my knees. The ladder was tugged out of my hand.

I heard one of the burning chunks hit the water and sizzle and my focus came back.

I bent to drag the linens that Jacques shoved at me in the water, then covered us the best I could. I knew I had dropped a few things into the water. As I pulled my petticoat out of the water the wind whined at such a violent level that my ears felt full. It didn't come in waves, instead it pushed through like a train that wasn't going to stop.

The heat didn't lessen with the wind, instead it felt like standing in front of a stove with the door open. Every time I lifted one of the linens to wet it again the heat nearly knocked the remaining breath out of me. I couldn't see well and was afraid to keep looking up to the opening of the well. I couldn't be sure if I had Atlan covered. These sheaves of heat would harm the tiny boy.

I felt something land on top of me and slide down my back. I tried to reach back to see if I was on fire, but it didn't seem like it. The coverings slipped, and I bent to wet them all and quickly cover us again. I could feel chunks of damp items floating in the water, but if they weren't on fire, I didn't care what they were.

I don't know how long the gale of fire went on. Many later said, in our area, that the worst of the tornado passed through in minutes, leaving so many new and rekindled fires. In the well, my ears now felt hollow, like something that had filled them beyond full had leaked out without my notice. I thought this was the end. I thought, I should pray. *Grand-mére* and *Mame* would pray. If I was dying, then I need to be ready. If this was the end of the world, I should have been praying. But I couldn't focus long enough to string the words of a prayer together correctly.

There was suddenly a small bit of reality; I didn't think Atlan and I were alone in the well. There was some movement around my feet. If it was someone else, they were small. Possibly one of the little girls.

Maybe letting go and knowing in my heart that this was the end of the world and that Atlan, and I were not alone in the well had helped me relax. I realized that my knees had been locked the entire time, and I slowly slid with my back against the wall of the well, into the kneeling position. I was now in water to my waist and didn't seem to have to dunk the linens as often. The angry orange glow in the well had dimmed and was nearing pitch black when I felt the pings on my head. At first, I thought it was more fire and brimstone falling from the sky but then realized it was rain coming down hard and fast.

I slumped over Atlan but kept the linens over our heads. I tried to tell by feeling around my front if his body was moving, but Jacques had saddled him so tightly to my front I couldn't be sure. Then I started taking stock. Jacques was the only one who knew I was in the well. Without the ladder I wasn't going to be able to get out with Atlan. What if everyone had died? One by one, the faces of those in my little Wisconsin community flashed in front of me in the dark. The last face I remember before I must have passed out was Sofie. She smiled at me and touched her hand to her heart, then faded.

October 9, 1871

The first thing that hit me was how cold I was. After feeling like I might combust into flames for so long because of the intense heat it was so unnatural to be physically shaking with teeth rattling cold. I'm not sure how long I had been sitting on my haunches, incoherent. The water around my waist felt terrible. I pulled down the shrouds remaining over our heads and thought about how I felt.

My neck was tight and stung, my knees felt like they might never work again. Everything else felt cold and stiff. When I brushed my hand down to my back to undo the ties holding Atlan to my chest, I realized it was John's dog, 'Spring Trout,' in the well with me. He licked my hand and whined a tiny bit. He, too, was cold and shivering. I wanted to cry. I could feel it brewing in my core.

"Trout, how were you down here?" I said it out loud to test my voice. It felt like I hadn't spoken in years, and my voice sounded unnaturally loud.

I knew that I was going to have to get out of the well and it was likely going to be easier if I kept Atlan strapped to my chest. I was struggling to make the move to confirm whether he had made it through the night. When I finally slipped my hand into an opening of the wrap the little form moved as much as he could. He was a ticklish little boy, and all those times I had struggled to change his diaper seemed so foolish now. He was moving.

Trout let out a yip that was hoarse at best. My first instinct was to tell him to hush, just like we always did when he barked at nothing. Then I realized he might be able to alert any others that we were in the well. It wasn't until I dropped my other hand to my side, that I realized that there was another critter in the well with us. Feeling around, I discovered there were several other objects down there too. After Jacques had pulled the ladder up, he had grabbed things within sight and slid them down the sides of the well. One of them was the young gander from the barn. Normally, he was such a loud, obnoxious creature; his silence now was even more unsettling.

Now that I was awake it just kept getting colder and colder and I was so thirsty. Reaching down to pull a cupped hand of water, I brought it to my lips. It tasted terrible, like crude soap, and I spit it out. Had the well turned to lye? Without being able to see clearly, I realized that there would be dead things in the water, and I'd better not drink any more.

It had been deathly quiet for some time, and it seemed like the light at the top of the well was fuzzy, like morning light. Even though it had rained hard the well wasn't much fuller than above my kneeling waistline now and the dry smoke smell had shifted to a damp and acidic stench. I started feeling around for any sort of hold or steps I could use to get out of this well. The bucket and rope were gone.

Atlan had made it through the night, but if I didn't do something to get us out and get him warm and fed, he might not survive the aftermath. I started trying to shout. I shouted in Walloon, French, and English, but my throat hurt so badly from being dry and the heat and smoke from the evening. It was pathetic. I groped around the water to find something I might be able to throw out of the top of the well. Shivering, I grasped some kind of tool. I tried to toss it toward the top, but it only landed back in the water.

I felt sick. I didn't want to be sick in the well. There was enough wrong with the water already. I pressed my back against the wall of the well and tipped my head toward the opening at the top. There had been no sound from above. No birds, no wind, no living things. It crossed my mind again that maybe I had died, and this was purgatory. I must have dozed off again, because I dreamed that Trout could fly, and he and the gander left me here in the well and flew away.

When I woke, I felt slightly better, whatever that means when you have spent a fire tornado in a well. The light above was brighter, and my stomach growled, confirming it was likely morning.

It was Uncle Frank who got us out of the well. He had stuck a long, charred tree pole into the well and skimmed down it, not knowing what he would find. It took a few attempts, but he managed to get all of us out, and on the last trip he pulled out the floating items tied inside my petticoat.

When I emerged from the well the light was painfully bright. My eyes hurt from the smoke and heat and the ground felt sandy under my feet. When I blinked, my vision cleared for a few seconds and nothing around me looked like it did when I went into the well. The odor was much worse above ground with the additional smell of charred flesh and blackened earth. Trees that were still standing looked like black kindling sticks and there were still fires burning where the thick woods had been just a day ago.

Uncle Frank was saying something, but I couldn't focus. Instead, I stumbled behind him toward the flat rock next to the barn. The barn was still standing. One corner had clearly suffered fire damage, but the rest seemed intact. I turned my body to see how the house had fared, and the entire motion felt as though I were underwater. When I came to the surface, I nearly fell at the sight of the smoldering pile of black ash and rubble of stone from the fireplace. Behind the heap that had been the cabin, the thicket of trees, which usually harbored shapeshifters, now looked like the teeth on a saw. The dark trees had always made me uneasy, but this new view was something you would conjure in a nightmare.

There were lumps on the rock. These lumps were people, the color of tar pitch and had tears in their clothing revealing cuts and burns. When I got closer to the rock, none of them moved. Instead, they stared with blank eyes in the direction they were facing or at the ground by their feet. It was as if the cold air had literally frozen them in place. If their chests hadn't heaved or a cough hadn't broken out, I might have believed they were dead. Getting closer I could see that there were different states of burned flesh from pink to bleeding wounds.

Sometimes when there is an unpleasant smell you get used to it and no longer notice it, but that didn't happen here with the stench the fire left. The death and destruction had commingled into a grievous reminder of what had just happened. It was a combination of smells that would separate and morph with the breeze. Each scent was terrible to the point that you wished the other would return so you wouldn't have to face the reality of the current.

At the barnyard rock stood *Pére*, John, Uncle Frank, and a man I recognized as a neighbor whose place was east of *Pére's*. There were also three unknown women. The neighbor man was the only one who tried to speak. Each time he would straighten from his slumped posture on the rock and open his mouth, but the only thing that came out was a puff of air. He would then slump back. I can't say how long we inhabited the rock that way. It was one of the women I didn't know who broke the spell. In a voice so smoke damaged she rasped,

> '*Otce náš, Jenz jsi na nebesich, posvet se jmeno tve prijo' kralov stvi tve.*
>
> *Bud' vule tva jako v nebi, tak i na zemi.*
>
> *Chlen nas vezdejsi dej nam dnes.*
>
> *A odpust nam nase viny,jako i my odpustime nasim vinikum.*
>
> *A neuved nas v pokuseni, ale zbav nas od zleho.'*

Until she ended her speech with what sounded like amen, I didn't realize she was praying in her language. The act of praying broke something in this woman, and she began quietly sobbing. No tears came out, and no one reached to comfort her. It was like watching a modern-day movie of difficult things happening to other people.

Throughout the morning the group on the rock grew with charred, ghostly people emerging from their hiding places. There were injuries that were hard to erase from my mind. A broken arm being held close to the body, tight angry streaked skin that radiated heat, and some whose skin was crackled with black coal marks and weeping openings. I wished I had barrels full of *Grand-mere's* simples to ease the suffering.

There was a young man called Tom who came with a small girl who didn't seem able to speak. They didn't act like they were related to each other but had somehow ridden out the fire together. Antoine, and Cédonie's husband Pierre Baudot, stumbled up the hill. When

Uncle Frank asked about their places, Pierre Baudot fell to his knees and started pounding the ground in front of him with a red fist. It was Antoine who announced that he would need help burying their families before dark, if they could find a shovel.

A husband, wife, and five children struggled up the hill to the rock. They had survived by burying themselves in the field by their destroyed farm. The mother and father's backs were fully burned. The children had an unsettling, distant stare from filthy faces. From the north, a tall thin man carrying a boy in his arms stumbled to the rock. He said his name was Wencel and the boy was Jacob. Both had been crying, with streaks through their black-stained faces. They had been traveling to Forestville to get his wife and daughters when the fire overtook them. They were Bohemian but had lived in the U.S. long enough to speak some English. The man wanted to leave the boy with us so he could go get his family. Uncle Frank convinced him to rest before he headed north. This pitiful parade went on until we had nearly thirty people, all freezing cold, and frightened, and huddled upon the rock.

Things were still jumbled in my mind. Stuck in the confusion, I sat on the rock and started an inventory of what I knew to be true. Magdaline, Leopold, Marie Louise, and Odile weren't at the rock. My heart started thudding again. Sofie, Cédonie and the children were dead. Dead. Gone. We should have never come here. If we had stayed back home, they would be alive. I started seeing dark spots in my vision. It was *Pére* collapsing in faint that brought me back to the rock and slowed my breathing.

Pére, Jacques, John, and Uncle Frank had fought through the firestorm to keep the barn standing. They had tossed water on themselves and on the barn, beating away flames that popped up. Uncle Frank later described running into our yard after his buildings had all caught fire. John had instructed his sister Marie Louise to run to the creek at the bottom of the hill and to stay as wet as possible.

In the confusion, they lost track of Odile. When Uncle Frank and John saw *Pére's* barn was not touched by fire they threw all effort into keeping it standing. According to John, at one time he came around the corner and *Pére* had fallen and was coughing. He pulled him toward the door of the barn where *Pére* passed out. During and after their battle, they had not seen Magdaline, Marie Louise, Odile, and Leopold. The hope was that they were safe somewhere, maybe struggling to find their way back without the known landmarks.

Later, Marie Louise stumbled up the hill from the creek where she had spent the night. She was covered completely with reddish-brown drying mud and ash. Her entire body was shaking with cold, and she stared at the rock's inhabitants with giant red eyes. When she tried to talk, it came out in a croak, and she started coughing so hard that her filthy hand came away from her mouth with a small pool of blood in the middle. When she saw the blood in her hand, it was as if she thought it was inevitable, no shock darted through her eyes. It was John that picked her up and held her on his lap as if she was a toddler, instead of a girl. They swayed slightly while trying to warm her limbs.

It was decided to turn the wall along the larger section of the barn into the hospital. The log barn was made up of two different sections. The older section was roughly 12' by 6' and had a low roof. There was a wooden door and a window in one corner. It had been built in the 1850s for the family to live in the first winter until they could build a larger home. The larger addition to the barn was roughly 8' by 20' and had a much higher roof and two small windows along the one wall. The skirt, petticoat, curtain panels, and a rug that Jacques had shoved at me were being used to cover those who could tolerate the weight of cloth where the fire had torn away parts of their normal costume. The gander and the dog were the only living animals we had seen since the fire. I remember looking around the barn and thinking, what would we do without chickens and the milk cow?

John brought Marie Louise, Antoine supported *Pére,* and the man carrying the young boy inside—all of them were placed in the new barn hospital wall. The man, who had come to the rock with the speechless girl insisted she take a spot. She was clutching a slate that was tied with a string around her neck, her hair was pure pandemonium. Half was burned and matted with dirt, and the other half hung like strings. The more the man pointed at the ground the more upset she became, but she didn't say a word and the man didn't win the argument.

Jacques had already taken off on foot to Ahnepee for help. We calculated that if he could, he would make it there in about three hours. No one thought it was noon yet. We were hopeful that he would get to Ahnepee in time for someone to come with a wagon and help by tomorrow morning.

I assigned Marie Louise to Atlan's care and urged her to ration the milk that was in his bottle. I feared that it was curdled from the intense heat, but she shook her head when I asked.

John and I were assigned to finding water, food, firewood and making a list of who we had in our survivors' group. I poked around the smaller section of the barn and found a nail and started scratching names into the logs. My right was for the survivors, and the left was for those who had died. I did the best I could with the spelling of their names. I counted thirty-eight survivors. Seven, along with an unborn baby, had died; Odile, Magdaline, and Leopold were missing along with twelve to twenty others.

When they got the fire started, one of the young children I had thought was German started shrieking in horror. If it weren't so bone-shattering cold, I'm sure there wouldn't have been any appetite for fire, but we needed some warmth.

The struggle to find clean water continued, but everything was contaminated. A man who lived a mile away told how he found a dead man in his well the morning after the fire. He and his family had sheltered in the root cellar assuming they would all die when the door to the dark earth room blew off. When he crawled into the well to identify the dead man, he had never seen him before in his life. Realizing that they had no other way to bury him, the entire family worked a handful at a time to fill the well with dirt. When he told the story he would end in a flat, distant tone by saying "at least the hard work helped keep them warm."

When I remembered the crates, we had buried I started clawing at the land under the flat stones. When I finally found the crate with the flour, I went to lift the fabric flour sack, and it turned to dust in my hand. Nothing in these stores was useful after the intense heat.

I carefully made my way to Uncle Frank's farm looking for anything useful. Along the worn path, there were large lumps that I guessed were dead animals. I couldn't bring myself to move closer to confirm. When I got to the yard, the side I knew to be their root cellar had a jumble of burned furniture and parts of the house. The only things left that helped me identify his place were the foundations of the buildings. When I reached to grab a crock that was still intact, I immediately yanked my hand back. It was still very warm to the touch. I grabbed what looked like a spindle from a chair back off the floor. It felt sturdy and cool enough, so I hooked it through the crock handle. The garden had been mostly harvested but I could see a few potatoes just under the dirt that had been missed. With my pockets full of potatoes and a crock on a stick, I walked back to the barn. These finds needed to feed thirty or more people.

I should add that my neck and shoulder had been burned by the flying debris on the race to the well, but the shock of the hours above ground made it feel almost like an out-of-body experience. It was tight and stung but fell so low on the priority list that it could have been happening to someone else.

The desperate sight on the flat rock hadn't improved through the day. Waves of shock, pain, and grief shook the refugees. Eerie visions kept confusing my sight. A small family had stopped in the farmyard on their way to Ahnepee and were sitting on the edge of the flat rock near the fire. The cleanest of the group was a completely bald baby who was old enough to sit up. As I made rounds to the people near the fire, the baby stared at me the entire time, and then I thought it started talking to me. Later in the day, I nearly started running toward the ruined tree line because I saw a group of people walking through what was left of the trees. Just as I was about to alert the woman near me, they faded into nothing.

At some point that afternoon, John started running toward the south. I almost told him that they were fake like my visions, when I fully stood up and realized it was a group of two boys and two women. I could hear John croaking as loud as his throat would allow. As I started walking toward the group, I realized it was Magdaline and Leopold. I took off on a clumsy run and had to stop myself from scooping them up and running all the way to Milwaukee and Magdaline's brother. John was sobbing dry tears and trying to hug Magdaline and Leopold gently.

My poor brother had tight, pink, burnt skin on his left arm and his shirt had burned away so it was only covering three-quarters of his body. His knee was red with blood. Magdaline had burns stretching from wrist to elbow on the backs of her arms, and her golden hair had been singed off in the front. Their leather shoes no longer had soles causing them to walk in a slow, uneven gait.

With them was the woman we called Madam Crow. She was the Indian woman we occasionally saw in the woods. Her leather-clad feet didn't make a lot of sound when you came across her in the trees and her long gray-and-black braid normally hung in a thin string down her back. At first glance she looked like she had escaped injury from the fire, but as she breathed, she had the same rattling and wheezing that *Pére* had back in the barn. The boy with her I recognized as the Indian boy that Leopold and John spent time with. The poor thing always seemed hungry and frail under normal conditions. The now soot- and dirt-covered boy was bent slightly forward like he was six times his actual age. John called him James. James cried out in pain.

I didn't want to hurt Magdaline more but wanted nothing more than to hug her close. She started sobbing and reached out her injured arms asking for a hug. With our burns searing, we embraced and cried harder and harder. It was the cry from the Indian boy James that pulled us apart. Doubled over, he howled, holding his middle.

"John, quickly go back and get Antoine or your *pére* to help carry this boy to the barn."

I squatted down in the same position I had held in the well all night. My legs and back screamed at me, but the distress of the boy was worth my additional pain. His deep black, red-rimmed eyes met mine and my heart went to him. I had no idea what was wrong or how to help. Magdaline bent down next to me but was still crying. She pulled up the remnants of his shirt and was trying to get him to identify what part was causing the pain. James moved his hand to the lower right side. Uncle Frank came rushing to join us and scooped the boy into his arms carrying him back to the barn. The rest of us did our best to move quickly to join him, but Madam Crow had to stop every few feet due to a coughing fit. When we reached the barn, she collapsed outside the door, and it was Uncle Frank who again carried her inside and placed her next to *Pére*. Poor James was crying out in pain again.

Leopold came to me and grabbed my hand with the hand on his unburnt arm. In Walloon, I assured him that I would do everything to help his friend and to make him feel better. Tears slipped through the grime on the boy's face.

I cannot thank the eldest girl, Regina, of the German Shoen family enough for the care she provided Atlan and Marie Louise that day. Hilda Shoen and her family had walked into the barnyard that first day. When the fire came, the father and eldest Shoen boy were on their way back from Green Bay. The mother, Hilda, eldest daughter Regina, middle child Peter, and youngest daughter Theresa had spent the fire buried in the dirt of the plowed perimeter they had made around their farm. Each had matted dirt in their hair, making their heads seem misshapen. They hoped they could stay with us until they knew where the father, also named Peter, and eldest son Klaus were. Marie Louise was too weak to take full charge of Atlan, so Regina Shoen walked endlessly with him back and forth around the barn and the charred yard. Her young sister trailed behind her, humming a quiet tune I didn't recognize. The dear little girl looked like a demon streaked with soot. I knew she was likely quite hungry like the rest of us, and I nearly cried, at the thought of such a dear child being hungry in what was now my home.

Hilda Shoen, and her children, had taken charge of the barn and had started making a pile of items that might be useful. Mostly it was the usual items you would find in a barn, but I admired their work. Magdaline immediately started talking to them in German and found out they were from a farm to the east.

When I think back to that day, pictures of people flash before my eyes. There was every different reaction to our current state you could imagine. Waves of shock, sadness and fear rolled through the charred farm. I was about to be drowned by a wave of fear when a man appeared in the farmyard. His clothing was singed, and he was filthy like the rest of us. He reached to shake Uncle Frank's hand which wasn't lifted to meet it.

The man said in French, "Frank, it's me Doc Antoine." I would never forget the look that washed over Uncle Frank's face. It was the first time I had seen hope run past his features that day.

Doctor Antoine lived in Bottkolville, one of the villages at the bottom of the hill. He would often stop and visit on his way to and from patients in the woods. On a normal day he always had a spark in his blue eyes and a mop of sand-blond hair that would start the day slicked away from his eyes but would end the day flopped just above them.

"Doc, ah, sorry." Uncle Frank stumbled but was clearly happy to see the doctor. "Are you okay, Joséphine? The children?"

A shadow that in the years ahead we would all recognize passed in front of the doctor. He looked at his feet. "My boy didn't make it."

We stood there silent, thinking of the eldest child of the doctor. He had been a smaller male copy of his mother. I guessed he had been two or three years old. The news that the tiny boy had died felt confusing. That's how those early days went. In your mind you knew that everything happening around you was very real and very dangerous, but you had so few things you could implement to improve the situation that there was no guarantee how you would react to another layer of sadness. It could be anger one moment, nervous laughter the next, complete shock the next.

The doctor was brought into the barn to look at the saddest of our group. Magdaline and Leopold followed him inside.

Doctor Antoine was a favorite in the communities he served. He had a way of making people comfortable and was willing to take goods and services as payment if a family couldn't cover his fees.

He was an avid reader and would consult with doctors around Wisconsin on ways to help his patients. Today he came to the barn without any of his trademark tools. There was no medicine to administer or ointment to begin the healing process to the burns. I think instead he realized we needed something normal to happen and a doctor would be who would help if this was a normal situation. He left instructions with Magdaline, Hilda, and me for each of those in the sick bay. Mostly it was signs to watch for improvement or worsening. Not that he or we had much that could add comfort or healing.

Doctor Antoine also told us that he had heard there was a group coming through helping with burying any dead. The church in GrandLez was burned, but the priest Father Crud would bury people in the graveyard. The Brethren Church in San Sauveur had also burned, but their pastor had been in Green Bay and was coming back for burials and to minister to the members.

I watched my brother Antoine's face harden at the news of burials. It had only been a few hours since we had learned of the gap left in our family and I could feel my false front cracking.

The doctor had also heard that there were wagons coming from Green Bay with supplies and possibly even on a ship into Ahnepee ports. At this point I didn't care if there was clothing or food in those packages, I needed water.

I have never to this day been thirstier. When we sailed to America, the sailors had told us all to not drink the sea water and spun what seemed like tales of seamen going mad from lack of drinkable water. The further into the day it seemed no longer like a yarn but a very real prospect for all of us. Every thought was followed with your mind saying, "but you are thirsty".

As that afternoon started to slip away more people came up the hill seeking the warmth of our fire and shelter in the barn. They were strangers and neighbors, but those labels didn't matter. I chewed on a small chunk of potato that had been cooked in the open fire and went to the smaller part of the barn to add Doctor Antoine's son to the list on the left.

If anyone slept that night, it was the children. I sat next to the fire letting Leopold lean against me on his side that wasn't burned. Every few hours I would get up to check on those in the barn. Both *Pére* and Marie Louise would tell me they were okay, but I knew they were struggling to breathe and their chests heaved uncomfortably during coughing fits. I knew Marie Louise was still coughing blood but had been hiding it by wiping her hand on the inside of her sleeve. The other patients either stared at the ceiling or just above their toes. Years later when Leopold was studying medicine, he showed me a photo of men in a hospital from the War Between the States, and those men had the same distant stare above their feet and heavenward. The stare of people hovering on the edge of shock, battling pain without comfort.

Young James had stopped screaming in pain but was so ashen that he nearly glowed in the dark. Doctor Antoine feared it was appendicitis, which would require an operation. He had explained to Magdaline that he hoped it could hold off one more day so he may have tools to perform the operation. Otherwise, they may need to risk sending him in any wagon that came this way to a town that had the tools. Magdaline tried to explain it to Madam Crow but if she understood we weren't sure. We could only wait for Jacques to come back.

October 10, 1871

The sun hadn't fully come up when Jacques and a wagon made their way into the barnyard. Anyone who could help, unloaded the small stack of items he had been able to secure. Ahnepee had also been struck by the fire, and many people had flooded into the town to seek help. Some kind women from one of the churches were helping divide the assistance as best they could. There was confirmation that there was more aid on the way with ships from Lake Michigan and wagons from Green Bay, but for now this wagon was much needed.

The woman driving the wagon told us her name was Mrs. Nancy Higgins. She had faded brown hair and tiny gold glasses hanging from a chain attached to her chest. She immediately took charge of the assembly line and started making a list out loud of items we would need. She offered to take Atlan and me and any of the other small children to her home in Ahnepee. I stood there seeing a ray of hope but was brought back to reality when James cried out again. There were those in greater need than me. We decided that Atlan would stay that night at the barn.

The supplies included water and some cooked food, blankets of all different kinds and some clothing. As each item was handed out, one of the people closest to the wagon would call over someone who would be the right fit for the item. When they got to the cooked food several women quickly took charge and somehow made it stretch to every soul on site.

We discussed for a long time if we should move James Crow to town. Mrs. Nancy Higgins was against it. She worried that if it was his appendix, it could burst in the wagon on the rough roads and creek crossings. They had to drive the long way back to town and even then, the path was strewn with the death of creatures and flora. She would instead find the supplies that Doctor Antoine needed to perform the surgery. It was decided that a severely burned neighbor boy and his older sister would ride with Mrs. Nancy Higgins and go back to Ahnepee for help. They made room for the Bohemian girl called Venda who had barely a stitch of clothing left intact. Her skin was a mix of tight, pink, and bleeding, and she was holding a bundle of cloth that she wouldn't let anyone look at. To this day we don't know if there was a baby or an animal wrapped in those clothes—maybe there was nothing. She had come to the barn like a spirit and left the same way.

Those first few days after the fire went so fast. Decisions were made in seconds and in the back of your mind you knew that the decision could mean life or death for someone in our barn camp. The nights were so uncomfortable. We were all still thirsty, even after drinking some of the water from Mrs. Nancy Higgins. My burn would become angry as the sun would go down. It tingled and throbbed, but there was nothing to do for it.

Waking up that second morning we discovered that Madam Crow had died in the night. She was sitting with James' head next to her leg and her back against the wall. James' pain didn't seem to allow him to understand that she had passed.

When we laid Madam Crow flat on the ground to be buried, I noticed that her usually crumpled brow was now smooth. No one knew how many years that Indian woman had seen, but in death it appeared her worries had been erased. She looked royal. Jacques and Antoine had gone to scout more aid and see if there were others who needed shelter. Jacques was the only one who may have known what the Indians would do to send her to the afterlife. We moved her to the smaller section of the barn. The man who had helped breathed '*Zdrávas, Maria, milosti plná,*' '*Hail Mary, full of grace,*' which I assumed was a prayer.

More reality came into the barnyard that morning when a group of men appeared over the hill. The most extraordinary thing about this group was that several of the men were shockingly clean. Their faces weren't smeared with remnants of soot, and their clothing wasn't singed and filthy. They had a wagon and shovels. They were the burial crew. They had been walking through the countryside helping bury people first and then animals. Sometimes these burials happened in cemeteries; other times families asked for them to be buried on their property. There were times when the fire had burned so hot that an entire family could be buried together in one casket. Mostly, there wasn't a casket. Instead, the men worked for hours digging holes big enough for the remains, then stood over their work, hats and rags in hands, wondering how their lives could have changed from cutting trees and farming to becoming undertakers.

Uncle Frank, John, and three men from our refuge joined this group and traveled around helping once our unwanted burials took place. John was such an animal lover that I worried about the things he would be seeing that day. The dead animals around the barnyard were heart-wrenching enough. He asked me to keep Trout around the barn. After spending the night of hell with the little creature in the well, we had formed a long-term bond. If he wasn't following John, it was me, he followed. Trout spent a lot of time with those in our hospital corner, offering something soft. With Marie Louise he would lay his head on her shoulder, and it seemed to slow her coughing. Remembering his pure spirit brought tears to my eyes.

More aid arrived that day from Ahnepee. There was more cooked food, water in barrels and clothing of various sizes. The chill had remained in the air and most people walked around at all hours of the day and night to try and keep warm any way they could. Nobody cared what the clothing looked like. There were girls wearing boys' trousers and boys wearing ladies' shirtwaists. If it fit well enough, you put it on and were beyond grateful. The cooked food was so welcome. We had nothing but the open fire to cook with and no real food to prepare.

Today it was Mrs. Higgins' husband and a hired boy who arrived in the barnyard. He had brought two wagons full to our camp. In one wagon there was an assortment of parts for a stove, kettles and pots, flour, salt, spoons, soap, rags and a few lanterns. He immediately started poking around the ruin of our cabin to see if the remnants of the wood stove were cool enough to move to the barn. He started taking the pieces apart and the little Theresa Shoen seemed to be happy to carry the pieces she could lift to the barn, following Mr. Higgins like a chick. Within a few hours he had the stove back together and the piping through the damaged side of the barn. He even had some sheet metal to cover the rest of the scars on the barn.

James Crow had slipped into a murmuring stupor at this point. We were able to send two of the young girls in the barnyard down to Doctor Antoine in Bottkolville. By the time he got to the yard, Mr. Higgins was ready to go back home, and they decided that they were going to try and move James to Ahnepee. I had saved a scrap of the fringe from his grandmother's shirt and handed it to Doctor Antoine. When he met my eyes, I knew he was exhausted and that each scene he had witnessed in his community was an additional stone to carry in his pocket.

We kept the fire going outside as well as in the stove that night. Some of our camp seemed uneasy with being indoors and would jump at the slightest change in atmosphere. There was more sleep that night, but it still came in fits and spurts.

October 11, 1871

Things shifted on the third day. I think people started to come out of shock and some may have started to realize that we had just been existing since that godforsaken night and would need to figure out the future. Maybe it was simply that we had more clean water and food the last twenty-four hours. Either way the children were moving around more, and the adults were talking more.

The men grouped together on one end of the yard and the women clustered around the stove in the barn that day. I remember most that the women standing around the stove all looked like they had aged ten years. A twenty-one-year-old woman named Joséphine's hair had turned completely white after the night of the fire. She was to marry a man who was working at one of the sawmills, but no one had seen nor heard from him. I had heard her quietly tell her mother that she feared when he saw her, he wouldn't want to go through with the marriage.

In these separate meetings, it was decided that teams of people would be set up to help get the group back on their feet. Everyone would have a job, even those in the sick bay of the barn. Tasks included gathering water, cooking, sorting the aid donations, collecting fuel for warmth, and sharing information. A group of men planned to walk to the closest lumber mill to see if they were hiring. This would help bring in cash for much-needed items. Some of the boys were tasked with going back to the barnyard survivors' homes and finding anything that could be used in the future, no matter how small. Caring for the young children and the injured was assigned to those who needed to stay close to the barn, and those who were less burned or inhibited were assigned tasks that might take them away from the barn during the day.

I was assigned to gather aid and help Hilda Shoen ensure it was used to the fullest. Hilda had already started the process by sweeping the barn and other burned buildings for anything useful. We didn't speak the same language, but she was so organized and clear with her body language that I was never confused about her intent with an item. When needed, Magdaline would translate. Hilda Shoen was such a loving woman that everyone in the barnyard benefited from her mothering, even when they didn't speak the German language.

We had been told that there would be a group coming from Green Bay into GrandLez that day with some food, and we hoped for more warm clothing. It had been so cold, even when the sun did its best to come through the remnants of the fire haze.

Leopold and I found a remnant of fabric that wasn't currently being worn and decided it would work as a sack to carry a few items, if they had things we needed, and started down the hill. It was funny to think about now, but we walked the same path we would have when there were trees. We didn't need to because we could see the remains of GrandLez from the top of the hill.

When we reached the village, it felt so unusual to see other people—people who hadn't been shuffling around the barnyard. I recognized a few of their forlorn faces. Mr. Oleson was from Norway. The first time I met him was after church one Sunday. He was not Catholic but attended services because it was too far to go to a Lutheran church each weekend. He spoke in a lilting voice in a language I didn't understand. The day I met him; he stood straight and lean with a shag of warm blond hair waving from under his black hat. Today he was leaning dangerously to the left with his long-fingered hand clutching his side. Coming out of the neck of his filthy white shirt was a shockingly clean bandage that went up the side of his head and tied under his chin. Pain walked all over his body. When he saw us, he attempted a greeting in his lilt, but it came out in stiff jolts. Leopold greeted him in Wallonian, which made him stop inflicting pain on himself. Our lives had been confined to the square footage of the barnyard for only a handful of days, but seeing Mr. Oleson made it feel like it had been hundreds of years. Leopold helped Mr. Oleson to sit on the ground outside what was left of the general store with his back to the toasted wall.

In the short time I had lived in the area, GrandLez was one of the few towns I had visited regularly. The church, saloon, and houses today looked familiar but severely scarred. I was relieved when *Madam* Waulet from the general store came out to greet us. She immediately started speaking in Walloon, asking at a mind-freezing pace about everyone in our family. Leopold did his best to explain, but openly started crying when he talked about Sofie, Cédonie and the children. In my rush to comfort him I patted his burnt arm causing more pain to the boy. *Madam* Waulet burst into tears as well and let them just fall from her eyes without even moving to dab them away.

While still crying, she said, "Mr. Oleson here has had word from his people's church in Green Bay that they were on their way here with supplies." She touched his shoulder with the lightest of taps. "He has been such a help here in town." He didn't move any part of his body aside from blinking with his right eye in a slow tired motion.

Madam Waulet invited us to sit outside or come into what was left of the store. They had managed to save what had been the small storage area, about eight feet square, built to the left of the larger store. She was housing her family as well as several others at night. During the day she worked to disperse information as she got it through her two sons, who had escaped injury from the fire, by running deep into the swamp and burying themselves in the somewhat dry mud. Later, these two men would talk about how the trees sizzled that night all around them, and they were sure that at any minute, the fragile roots of one of the swamp trees would give and kill them in their mucky beds.

We opted to sit outside and wait for the Norwegian church aid. I think Mr. Oleson passed out or fell asleep because he didn't move for such a long time. Before the fire Leopold would have tried to have a conversation with Mr. Oleson. Today he sat quietly in the weak sun on a small, smooth stone. This was the first time we were able to just sit and not be solving a problem.

Magdaline had made some bandages with the aid that came yesterday, but Leopold had refused to get in line, knowing there were others who needed the coverings more. I was equally proud and scared that he had sacrificed for others. I knew his burns needed care today. Maybe there was more water and things for bandages coming today. It was amazing how this little village was still moving at a faster pace than on the farm. Uninjured people and animals, seeming to have no owner milled around, but they still appeared wary.

A boy who was maybe the same age as Leopold but much shorter came running into GrandLez in bare feet. His mismatched clothing was clearly donated items and fit him enough. He skidded to a stop in front of us. "Was *Madam* Waulet here?" he asked in Walloon, wrinkling his nose and wiggling his shoeless toes in the dust. I pointed into the doorway.

The boy didn't need to bother going into the store, he shouted his news so loudly that much of the village heard. He had come from a mile ahead and there was a chain of wagons from Green Bay coming this way. Mr. Oleson was so pleased with the news that he inched himself up to his new crooked stance and looked off toward the southwest.

I spent the time thinking about what items our group really needed instead of relaxing my mind and watching the village.

    Bandages

    Water

    Flour

    Salt

    Milk

Leopold had tipped his head back against the building and was snoring softly.

    Magdaline needs a shirt and shoes

    Leopold needs a shirt and shoes

    Regina needs a warm coat or wrap

Uncle Frank needs a warm hat

Marie Louise needs her own blanket

The mute girl, Lenka, needed some scissors to cut her

singed hair and chalk for her slate

This was only six of the nearly forty people who had been staying with us in the barn. Where was I going to find clothing for forty people? That morning, we had something called Johnny Cakes. Tom, the man who brought the mute girl to us had fought in the War Between the States as a Yankee. He had explained that they would make these during his war days when they had flour or cornmeal. I found them tasteless, but they stretched to the entire group. Magdaline explained that some people ate them with sugar or molasses. I added more flour to my mental list.

I could feel the panic coming from my toes. Even if the wagons were stuffed full there was no way I would get even a portion of the items we needed. As I sat there feeling like I was being sucked into a black abyss, I noticed a small clutch of children coming toward the general store. They were all different heights and various levels of cleanliness. These were likely the orphans from the home here in GrandLez. They amazed me with how resilient they seemed. Even in their smudged skin and torn clothing, they still helped each other carry a water barrel through the street to what was left of the foundling home. There was only an open shell of a building with a fire burning in the middle. Poking around the rubble was a grim figure who could have been either a man or a woman, based on the donated clothing.

I looked over at Leopold and didn't have the heart to wake him. I knew the boy hadn't been sleeping well at night because of his injury and he was so brave during the day he always offered to help right away in the morning and kept moving all day.

Yesterday, when the men who helped with burials returned, they collapsed on the rock next to Magdaline, who was trying to make sense of one of the children's burnt hair. I was across from her tending the outdoor fire when I noticed John's face was wet with tears. Magdaline's charge turned, with eyes as large as saucers and reached out to pat John's filthy hand. Magdaline stopped with the child and pulled John close to her, wincing with pain from her forearm burns.

"John, oh John," I stopped with the fire and sat on his other side. "The work you did today was so important." I leaned into him on the other side hoping that between Magdaline and me, we could erase some of the anguish. The child on Magdaline's lap slipped over to John's lap and gave him an awkward hug around his torso.

Magdaline continued, "John, you did the Lord's work today. You made sure that those dear souls were given respect. You helped protect them from further harm on this earth."

He nodded, but the tears continued. "I didn't find my *mame*." His statement shot through me and likely went through Magdaline and the child after leaving my body.

Jacques had alerted the authorities in Ahnepee with the names of those we knew were missing from our barnyard community. John was old enough to be aware of his mother's delicate emotional balance and had seen how people he had known his entire life who were considered rock solid had faltered. We could only assure him that we would continue to look for his *mame*.

I had been lost in thought about Odile but snapped back when people around me started to stand and shuffle toward what sounded like several living horses. The wagons had arrived. Mr. Oleson stood as straight as he could manage while leading his countrymen into the cinders of GrandLez. They hadn't even stopped their carriages when he started speaking rapidly to the lead driver. Norwegian had such an up-and-down quality under normal circumstances. Today it was flat and met equally flat between these two men.

As soon as the wagons stopped several people got off the backs of each and began unloading supplies. Leopold and I stood in the line to get whatever we could load into our makeshift sack. It was a huge relief when one of the men from the wagon realized that there were many of us hoping to just take what we could carry and instead of dropping the supplies in GrandLez, they were going to bring the wagon up the hill to our barnyard and then continue to Rosiere while the empty wagon took those in need of a hospital back to Green Bay.

While we waited to walk up the hill with the wagon train, I noticed a young woman who seemed so impossibly clean and bright. It felt as if I were seeing an angel. The blonde hair poking out from under her bonnet was nearly the same color as her skin and her eyelashes were like little snowflakes surrounding the palest blue eyes I had ever seen. When she saw me, she immediately made room in the back of the wagon she had been riding in for Leopold and me. She draped a blanket around the two of us, trying to be careful of our injuries. Leopold's head dropped to my shoulder, and I felt relieved that maybe he would sleep for a few minutes more before we got to the barnyard. When the children from the orphan home passed our wagons carrying another barrel of water, the angel woman breathed sharply. The back of her hand tried to brush away the tears that had started but also hide them from me.

Once the aid had been left for those in GrandLez, the wagons with the remaining items started moving toward the barnyard. I think I fell asleep for a small portion of the ride, because it felt like it only lasted a few minutes.

When we reached the barnyard there were a few new people standing and talking to Antoine and Uncle Frank. At this point we were so used to the transient nature of our camp that I didn't take much notice. It wasn't until the angel woman rocked and slipped to the ground that my attention shifted from helping organize the aid. News traveled quickly in various languages that the young woman was engaged to a man who had died in the fire. She had just arrived from Norway and had offered to help with dispersing the aid if she could also look for her fiancé along the route.

That day we didn't have much time to add her sadness to our sorrow, because they trundled her back into the wagon and announced that they hoped to make it to Rosiere before dark.

As they rode out of the barnyard, day three continued its surreal path. Magdaline started running toward the north, to greet a shadowy figure that was at the crest of the hill. When I caught up, I realized it was Odile. If the Norwegian woman was an angel, Odile was a demon. Her face was blackened and streaked, as though she had clawed at it with her fingers. Her hands were balled into fists and the clothing from her knees down had been burnt away. Her shins and feet had to be in immense pain based on the blood dripping between her bare toes and swollen skin. When she finally looked up, it was me who started shouting as loud as I could for someone to get Uncle Frank. Odile stood there swaying as if there was a strong wind pushing her in every direction. Magdaline was trying to speak to her, but she didn't seem to hear. When Uncle Frank came racing toward us, Odile broke from the trance and started shrieking and railing at Uncle Frank's chest. The hellish sounds she was making drew additional help from our enclave, including her son John. He stopped about five feet away from his parents with his hands in the air and mouth open. Magdaline thinking quickly ran to steady him.

It took three adult men to get Odile into the barn. She raged the entire time pulling at her hair and shouting in a language unknown to anyone. When they got her seated in the barn, she sat with her legs ramrod straight and her back stiff but screamed the entire time barely stopping for a breath. Her daughter, Marie Louise, sat on the floor next to her and *Pére* started loudly praying. John's chest was heaving, and Magdaline was doing everything she could get him calmed.

Uncle Frank stood before his wife, looking from face-to-face pleading with us to help him help his wife. No one knew how to manage the situation. Hilda Shoen sent one of the people standing nearby to try and find the doctor. She then crossed herself and started mumbling prayers in German.

When the screaming finally stopped, it was just that the noise coming out of her mouth ended. Her torture continued but now each time she opened her mouth, no sound came forward. We had all seen the terror of burns and the anguish of the death of loved ones from this fire storm, but this was a new level of fear. This was something unseen by the rest of us.

It wasn't until she lapsed into a trance-like state that we were able to clean her the best we could. That was when Magdaline was able to pry a shard of wood from her fist. While it had been burnt, it still showed careful carving on one area. When Uncle Frank saw it, he ran out of the barn and got sick next to a charred tree stump. After he had composed himself, he explained that Odile's brother Jean Baptiste had carved crosses for each of the family members who were buried on her parents' original Wisconsin farm. Jean Baptiste had sold the family farm several years ago hoping to make it rich out west.

The first Wisconsin home Odile knew was located a few miles northwest of Uncle Frank and Odile's farm. We all knew Odile would make the walk to visit those cemetery plots when she could find the time. Odile had walked to that graveyard during or after the fire and had lost her mind along the way.

By the time the sun started to set, everyone's nerves were on edge. Some had found slightly warmer clothing in the donations. We had more food and water than the day before. You would have thought we would have all slipped into sleep due to exhaustion, but instead a fight broke out between two of the younger men. At least one punch landed before Antoine stepped in to separate the men. I never fully understood what the fight was about and years later these two men were still friends.

After October 11, 1871

In the weeks following we continued to receive aid from various donors. Some of the gifts were more useful than others. A well-meaning person had sent a box of fancy silk dresses, top hats, and tailcoats. Thankfully, shortly afterward, a box came with sewing items, so we could rework donations to be better suited. The gifts of fowl and livestock were equally appreciated but came with the unknown of how we would feed them through the winter. I would forever be intensely grateful to every person who packaged something and sent it to a faraway place to people they had never met before. There were some who began to complain that there wasn't enough aid and there were those who felt slighted if they didn't get the same as their neighbor. I guess this was a sign that human nature would always come back to itself.

As planned, most of the men went to the mills to work after that third day. Before they left, Uncle Frank taught the younger children how to make shingles. Even though the wood wasn't as available as before the fire, there were areas that had escaped total destruction. The children were taught which logs could still be used even if they had been slightly burned and which weren't useful. Shingle making had been a vast industry in those early years of Belgian immigration in Wisconsin. It boosted spirits around the barnyard. We were doing something to generate the needed money to feed humans and animals. Hilda's daughter Regina, the white-haired Joséphine and two other girls in the barnyard took jobs in area towns to help earn money for their families. Regina was working at the orphan's home in GrandLez, which meant we got to see her more than the others.

Pére had seemed to consistently gain strength and get better after the fire. Most days he felt well enough to oversee the shingle production with the children, helping them make neat piles for sale. He was still the first to go to bed at night and the last to get up in the morning, but we all assumed that the sleep was healing him. He rarely spoke. Marie Louise seemed slightly better too. She would help with sewing projects and the care of her mother.

Odile was nearly mute and hard to predict. Without chalk for her slate, Lenka had been scratching pictures and words into the dirt with a stick to communicate. She tried to share her stick with Odile and was met with a slap across the face. The poor girl just backed away and avoided the area as much as she could. No one had known Odile to lay a hand on anyone, much less a child, which made the event weigh on all our minds. Nearly everyone took the same path as Lenka and provided only the basic care Odile would tolerate.

Magdaline and I had started walking the barnyard to discuss how we needed to handle certain situations. It had been nearly a month since the fire when, on one of these walks, Magdaline's brother Leo appeared. He came over the hill with a heaping wagon of items he had brought from Milwaukee. He snatched Magdaline up like she was a piece of cloth and locked her in a fierce embrace. When he set her down, he was sobbing and then grabbed me in the same greeting. The friendly giant didn't calm until he held Atlan.

He explained that at first, they had heard in Milwaukee that the fire was only on the west side of the bay of Green Bay and that surely his sister in Kewaunee County was just fine. The same night as our firestorm, a fire had broken out in the big city of Chicago and Milwaukee was called upon to help aid the victims in that city. News then came that the entire village and area around Peshtigo and the Door peninsula had hundreds of dead. It was several days before it was confirmed that his sister may have been in one of the burned areas and it took time for him to organize the items in the wagon and secure the trip all without knowing if his only relation in America was dead or alive. When he arrived in Ahnepee, one of the first people he saw felt familiar. When he approached the man, he was the *Métis* named Jacques his sister had written about. Jacques helped lead Leo to the barnyard.

Leo and his shop assistant had thought of everything we could possibly be missing as we helped sort the items. Leo noticed Lenka, standing with her slate tied around her neck. When he greeted her, her only response was to tilt her head to the side. Magdaline explained that they thought she was mute and likely deaf, but that she used her slate to write words when she had chalk. Leo's eyes lit up as if he had been offered the grandest prize and he started rooting through one of the rough sacks. Out popped his hands, each holding small wooden boxes of chalk. Lenka threw herself at Leo and kept making the same hand gesture that we all assumed was for thank you. Leo, the giant shopkeeper from Alsace and Milwaukee cried again while patting the little girl's back. He then pulled out a small leather-bound pad of paper and pencil and made a note.

He looked up after scribbling, seeming pleased with himself and said, "for Lenka, a doll, a ribbon for her slate, chalk and I will talk to the doctors in Milwaukee."

"Leo, would you?" Magdaline let out a whoosh of air. "She seems to be such a bright child, but I can't always communicate. Maybe the doctors have something we could use or give her." In one breath, Magdaline had let out nearly all our worries for our small charge.

"What about her relations?" Leo had stolen the thought from my head.

"We fear they were part of a Bohemian settlement north of here that was completely wiped out." Magdaline grabbed one of the crates on the top of the wagon.

"Dr. Antoine has been asking on his visits if anyone was seeking their young daughter who didn't speak, but there have been no developments." I added.

Leo looked over at Lenka, who was counting the sticks of chalk in the little boxes. "I will place an ad in the papers asking if anyone knows her. Maybe if her parents passed, there would be aunts, uncles, or grandparents."

Magdaline and I had made a pact that unless her real family came for her, we would keep her. There had been the suggestion that we take her to the orphan home in GrandLez, but I knew from my trip to town for aid that they were doing the best they could with even more meager resources. Having one more orphan would not help their situation. We both hoped we could find her family, but we both knew that as each day passed the chances were getting smaller.

Leo's help extended beyond the supplies. He went with Uncle Frank into Green Bay to make a claim on the insurance for his farm. The paperwork had been lost in the fire, but Uncle Frank hoped that having a distinguished shopkeeper from Milwaukee vouching for his farm would help get past the missing documents. Leo was also able to secure some feed and hay for the meager group of animals we had acquired through donations. He seemed to be loved by all, and his negotiation skills ensured that both parties felt they had the better end of the deal. He had not been there for the fire and was now clear-headed and could see what we would need in the future after the immediate needs were met. The weather felt more and more unpredictable each day. Winter was coming to Wisconsin, and only those who had lived there through a winter knew what we really needed to survive.

Hilda Shoen taught us how to make sausage from her childhood in Germany. That first winter it was composed of wild game, some pork and herbs Leo sent in the mail once he was back in Milwaukee. She made a quick version and fried it up, then layered it in storage jars. The rest she stuffed into intestines and smoked in a rough little building made into a smoker. She sat by the smoker or had *Pére* sit by the smoker to ensure none of the precious hardwood would be wasted. Jacques taught us how to make a version of preserved seasoned meat by rolling the mixture thin then drying it flat until it was little meat slabs.

Leo's shop assistant had secured a free sewing machine from a soft-hearted salesperson. I had seen a photograph of one of these machines in the newspaper but never thought we would have access to such an expensive tool. Hilda Shoen's daughter, Thérèse, quickly learned how to make the sewing machine perform and would spend several hours each day altering the clothing received as donations. With the scraps Lenka started piecing together quilts in randomized patterns. Other survivors learned of the girls' talents and would bring clothing for alterations and scraps, hoping to have Lenka make a warm blanket for them too. Sometimes the girls would get paid a small amount from men in the logging camps for their work.

The girls who went to work out of the house knit as fast as donated wool could be spun. It wasn't unusual for Hilda's daughter Regina to knit while she walked back to her job at the orphan's home after her Sunday day off.

Leopold spent nearly all his time finding and dragging wood that could be burned in the stove for the winter. The others who were able took their turns with the ax, and it became a nearly constant background sound of wood being thwacked into manageable slices.

When he wasn't sourcing fuel, he liked to tend to our sick and injured. He even started taking daily notes in the margins of a scrap of newspaper, which he would then share with Dr. Antoine when he made his rounds.

The injuries to Magdaline's arms were improving, but they made it hard for her to complete some tasks, so she spent much of her time cooking and sourcing food. She and Hilda would mix potato, flour, and water together then roll it into a long line and cut it into pieces. The pieces would go into a stew to stretch it further. They called these dumplings *knoephla* and while the ingredients in the stew might be different each time, it was a welcome dish that sat on the stove warming all day for any weary travelers coming through. Those of us from Wallonia called the stew *bouillabaisse* (booyah). These women with German backgrounds also introduced us to how you make sauerkraut since late harvest cabbages were often donated. The fermented cabbage helped provide vitamins in the winter since we didn't have other vegetables preserved.

Things improved each week. When the men weren't working at the mills they worked around the farms. Antoine called a meeting one day to discuss his thoughts on how the reborn farms should be laid out. He invited Jacques and Pierre Baudet. His idea was to build the houses of the three Gaspard farms at the corners where the land joined. He then suggested that Pierre Baudet and Jacques build their new houses and new farm buildings at the edge closest to the Gaspard land. That way if a fire ever came again, it would be easier to get between the buildings of the farms and work together to save the people and buildings. Everyone agreed, and Jacques and Pierre Baudet staked where their houses would go an eighth of a mile from the four corners where the Gaspard houses and barns would be situated.

The first house followed the design of men who had come from the south, offering their skills and layout for a nearly square, two-story house. We started gathering the materials needed to build the home of logs first, and then it would be clad with bricks from the nearby brickworks. The idea was that if a fire came again the shell of the house wouldn't burn and we wouldn't need to completely start over.

Once the house was erected in the spring of 1872, we barely waited for the windows to be installed before moving most of the people who had been sheltering in the barn into the new home. The barn was then put on rolling logs and moved perpendicular, behind the new house. We still had a few men that would sleep in the barn when they weren't working at the mills or on their own farms. As the work continued adding plaster to the walls, trim to windows, and rugs to the floors—the first house became a catchall for activities both happy and sad.

Illness came that winter and we first lost *Pére*, Christmas of 1871, and then Marie Louise in the spring. The front room was used for Marie Louise's funeral as well as several others in the neighborhood whose lungs hadn't fully recovered before typhoid fever, influenza, and even common colds invaded.

There were happier events in the house. The soldier Tom, who brought Lenka to us, and Hilda's daughter Regina were married in the front room, there were at least three local babies born to women who came to us to give birth in one of the closest solid structures and we hosted the first teacher who conducted classes around the kitchen table.

This was the last page in the pile from Emilie, but not the only pages in the box. Edna Mae had gathered stories about and from other women who were in the fire.

Chapter 16: Women of the Fire
Marie Thérèse Lateau Gaspard's Story

Marie was born in *Bois-d'Haine* but moved as an infant with her parents to *Grez-Doiceau*. The Lateau family had what would have seemed like unusual skills in the 19th century. Her father was a dowser of some fame in the community, and her grandmother was said to have the power of healing through herbs and some said through her hands. The most unusual family member, Anne Louise Lateau, was a cousin who had been born in 1850 in *Bois-d'Haine* and at the age of thirty-three she had her first experience of stigmata and ecstasy. Through the years the Catholic church and other health organizations observed Anne Louise with mixed results.

Marie, however, seemed to have the unusual skill of knowing things without seeing or hearing them and she inherited the art of healing from her grandmother. What was particularly striking was that the gifted members did not behave as if they were different, nor did they seem to think of themselves as special. They used their unusual skills daily without fanfare. Of course, there were people who talked about how these gifts felt supernatural, but they were usually the first to seek their assistance for a new well or medical aid.

The gifts had been passed to her children. Uncle Frank may not have realized that his ability to locate a water source beneath the thick limestone in Wisconsin was a family skill. When Atlan found a water source the first time Uncle Frank brought him to help a neighbor find a new well it seemed the next generation was in line to inherit. Emilie was approached by a group in the mid-1880s. They had heard a rumor that her ancestor was Anne Louise Lateau and that her dead mother had visited her the night of the fire. It seemed like she would benefit their Spiritualist Church in Luxemburg, Wisconsin. A year later, another Spiritualist Church was built near Brussels. Emilie attended that one once out of curiosity but felt no connection with the people or the message they were projecting. In the early 1900's one of their members sought to test the power of the church and cut off his own hand, after he died from his wounds both the Luxemburg and Brussels area Spiritualist Churches disbanded.

On October 8, 1859, a young woman named Adele Brice was bringing grain on foot to the local grist mill. In a field near current day Champion, Wisconsin in Brown County, and near Kewaunee County, she claimed to have been visited by the Virgin Mary. The next day, on the way to and from Mass, the Virgin Mary visited Adele twice more and Adele said that the apparition had taxed her with bringing Catholic education to the local children and atonement to sinners. Adele had been called a Spiritualist, but she strictly stuck to her Catholic faith even when the Church sought to stop her mission. Emilie thought it was odd when people in the Spiritualist church tried to draw a comparison between her and Adele. Emilie had been jostled awake during a firestorm by what she thought was her mother. She had not been given a life calling by the Virgin Mary.

Emilie learned about her *Grand-mére's* experience during the big fire via a letter from her sister Eugénie across the world.

According to the letter, *Grand-mére* sat straight up in bed at 3 a.m. shouting that there was a fire. *Grand-pére* was so startled that he had jumped from the bed and ran around the house looking for the source of the fire. Not finding anything, he returned to their bedroom to find his wife speaking under her breath and wringing her hands. *Grand-pére* was trying to get additional information from her when she sobbed and fainted to the floor. *Grand-pére* struggled to get her to revive and when she did, she looked him in the eyes and said without flinching. "Four are gone, one was lost, two more will be leaving." *Grand-pére* had lived with her for so many years that he had grown so used to her strange comments and he was rarely surprised, but this was a riddle that needed daylight and strong coffee to unravel.

She refused to go back to bed and instead sat in the sitting room by the cold fire, tears streaming down her face. *Grand-pére* stumbled around the kitchen to heat water in the kettle hoping it was just a bad dream. He managed to get the hot liquid into cups and joined her in the sitting room. After a few sips he asked her again what the dream had been about. In the dark room, *Grand-mére* spoke slowly and evenly stating, "There was a disaster in America. Someone was missing, and she couldn't find her way back. Jean Baptiste would leave earth soon." She paused and with a sharp intake of air continued, "Sofie, the children… gone, gone, gone and François' child will follow." The tears ran like rivers down her wrinkled cheeks. *Grand-pére* said he had never felt more disturbed in his life but there was no way to quickly find out what was happening to his family in Wisconsin.

The next day he sent for their grandchildren Eugénie and Joseph to try and rouse her from the sitting room. When *Grand-mére* saw Eugénie enter the room she said, "Emilie needs us, she doesn't have the simples she needs for all of the people." Eugénie knew her *Grand-mére* had an eerie way of knowing which herb to use when needed, but this seemed so out of character that she wondered if she had apoplexy or had maybe lost her mind. Before she could finish the thought, *Grand-mére* turned and met Eugénie's eyes, then shook her head slightly. Eugénie later said in the letter it was almost as if *Grand-mére* knew what she was thinking and wanted to assure her that she was not ill or crazy. *Grand-pére* told Eugénie that the night before he could have sworn, he smelled smoke but when there was no fire, he too feared that she had lost her mind.

Eugénie stayed in the room in the eaves for the next few days to help *Grand-pére* manage. It was over a week, when the news reached Wallonia that a settlement of their immigrants had been in a tornado of fire. Many were dead and there were so many who had no clothing or shelter. Eugénie said she was struck dumb when her husband delivered the news to her grandparents' house. What was strange was the confirmation seemed to rouse *Grand-mére*, and she got up and started collecting items around the house. When asked what she was doing she explained that her family was going to need these.

She was correct, they were going to need these items and the country of Belgium also recognized that their immigrants needed help. The Belgian government sent money and shipped crates of linens, clothing and other items to Wisconsin.

Eugénie and others in the village were worried sick and quickly sent letters and packages to the locations they prayed their relatives were still located. Jacques carried that letter to Emilie many weeks later. Thankfully the local mail in the region had started again quickly after the fire. Of course, transatlantic missives in those days took several weeks to arrive. In Eugénie's letter, it stated that she and Joseph spent as much time as they could with their grandparents. *Grand-mére* was constantly collecting things to send to her family in America not realizing how long it would take them to arrive. *Grand-pére* extended his walking circle around the village each day in the hopes of getting news about the people they knew in Wisconsin. *Grand-mére* was so certain and had repeated the same premonition over and over causing everyone additional unease.

When Eugénie finally received word from Emilie the accuracy of *Grand-mére's* prediction was alarming. She was correct about there being four dead immediately after the fire. Her son was indeed injured and died in December from wounds and smoke inhalation from the fire, granddaughter Marie Louise died in the spring. She likely had what they called smoke pneumonia, so when she caught bronchitis, her weak lungs couldn't fight. Finally, daughter-in-law Odile, a woman that *Grand-mére* had never actually met, had lost her mind.

Died in the fire October 8, 1871

Sofie Agathe Defaux Gaspard 26 years

Adele Martine Gaspard 5 years

Rosilia Thérèse Gaspard 4 years

Honoré Louis Gaspard 3 years

Died with Sofie in the fire October 8, 1871

Cédonie Marie Thérèse Cuvelier Baudot 28 years

Juliette Marie Thérèse Baudot 6 years

John Baptiste Joseph Baudot 3 years

Baby Baudot

Died from burns and smoke illness from the fire
December 25, 1871

Jean Baptiste Joseph Gaspard 48 years

Died due to complications from smoke inhalation and
bronchitis from the fire March 11, 1872

Marie Louise Gaspard 12 years

<u>Died in the Wisconsin asylum after experiencing a mental break during the fire April 17, 1875</u>
Odile Joséphine Meurice Gaspard 46 years

Chapter 17: Women of the Fire
Odile Joséphine Meurice Gaspard's Story

Odile Meurice was born in 1829 in a village just a few miles from the Gaspard family's home village of *Grez-Doiceau*. When she was twenty-four, she sailed with her parents and younger brother to America with the goal of aiding the family in farming in Wisconsin.

Odile was considered very pretty with her pert nose, large greenish eyes, and dark hair. She was tall for a woman, but her mannerisms and charm typically made people forget that she was inches taller than most. When she was eighteen, she met a local man and planned to marry him. She never fully explained why she didn't marry and stay in Wallonia, waving off any questions saying that she was destined to be in Wisconsin and meet and marry Uncle Frank.

When her family arrived in 1853 there were only patches of Kewaunee County, Wisconsin where the sun could reach the ground. The trees were so thick that there was no way to see through them and most of the white pine were large enough around that three to four men joining hands with their full arm span may not touch the other man's fingers. Having lived her entire life in a village, the sounds and smells were new and at times terrifying.

The first few months they lived on the land her father had claimed, they slept in a canvas shelter with an open fire. During the daylight hours the brown deer and small critters would stop if they saw them and look with curiosity. Once they lost interest they would skitter away. The night was a different story. Without being able to see through the trees and moonlight struggling to reach the ground the sounds became sinister, with the heavy breathing of bears, snuffing of deer, the screeching of coyotes, and the most feared of all, the wolves. Nearly any settler in the region who came in the fifties had stories about the wolves. Their nocturnal roaming and pack howling would make grown men shiver on a 90°F day.

Odile once said that her mother was so shocked by where they had landed and the volume of work that it was going to take to earn even the smallest portion of comfort, they had easily in Wallonia that she stopped talking. She went about the hard labor each day, doing her share and more, but couldn't bring herself to say a word. Her father in contrast was overjoyed at the prospect of owning such a large parcel of land and having it to hand to his son. He came with no knowledge of how to cut down the behemoth trees, how to build a house, dig a well, or plow a field. He had worked as a clerk in their village and aside from the care of household animals this was completely new and exciting for him. Odile said her brother Jean Baptiste was eighteen when they arrived and probably had the most balanced reaction to the job ahead. He was excited but had a healthy amount of respect for the obstacles and instinctively seemed to understand what tools they were going to need and how to get them. He was the first to explore the area around their land and met the nearest neighbor, a very young man called Jacques.

Jacques had grown up with a father who was a French fur trader. His mother was an Indian woman, and he was always quick to explain that that made him a *Métis*, French for mixed blood. The fur trade as a career was waning by the 1850s and Jacques was tired of moving around beholden to the shrinking population of desirable pelts. Instead, he decided to try farming his own land and picked Wisconsin. Nearly everyone who had ever met Jacques had a story about him and most of these stories featured him as the hero. He was a guide, hunter, people connector, and strangely not a great farmer.

When he met the Meurice family he was the only person in the immediate area who spoke French, was used to living rough in the wilds of North America and was happy to help people as he traversed his new life.

Jacques and the Meurice family became a tight-knit unit. Jacques taught Odile and her mother about the plants on their land. The Meurice men and Jacques worked together to start removing trees on each other's property and building a better shelter for the family.

That first year was filled with constant back-breaking work and worry. Building a home that would protect their family through the winter without tools or any experience seemed unimaginable but was completely necessary. Cooking on a fire set in the middle of a forest and the daily trek to get water were just the tip of the sword for survival in Kewaunee County Wisconsin.

In a wooden box in her current log home Odile kept the work dress she wore those first four years. When she brought it from Wallonia it was a gray-and-ecru pin-striped dress with a full skirt, long sleeves and an ecru lace collar. After four years of nearly constant wear the dress was now so thin in some places you could see your hand through the material. The hem below the apron line was permanently stained a splotchy dark gray and the lace at the neck had been removed and sewn onto a baby dress and then removed again in case it would be wanted for a future wedding dress. For Odile she didn't keep the dress to hold on to happy memories. Instead, the dress meant that she had worked hard and built something. She had seen darkness.

In 1854 François Gaspard and Honoré LaCosse stumbled into the tiny clearing where the Meurice's had removed five trees and had built a five-foot wide by eight-foot-long log building. It had no windows, and the women had spent their spare time making the chinking that went between the logs to seal it from the elements. The only natural light came from the open door. The only luxury was the new cookstove. Odile's brother worked at a lumber mill twelve miles away to earn the money to buy the stove. He found that he liked the work and learned how to make shingles and rough furniture, both of which made the dark cabin more comfortable. When Uncle Frank and Honoré appeared in the clearing, Odile hadn't seen other white people who weren't Jacques or her family for months.

Uncle Frank and Honoré had purchased items in Green Bay they hoped to use as barter as they traversed the woods looking for their claimed land. When Odile's mother saw the cakes of soap they had purchased, she burst into tears. Jacques had taught them to make their own soap, but it was hard on clothing and hands. Her mother had barely spoken the entire time they had been in Wisconsin, something that only seemed to trouble Odile. With the cake of soap in hand she sobbed her thanks until it was incoherent.

Neither Odile nor Uncle Frank remember exactly how they decided to marry, but it wasn't long after they first met. A missionary priest wandered into the Meurice clearing one day and the next they were married at a makeshift altar covered with her mother's good shawl and a crucifix the priest had carried through the woods. Uncle Frank and Honoré hadn't built a log shelter for winter, so it was decided that the married couple would live with her parents and the bachelors Honoré, and her brother would live with Jacques. Ultimately all the men took jobs at the sawmill and lived in the company barracks leaving the two women in a windowless box in the dark woods alone nearly all winter.

With her mother's help Odile delivered a set of stillborn twins on a bitter cold January night. With the ground frozen and no way to dig graves, Odile and her mother laid the babies in the only wooden box with a lid, and they placed it outside the door with stones on the top in the hopes of keeping animals away. Every day Odile had to walk past her dead children on the way to retrieve water from the creek. Between work and poor weather on his days off, it was two months before Uncle Frank returned to find his wife no longer pregnant and his mother-in-law retreated deeper into her silent alcove. The money from the work was desperately needed for food and tools to continue work on the Meurice and Uncle Frank's land and was another sacrifice demanded of this new country.

This cycle of the men working the winters continued for several years. In November of 1855 Odile gave birth again to a boy while Uncle Frank was working in the mill. The end of October 1856 she gave birth to a girl in her mother's cabin that now had two small windows. The beginning of November 1857 she gave birth to another girl in that same cabin while the men were working.

The winter of 1857-58 was a nasty one for the people living in these small clearings. While they were making slow progress on removing the trees and opening land for farming an illness was rapidly killing people. Odile's mother and all three children became violently ill and nothing Odile did would bring down the fever or quell the coughing. Over twenty-four hours her mother and two daughters were dead. Without a box large enough for the three bodies, Odile was forced to move them to an outbuilding they used to store smoked meat and other provisions. For weeks Odile would retrieve items from this outbuilding and be confronted with her loss. When the men returned, they dug three more graves to go alongside the twins. Her brother made thick wooden crosses and carved patterns and each of their initials into the wood. After hours of this work in the evening he would go out and stake the cross above the body it belonged to.

With her mother gone, she would now spend the long winters in her own cabin with her son listening for the wolves and wind by the cookstove. Three more crosses were added to the family plot by 1859. Her father, whose sight was failing, died after a gruesome accident at a mill and another set of twins were added. Odile once said she completely understood why her mother stopped talking, what was there to say in this land that just kept taking and rarely gave back?

By the time Magdaline and Emilie arrived Odile was forty-two, her dull hair was a gray brown and her once smooth complexion was ruddy and wrinkled. Her son John was now sixteen and her daughter Marie Louise was ten. Uncle Frank had removed enough trees to plant nearly an acre of crops around the dying tree stumps. The one room cabin now had two additions with windows and there were animals in the barn and fowl roaming the patches around the house. Things had gotten better, but the toll taken on Odile was evident even to those who had just met her. She still worked incredibly hard but would stop and eye the nearby woods with caution or stop with her ear raised on alert for predators.

Many others in the area would walk on Sunday to the rough church buildings for service, but Odile was never in attendance. Church, she said was for people who had faith and hope. While she didn't feel she had either for herself, she did feel she had hope for her living children. She insisted they attend the closest school as often as possible and even had them help her learn to write her name and a few other words in English. The toil and sadness were not something she wanted for John or Marie Louise.

Odile knew the crops were going to fail again in 1871 and without the crops Uncle Frank would likely need to take a position at one of the mills and would take John with him this winter. Even with the windows and the one whitewashed room in her own cabin, spending the winter alone in the woods with her daughter felt like a cruel setback.

The trees had been a constant source of struggle for Kewaunee County residents who wanted to farm. Even after the tops were removed, eliminating the stumps was nearly impossible. Most resorted to burning them out and this year it only added to the thick pall that hung over all Northeast Wisconsin. By the beginning of September most people were living with red-rimmed eyes and a nearly constant cough or tightness in their chest. There were fires burning in the woods to clear stumps and fires to burn off the unwanted refuse from lumber mills and in other areas of the state fires to help clear for a railroad extension. All of this felt like just another inconvenience to building this state, until things took a turn the week of September 23rd when the family and neighbors spent a difficult night protecting what they had built from the fires burning around them.

Stories came back from the village of Ahnepee of people fleeing their burning homes to piers stretched out into Lake Michigan. They had struggled to find a road without a bridge that was burned-out and large fires were still burning in the south of Kewaunee County. Livestock were roaming freely after their homes and fences were destroyed. People who still had wagons were dodging fires and burnt-out corduroy roads. Odile took in the news the same as the rest, but she struggled to hide her frustration. They finally had a home with windows, out buildings, animals to help with the work and now additional family to lighten both the work and mental burden. The thought of it all being wiped away made her anger simmer to the very top.

Jacques showed up at Odile's house a few days later and delivered a message from his mother's people that things were going to get worse. The Indians had been in the area far longer than any white person and felt the behavior of the animals and the streams drying up was an omen. Odile trusted Jacques. He had become more than a teacher through the years. She considered him another brother.

After the family fire-preparation meeting that week, Odile and her daughter Marie Louise began wearing men's trousers and sat while Magdaline tightly plaited their hair into coronets. Odile had folded a few sewing needles, the lace from her first Wisconsin dress that had been placed on the baby dress, a tin cup and a small bag of salt in her waist bag. She helped bury a kettle, tins of flour and sugar and a few other household items they may need. Taking her turns with each task on fire-preparation the general observer would have only seen a hard-working wife.

The day hell came to her corner of the county Odile was on fire watch with her husband on their farm. The layer of smoke had been around so long that it was hard to say if it felt much different than the day before. Aching backs, burning eyes and throat and the stress of still completing daily chores while saving everything they had built was just what life had morphed into.

When Uncle Frank and Odile's barn roof caught fire in two places, they moved to protect the house, but the flaming debris from the sky was dropping on the roof and around the house faster than either could keep up. Within a few minutes it got too hot and instead of smoke breathing problems the intense heat sucked their breath from the lungs that had just been struggling with the smoke. They decided that Uncle Frank would run to his brother's farm to try and help save the barn or cabin and Odile would run to the freshly plowed field and get as close to the ground as possible.

Uncle Frank sprinted through the woods to his brother's farm, but to this day no one knows where Odile rode out the fire. She was not in the field the next morning when the search began for the missing. The fire had been so hot and fast that animals and people caught in the inferno may only be a pile of ashes that partially washed away when the rain started. No one wanted to believe it, but Odile could have been one of these pyres.

It was a full three days when Magdaline started running down the scarred hill toward a figure. Emilie followed and realized it was Odile. Like an apparition, she looked like she was floating. The bottom of her trousers had been burned off to her knees and her leather shoes no longer had soles. Emilie started croaking as loud as she could for Uncle Frank. The exposed skin below Odile's knees and her fists was red and angry. Through her blackened face and red eyes, it was apparent that there was more damage than just the burns.

When she was led to Uncle Frank she came to life and paused in front of him. After the trauma of the fire there had been every different type of reunion seen in the barnyard. Relief, depression, and everything between. Odile's reaction was different and terrifying. She lunged at Uncle Frank with her fists and coordinated pounding his chest with a howling worse than any midnight wolf visit. Kicking and screeching, Uncle Frank and three other men carried her into the barn and added her to the hospital corner. She sat on the floor with her fists clenched and only stopped screaming when she took a quick breath. After hours she lost her voice and continued to silently scream, which may have been worse. When she stopped screaming a wall slid down over her face and it became blank. Her daughter Marie Louise lay on the ground next to her gasping and coughing the entire time, but Odile didn't seem to notice.

It was hours later when they were able to get Odile cleaned up with the meager supplies. While inspecting her hands Magdaline discovered she was clutching a slice of charred wood about two inches long, and on one side there was clearly the carving from the crosses her brother had made. Odile had at some point walked to where her family was buried and had walked back with what was the only thing left to mark the site. When Uncle Frank saw the talisman, he couldn't believe that she had walked that far with her burns and none of the landmarks to aid in locating the site.

Doctor Antoine stopped at the barn to check on the sad hospital corner and spent some time with Odile. He ultimately recommended quiet and rest. He stopped back several times on his rounds to the few standing structures over the next few weeks. There had been no improvement, and she had stopped eating and was tearing at her hair. He told Uncle Frank that there was a hospital in Madison that she might benefit from. He would need to take her there via train and admit her as insane.

Odile was admitted to the Wisconsin State Hospital for the Insane in the spring of 1872. Everyone had struggled to make her eat and her self-harm had extended to tearing at her hair and peeling the damaged skin on her legs and hands exposing herself to infection. In one of the donation barrels from the relief agency there was a long sharp knife. It was intended for clean fish and game. The day before Odile and Uncle Frank left to travel to Madison, she had attempted to stab herself and to cut Marie Louise.

As Uncle Frank and Odile were riding toward Green Bay to catch the train she started laughing and waving and shouting *"å r'vèy"*.

Odile's daughter Marie Louise died from bronchitis that spring. She had lived through the fear of the fire, the death of family members and the loss of her mother's mind in her extremely short life. Odile probably had no idea.

Odile lived in the asylum for just under three years. Uncle Frank and her son John were only able to visit her once a year. They never spoke about those visits to the rest of the surviving Gaspards. There were no photos of Odile that survived the fire. There was no headstone marking where she lies in the Asylum graveyard. Her name appears on the U.S. census in 1860 and 1870, and there were nine unmarked graves in Kewaunee County, with names that never appeared on any U.S. census that were her family. The only immediate family member left in the U.S. was her brother who never married and died in Alaska after failing to become rich in the gold rush. It was not known where he was buried.

Chapter 18: Women of the Fire
Sofie Agathe Defaux Gaspard's Story

Sofie was born in *Grez-Doiceau* to parents who had suffered bouts of infertility and were eternally grateful for her birth. Their home was likely unique for the era in the fact that they doted on her and openly showed affection. She was a confident child, but most would describe her as plain looking.

Antoine would say that Sofie chose him when they were very young. After they married, she slipped into the Gaspard family and changed the dynamic slightly. When it came to her children and Antoine, she freely stood up for them. Because it wasn't normal for a woman to be quite so outspoken, her words often met a silent shocked response.

One of her biggest fears was her children not living to be adults. She did everything within what existed at that time to ensure they would grow and thrive. When waves of hardship and illness struck Wallonia her fear would spike, so when Antoine suggested they go to America she was hopeful these plagues would not be across the ocean.

The journey across the Atlantic was consumed with keeping track of her three young children while being separated in the women's area much of the time. Watching people get sick and hearing that three people had died during the journey added to her anxiety. By the time they reached land, she was so thankful to be off the boat and on to the next stage of their migration. Unfortunately, three weeks later *Pére* was held in immigration for some unknown health reason. The three children, Antoine, Leopold, and Sofie stayed in their temporary housing while they waited for word on *Pére*. Everything about the city was foreign, but Sofie set her chin and tackled the new surroundings the same way she tackled her life.

As the weeks went on, they became concerned that *Pére* would not be allowed to enter America, and they wouldn't have the money to continue to Wisconsin. When he was finally released the new concern was getting to Wisconsin too late to ensure they had what they needed to make it through the winter. They hadn't foreseen the true volume of labor that would be needed on the farm and the money needed for supplies for the winter.

Uncle Frank had secured the two farms before they arrived saving some steps to getting established in Wisconsin. Unfortunately, arriving at the beginning of September they had no time to plant a garden, or the fuel needed to keep two houses warm. After discussing the different options, they determined it would be easiest if they rented a place in nearby Green Bay while the men took jobs at a sawmill. Uncle Frank encouraged them to send Leopold to school to learn English. When the men had spare time, they would walk to their property to plan and prepare for spring. Sofie spent nearly all her time in the two-room rental with the children. When Leopold would come home from school, she insisted they all sit and learn the words he had learned that day. She thought Leopold was a fantastic teacher and was thrilled that her children were able to interchange between English and Walloon. At night, when it was quiet, she practiced her letters in English.

The two rooms felt oppressive when the weather turned cold and blustery and only got worse when Leopold came home from school one day listless and aching. Soon all the children were ill, and Sofie lost track of the kettles of broth and cool cloths she had prepared. With her determination there was no way that her children would succumb to this illness. They had traveled too far. She was going to make them healthy if it meant never sleeping again.

When she finally had everyone healthy, she composed a letter to the Gaspards in Wallonia with the instructions to share the news with her parents. She missed them so much that every time she tried to write her parents a letter her vision would blur, and she couldn't see the paper. When they were finally on the farm she would write a long letter.

The day before they were to move out to the farm Antoine surprised her by taking the afternoon off. He took her and the children into the city to purchase items they thought they would need. It had been so long since they had spent money on anything but food and shelter that it felt wasteful, but she knew it was a long walk, and they had so few things from the trip that would get them on their way as landowners. They purchased kitchen items, linens, seeds, tools and food dry goods. Sofie saw the Bible in the glass cabinet. It wasn't large, but she knew it was in English. Antoine saw her looking at the book and made an excuse to go back into the store to buy it for his wife. He knew she was adamant about the children being able to communicate in English as well as Walloon in their new country. Not every immigrant felt this way, but all those weeks in the giant landing city not understanding why *Pére* was being held and often not being able to communicate with people made Sofie certain she was doing the right thing. That first English book in the house was also the bible which meant she could look up the words in the Bible from home and continue her own studies.

Antoine and Sofie had planned with *Pére* to take the farm that had fewer improvements. *Pére* was older and Leopold was still too young to complete the full work of an adult man. So, their farm only had a twelve-foot log cabin with an attached barn that could fit a horse and cows. There was a garden plot that would need to be expanded once more trees were removed. They did have nearly three acres of land that could be used for planting, but not all of it was free of trees and stumps. The bachelor who had owned the farm first had left the hand-built furniture and cookstove. Sofie quickly went to work switching the living area to the larger barn area. Cleaning, airing, and making beds for the family. Through the woods, to the south of their cabin there was a path that led to Uncle Franks to the East there was a path that took you to *Pére's* farm. She appreciated that they were close, but getting used to not being able to see your neighbors was something she struggled to overcome. The trees were so close that it was several weeks before she knew there was a young mother less than an eighth of a mile from their cabin.

Cédonie Baudot had a son, and a daughter with another on the way. Her husband, Pierre, like the others in the neighborhood, spent his days alternating between farming and removing trees. The young children were beyond excited to have friends close, but both Sofie and Cédonie agreed that they would always walk the children back and forth through the woods since the oldest of the group was just six. They would often meet at the edge of the woods on either side and visit for a few minutes before heading back to their home.

Cédonie and Sofie were the ones responsible for the group attending the church in the village at the bottom of the hill called GrandLez. It was only about a two-mile walk, and the services were in French thanks to the French missionary priest. It was such a small village that it tripled in size on days where church service or vespers were happening. Cédonie often invited us to their home for fellowship since they had added on to their cabin and had enough space for a plank table that fit nearly everyone.

Everyone enjoyed the Baudot family, but Sofie and Cédonie were quickly the closest of friends. They shared big jobs chatting the entire time and invited Emilie, Magdaline, and Odile to their homes to join in the activities when they could.

When the fires escalated in the last weeks of September Cédonie and her husband Pierre, like neighbor Jacques, were part of the Gaspard plan. Cédonie was the one that had quickly sewed the bags everyone could tuck their important items in if they needed to stay somewhere while they waited until it was safe to return. The Baudots had worked out with Antoine and Sofie that depending on whose farm was most at risk, the other would come and fetch the children while both men and the wife would work to save as much as they could. The thought was that the plowed land near the tree lines would keep the fire away from the other farm.

When the smoldering debris started landing in Sofie and Antoine's yard on October 8th, she quickly dressed the children tying their bags around their waists. She and Antoine assumed that the debris was coming from their dear neighbor's farm and were ready to spring into action. They started toward the tree line when Uncle Frank's son John came sprinting through the opening of the woods. He needed Antoine to come as quickly as possible. The barn was on fire. Antoine told Sofie to take the children and go to Cédonie and explain that he would come and help as soon as he could. She was to take all the children to their house and go into the well if they needed to.

As the flaming debris became more intense, Sofie decided to run back to the house to get some wet blankets to keep the children from being hit. The barrel near the front door was half full and she quickly soaked two quilts and headed back toward the Baudet's.

A panicked horse burst through the opening in the trees and made a strange circling motion almost like a dog, then it snorted deeply and ran to the east. She and the children increased their speed to get to Cédonie and the children who must be heading to Sofie's for safety. The trees were exploding, and the wind was whirling even in the dense forest. It was getting harder and harder to breathe and the blankets were nearly dry when she stumbled over what she thought was a log in the forest. Brought to her knees she realized it was three figures lying on the ground. Slightly raising the corner of the blanket, they were under, she made out that it was Cédonie and her children. When she looked toward her neighbor's house, she saw a wall of fire that they were not going to get through. The only option was to get to the well on their side of the trees. Stumbling and pulling she urged her friend to get to the field. She had been told that the dirt wouldn't burn. When they cleared the opening, she pulled the blanket up and was shocked to see both her house and stable were fully engulfed in fire. There was no way they would make it to the well. Fumbling, they collapsed in the middle of the plowed field, pressing the children close to the earth and swatting embers.

When the rage of fire was over, Antoine found Pierre sitting in the middle of Antoine's field next to eight charred bodies. The six little bodies were still under their mothers. Cédonie had delivered her baby in the rage of hellfire. The heat from the fire had been so intense that all the forms appeared shrunken. Antoine had walked through dead livestock and wild animals to get back to what had been his farm, but nothing prepared him for this. Pierre's eyes were nearly sealed shut and Antoine couldn't stop coughing. Both were in the tatters of the clothing they had put on that morning. Both only had these tatters left.

Chapter 19: Women of the Fire
Lenka Aneta Zajic's Story

Lenka was born in Wisconsin in 1866 to parents who had emigrated from what would later become Czechoslovakia in the early 1930's. At the time of the fire, they were called Bohemians. The family lived within a settlement of other Bohemians on the border of Door and Kewaunee Counties. Like others who were working to be successful farmers they spent much of their spare time removing more trees. There were at least ten other families in this community, which allowed them to maintain some of their customs.

Lenka's mother was thrilled to have a daughter but also worried that she wasn't a boy who could help her husband. As the weeks after her birth passed, one of the neighboring women stopped in for a visit and she noticed that Lenka did not follow the sound of her voice. Lenka's mother began testing Lenka daily to see if she could hear, but day after day it became clearer that Lenka was likely at least partially deaf. Her parents decided that when the doctor came to their settlement the next time, they would pay to have him test Lenka.

When she was three months old, a doctor from the Door County side felt very sure that she could not hear. He explained that there were doctors and teachers out East who were teaching deaf people and their caregivers how to speak with their hands. He promised that he would find a pamphlet on how they did this and bring it to them. Stunned, Lenka's parents didn't know how they would manage a child who couldn't hear in the dark woods of Wisconsin.

There were still animals to be avoided in the woods, and household incidents, like open fire, that were difficult with hearing children. Aside from elder relatives who had lost some of their hearing with old age, they had no experience with deafness. Lenka's mother however did not want to send the girl away. If they could tackle the tall trees, mosquitoes, hunger, and harsh winters of Wisconsin, they could handle this.

The doctor did return with a pamphlet that showed how to make some basic signs with their hands, like 'eat' or 'sleep' as well as the English alphabet. It took months to find someone who could translate the pamphlet into their native language so that they could start teaching Lenka to communicate with something other than squeaks, shouts and pointing.

By the age of two Lenka had memorized all the letters and signs on the pamphlet along with her parents. As with others who have one weakened sense, her eyesight, sense of smell and touch were heightened. She knew a horse was coming long before anyone else in the house noticed because of the vibrating ground.

When she turned five, her mother walked her to the local school cabin and sat with her in the back of the rustic room. Lenka was enthralled with the activity around her. After the class cleared the room for the day, she stepped up to the slate hung on the wall and started tracing the letters on the wall below with her fingers. The schoolteacher took notice and offered to have her sit in on his class as long as she was quiet and behaved herself. Lenka's mother knew her daughter would be fine in school but made the time each day to walk her the mile and a half each way when she attended. Lenka's mother held her head high on those walks and was so proud that the daughter they thought would never be able to go to school was in attendance. Equally proud Lenka's father presented her with a small 8" by 5" oak trimmed slate of her own with a box of shockingly white chalk. He quickly noticed that his daughter constantly had the slate in her hand making it hard for her to do other things, so he drilled two holes in the oak frame, and her mother fashioned a ribbon strap so she could hang it around her neck. Lenka was thrilled.

The schoolteacher was amazed at Lenka's thirst to learn. He realized that he needed to help her associate the simple words she was copying on her slate with the objects. One of his older students liked to draw, so he asked him to draw small pictures of things like cats and houses. Lenka absorbed all of it and would take her new drawing and word home each night to practice. Her parents were thrilled that she was proving to be clever enough to overcome her lack of hearing. They all started using her slate and the hand signals to communicate creating their own language.

By September 1871, Lenka's heightened sense of smell was nearly overwhelmed with the constant dense smoke. The reports of fires around the counties scared the Bohemian community and they began preparing in the ways they knew how. Fields were plowed; barrels were filled with water and placed next to entrances of buildings and children were given orders on where to go if a fire came to their house. All these preparations for a normal fire made complete sense, but what arrived on October 8th wasn't normal.

Lenka's father, like all their neighbors, had hardly slept those last few weeks. They spent the nights watching for pop-up fires and any sparks that could ignite causing a larger blaze. When he threw open the door that evening of October 8th, Lenka could tell her father was shouting even without hearing the words. The panic on her mother's face was nothing she had seen before. Her mother gave her the symbol for stay and ran out of the house with her father. Watching out the door, Lenka couldn't believe the chaos. Her super sensitive nose scrunched at the large waves of black smoke. There were birds swirling and diving toward the ground all while it looked like it was snowing. The smell all around was now bitter, and the heat was like standing too close to the cookstove door. She saw her parents rushing around the barn trying to wet the roof, but the back half was already in flames. Lenka automatically crouched to the clearer air near the floor. Her mother went to pull her father off the ladder when she was blown over by a gust of heavy wind. Her mother's skirts caught fire. For a terrible moment, Lenka thought her mother looked like a blazing candle before she collapsed. Lenka lost track of where her father was in the yard. Scared, she stood and started running toward her schoolhouse. Her teacher would help.

When she arrived at what she thought was her beloved school yard, there was nothing but a wind pushing her from all directions. The flames behind her were racing and so close. Tipping her nose in the air, she started scurrying toward what smelled like slightly fresher air. It was getting harder and harder to see and the wind was making it hard for her to stay on her feet. At one point she thought she was being swept away, but it was a man who had grabbed her under her arms and was running with her. They fell together into a creek she wasn't familiar with. It wasn't very deep but the man who had picked her up insisted on nudging her to keep rolling in the inches of water and to keep herself coated. She could smell the steam from their clothing when whatever side was out of the water would dry almost instantly. As they continued to work to keep themselves wet Lenka began to wonder what all of this meant. She clutched her slate in one hand to her little chest and continued fighting to save herself.

Lenka smelled the shift in the air before they felt the first raindrop. After feeling so hot for so long it was alarming to feel so cold. The man who had carried her had stopped rolling and was trying to judge if it was safe to get out of the water. He tugged on her arm to get her up. Her eyes were nearly sealed shut. She could feel how heavily the man was breathing when he flopped on his back on the small bank of the creek. His lips were moving. It was raining, but both were so exhausted that they stayed on the bank for a long time. Lenka wanted to sleep but was too cold and too scared. The rain had changed the smell to a terrible mix of roasted flesh and acid, but the absence of any vibration of sound aside from the rain falling was immediately more disturbing. Where was everyone? Where were the birds?

When the first prick of light came to Kewaunee County that morning, they both roused from their slanted perch on the creek side, realizing they had nodded off at some point. The man wriggled to the water and leaned in to get a drink. He quickly spat out his mouthful. Lenka thought she could smell the soap her mother used on wash day. They sat by the creek a bit longer letting their eyes open further. When she reached to rub her eyes, the man swatted at her hand. It took several minutes before she could finally take a better look around. In the gray light she realized that nearly all the trees were now charred picks, and some were still smoking. She had no idea where she was or how she would get back to her parents.

The man got to his feet and motioned for her to come with him. She stood up on jelly legs and started walking behind him on the new lunar landscape. They walked for a long time not seeing another living person or animal, just many smoldering buildings and carcasses of living things that got caught in the fire. There were several times the man grabbed her and tried to hide her eyes. He wasn't always fast enough to shelter her from the sight of lifeless legs behind a rock or charred tatters of once bright colored quilts covering forms in the middle of a field.

It was very late in the afternoon when they walked to the top of a hill where a lone log barn was standing. Part of its roof was burned and there was a hole in the side from a fire. Perched on a large flat rock a few paces from the barn there was a group of people huddled together each staring into different directions with blank blackened faces.

The man slowed his pace toward the group of people and Lenka did the same. The forms on the rocks didn't turn when they got closer. Lenka joined the group sitting on the backside of the rock. The man walked into the barn, but Lenka couldn't follow, her chest hurt from the walking and coughing. She was shocked when a woman wearing trousers came out of the barn with the man. On instinct she reached into her smock pocket for her bit of chalk, but after being in the water for so long there was nothing left. She started signing, but the two people in front of her just looked at her moving hands without recognition. When they began talking, she could see their lips moving, but they weren't making the same movements as her parents or teacher did. The fear bubbled, but exhaustion was fighting for her attention.

It was more than a week when one of the aid barrels had a sheaf of paper and a pencil. While helping with the unpacking she gestured to have a piece of paper. Lenka had tried several times to make them understand her hand signals, but if it wasn't something simple like grabbing her middle they didn't understand. She wrote the words she could spell in an uneven hand on the paper. It had been so long since she had written anything. At the bottom of the page, she slowly made the letters from her name. The woman in trousers saw her letters and pointed to the Lenka on the bottom. Lenka pointed at her chest.

It took Dr. Antoine visiting to tell her caregivers that she was likely deaf, but he couldn't tell if it was because of the fire. He thought probably not since she was making letters on paper. He agreed to ask around about a young girl maybe named Lenka.

As the refugees' days became a pattern and the weather turned cold there were still so many health problems continuing in the barn. Lenka was not burned and while she couldn't speak, she helped around the barn where she could. Lenka wanted to find her parents but didn't know how. Her mom could be lying in a barn somewhere near, like the other burned members in this group. Dr. Antoine came up the hill on a cold day with a puff of breath. That was the day he told the young woman in trousers that he thought she was from the Bohemian settlement several miles from here that had been completely wiped out. He wasn't aware of any survivors. He did talk to one of the doctors from Door County who remembered a colleague treating a Bohemian girl who was deaf. That doctor was now practicing in Manitowoc.

Lenka didn't understand that Magdaline was gifted with languages and Magdaline hadn't realized that Lenka was Bohemian. Now that she knew, Magdaline had instructed everyone in the barn yard to ask all passersby if they spoke Lenka's language. Magdaline would walk sometimes into the various villages seeking someone who could help. It took much longer than anyone imagined. One day Magdaline brought a woman back to the barn. She was wearing the same type of mismatched clothing everyone else who had lived through the fire were thankful to have. The woman tried writing the letters she knew on the paper and speaking slowly to Lenka, but nothing seemed to get through. Magdaline thanked the woman and walked her back.

The group in the barn shifted that winter when the men who were able bodied went to work for the sawmills and would only come back on their time off. They used the barn as a home base to store things for when they rebuilt their farms. Some of the women went to the surrounding communities to work doing laundry and other support jobs. Even with still more than 20 people daily in the barn, Magdaline had a bit more time to ponder how to communicate with Lenka.

Magdaline tasked Marie Louise with drawing simple pictures and their names in English and Walloon next to them. As they had time, they would work with Lenka on being sure they each recognized the image and word combination. Marie Louise seemed to brighten with this task and was thrilled with the progress. The girls would incorporate their learning all day, stopping during a chore to write the name of something. Lenka was so eager to learn that she was starting to write simple sentences in English and Walloon.

The snow was still crunching underfoot and your breath hung as a mist in the air the day that Mrs. Antoine came to the barn. She came bearing the news that her husband, the doctor, had died, but she had promised him she would still make rounds and help people when she could. There were still people with burns and lung issues who needed care. He had helped keep the barn group calm while everyone did their best to survive. Mrs. Antoine herself was still coughing and hadn't lost the ashen hue that some of the survivors carried. Magdaline placed a blanket on the box closest to the stove and brought the grieving woman over to sit. She sat there with tears wending their way to the collar of her too large shirt. The crying was making her cough harder. When the visit ended, she left a few new bandages and salves and walked to the next structure that was inhabited.

The day of Mrs. Antoine's visit, Lenka was practicing her letters on her slate. When she saw the woman crying, she drew a sad face and the words '*malureu*' and 'sad' next to it. Through the sadness of the death of the favorite doctor, this simple gesture shone a beam of hope. With a teary smile, Mrs. Antoine leaned over and gave Lenka's shoulders a squeeze.

"The doctor would be so proud."

Chapter 20: Women of the Fire
Hedda Karlsen's Story

Hedda Karlsen was 17 years old the day she set foot for the first time in Green Bay, Wisconsin. It was October 9th, 1871. When compared to other immigration stories, Hedda's trip across the ocean was smooth and she had arrived in Wisconsin only two days later than predicted.

Hedda was meeting her fiancé Aksel Haugen. He had immigrated the year prior and dreamed of owning land and farming. Something that would have been nearly impossible in Norway. Both Hedda and Aksel grew up in Christiania, Norway, a major city in the 19th century that would eventually be renamed Oslo. When Aksel arrived in America he needed to earn money to pay for the land he hoped to buy. Like many, he had heard stories about cheap land in the middle of the country available to anyone. Eager to work hard to make this dream come true for himself and his future wife, he ended up working first in Michigan in a lumber camp. During his free time, he would scout areas for his farm. Not finding what he wanted he followed some of his fellow lumbermen to Wisconsin. Several of these lumbermen took jobs in a community called Peshtigo. Aksel and two others went to Green Bay and ultimately took jobs with a lumbering company that had several sites on the Wisconsin peninsula northeast of Green Bay.

Aksel sent word to Hedda to come to Green Bay with the goal of being there in the fall of 1871. He had found an area he thought would be good farmland, and they could both work in the winter to support themselves while clearing the land.

Hedda was anxious to start her new life in America. She said goodbye to friends and family and landed in Green Bay that grim October day not fully understanding how much her life would change in America.

A noxious smell of smoke and charred wood lingered over the city of Green Bay and mingled with the damp from the rain that night. The city felt unsettled, but Hedda had no idea how unsettled it was.

Aksel was supposed to find her, if he was not there, she was supposed to find lodging for the night, and he would come to her. She had written down the name of his employer and the words Kewaunee County, which was where several of the company's lumber mills' facilities were located. By sheer luck, she crossed paths with a Norwegian woman that day.

Solveig Jensen recognized Hedda's clothing as being from her homeland before the girl even spoke. Solveig had been in America for the last two years and spoke some English. She approached the confused-looking Hedda that day and cemented the beginning of their future relationship.

Speaking quickly Hedda explained that she was to meet her fiancé Aksel and showed her the paper with his details. She was shocked when Solveig told her what she knew about the previous twenty-four hours.

Green Bay had gotten word from ships on the Bay that massive fires had destroyed communities. There were thought to be about three hundred people dead on the west side and maybe thirty-five on the east side. At that point Solveig told Hedda she should assume that Aksel would be delayed. Hedda felt unsettled and anxious. Solveig took her back to her modest home hoping that her husband could help keep the young girl calm. Instead Hedda became more insistent. She needed to get to the mill. She needed to get to Aksel.

After a sleepless night, Hedda begged Solveig and her husband to help her get to the mill. They ultimately agreed and walked to the Green Bay Trinity Lutheran Church to see if they could get some help with Hedda's request. The church building was still considered new having been completed five years before by the Norwegian congregation. The trio found a swarm of people and things being shuffled on the front steps and in the rear of the church building. One of the whirs explained in Norwegian that they were collecting items to bring to the burned areas. There were families that barely had the clothing on their bodies.

It was agreed that the men who were going to bring the supplies to the east side of the bay would bring Hedda with them if she agreed to help distribute the aid. The next morning, gripping her paper she rode in the back of the wagon squished among the supplies. She was surprised to see a long line of wagons heading in the same direction that were not part of this Norwegian train. All the vessels were heaped with a mix of items. The wagons contained cooked food and various donations. Even being a part of this wagon train didn't alert Hedda to the size of the disaster they were driving toward. She was focused on finding her fiancé.

It took so long to get to an area they called New Franken where they stopped in the middle of a group of charred and burnt-out buildings. There were a few figures moving around as if they had lost something and just needed to look harder for that item in the rubble. The wagon in front of them started unpacking a few of the items on their load, which was the nudge Hedda needed to start handing out the wagon's contents. She was surprised at how quiet the transaction was. One of the figures was crying quietly, others croaked what she assumed were words of thanks. They were all filthy. Some were dirt covered, some were soot covered, many were both.

Unfortunately, this was the best of what they saw over the next twenty-four hours. The ghosts in the rubble encouraged the wagons to continue north. They had heard a few stories from residents passing through who were severely injured and seeking medical care in Green Bay. These stories made their plight seem less urgent than their neighbors. The train started rolling along again trying to avoid animal carcasses and burned-out roads and bridges. They reached a chapel with a fence surrounding it. Everything around the building and the outside of the fence was burnt black, but the chapel and the inside of the fence around it seemed untouched. They were greeted by a woman in a black habit who was speaking what she was told was French. Hedda couldn't believe how calm this figure was even without understanding a word she was saying.

The train of wagons camped at this chapel for the night along with fifty or more refugees from the surrounding farms. Hedda was not Catholic but understood when these people started praying and tried to let it calm her growing fears. After the prayer session more people started arriving at the oasis, mostly on foot. Some came with the barest of items they could spare for those in greater need further north. Hedda's stomach gripped at the sight of these people. How bad was it that people who had lost nearly everything were willing to give half of what was left to their neighbors.

When a wagon was empty of the supplies it would head back to Green Bay with people who had arrived at the chapel in need of doctor's care. The others continued north.

Hedda felt actively sick. The further they went the more charred the ground was and the more piles of rubble some still smoking stretched ahead. The people she was traveling with spoke Norwegian, but nobody said a word.

When they stopped again it was in a town, she was told was called Thiry Daems. She would forever remember the unusual name and the struggle her fellow Norwegian travelers found in pronouncing the two words. Like New Franken it was a mix of completely burned buildings and a few rustic log structures that had survived but were singed. It felt like there were more people than shelter at this stop. Word had gotten out that there was aid on the way. Those who could walk for the much-needed supplies had set out on foot stopping at locations that had been village centers. The suppliers followed the same procedure of unloading a wagon and filling an empty wagon with those in need of medical care in Green Bay and then moving forward with the remaining supplies.

It was in the next village called **GrandLez** that Hedda noticed the very young woman and boy standing slightly off to the left of the burnt general store. The woman was unmistakable because she was wearing men's trousers tucked into blackened leather boots. Her shirt had a weird bunching around one of the shoulders and her hair was tightly plaited around her head. The boy's face was wan, and his brown eyes didn't seem to blink. One of his arms was an unnatural pink color and seemed almost shiny through the tattered sleeve of his shirt. One of his knees had an angry red scrape where the pants had torn. You could feel the exhaustion radiating off them and the others who had gathered.

As they worked to unload supplies, they learned that many of those who had walked in were living huddled together in the handful of shelters they had managed to save. The boy and young woman were in a log barn that had some damage but was now housing more than forty people. The empty wagons again loaded those who needed doctor's care in Green Bay while the others formed a plan for their next stop. After a confusing conversation in multiple languages, it was decided that they would squeeze in some of these walking refugees and bring them closer to their current shelter dwellings. Hedda quickly moved toward the young woman and boy and motioned for them to get into the small space she was able to make in the back of the wagon she had been assigned.

When they crawled into the wagon, they sat so close to each other that there was no perceptible space between them. The boy winced at being jostled and the young woman's eyes clouded when she leaned back against the wagon wall. With everything packed Hedda wasn't sure where to find comfort in their supplies for these two. It was one of the men from a wagon ahead of them that came back with a quilt that was a riot of colors and stitched shapes. Sheer relief oozed from their young shapes at the sight of this simple item. They painfully both moved forward and draped the quilt over their heads and shoulders with the boy gingerly moving his painful arm in front of him. As the wagon started moving, she noticed the boy's head leaned slowly to the woman's shoulder. Something that would have been frowned upon based on his age under normal circumstances. The young woman pulled the quilt a bit further around to give him more shelter.

Hedda hadn't realized she was crying until the young woman met her eyes. She quickly rubbed away the tears feeling embarrassed that she would cry when clearly these two children were injured and tasked with finding supplies for the estimated forty people waiting for them in a wounded barn. Hedda didn't forget about Aksel, but the layers of her worry now included these two nameless foundlings.

The scene continued to play out with more destruction and there were fresh mounds of various sizes lying near burnt out remains of farms and in some cases along the road. Hedda knew without asking what was under those mounds. When they stopped on the outskirts of GrandLez she thought she might lose her mind. Meeting them at their stop was a group of small children all in various stages of tattered dress. They were from a small orphan home located in this town. She was told most of these children survived because they were buried in the field behind what was left of their home by their caregiver. That caregiver was burned and experiencing breathing problems, so the children were doing their best.

It had been days since they had left Green Bay and **GrandLez** was the first town they came to that seemed to have more first-hand news from the areas around them. A group of men from Ahnepee had come and helped bury the dead humans and animals and brought news. A mill in Door County to the north was completely gone and seventy or more people including family members of the owners, were dead on site. The Bohemian settlement to the north and west had more than 10 large families in residence and only a handful of people had survived. Villages called Rosiere and Misere were nearly wiped from the map and other Belgian settlements in the fire's path were equally harmed. People had tried to save themselves in root cellars, fields and wells. Some succeeded while others were nearly completely removed from the earth. There seemed to be no reasonable explanation to who lived and who died. There were people who lived but had no home or shelter left and there were homes only partially destroyed with no family left to take refuge.

After a slow climb up a hill, she was unloading crates and trying to hide the tears that were freely flowing when her driver pulled her over to a group of five people talking around a large flat rock. He pointed at the Scandinavian looking man and said in Norwegian, *"Fortell henne hva du vet." 'Tell her what you know.'*

That was when the dream blew to the wind like the ashes of these people's lives. Aksel's name was listed as one of those who died at a mill in the neighboring Red River Township. He had been sent to that location to look out for fires and help save the mill if needed. He had died with twelve others, mostly Belgian immigrants but there were two clearly German surnames and his Norwegian on that death list.

Chapter 21: Atlantique Afterword

It wasn't until after Emmee passed away in her sleep at the age of eighty-nine that I took the time to read the papers in the box that had arrived from Edna Mae's brother so many years before. After the article was published to commemorate the anniversary of the fire, both Edna Mae and Emmee felt that their work had been edited into a glossed-over retelling of what was a horror story. At the time, a woman named Rose Wilder had worked with her mother to write a book about her childhood in western Wisconsin. Edna Mae knew the publisher and convinced them to read a book about Emmee's fire experience. Ultimately, the book was published for a younger audience—readers closer to the age Emmee was during the fire. Many schools in the Midwest required it as reading and while names had been changed and language had been altered to suit the audience, it was still at its heart Emmee's story. Edna Mae had negotiated payment for the book for Emmee, and she received checks for her work. Emmee, being Emmee, always felt that Edna Mae should take all the money, since she "really just took my rambling notes and made it a story". The box contained all the pieces that went into that book. Stacks of written and typed notes, scraps of newspaper clippings, even a copy of *Little House in the Big Woods* by Laura Ingalls Wilder dog-eared, stuffed with paper markers.

My lovely little wife Effie and I sat at Emmee's marred oak kitchen table and openly wept as we lifted each item from the box that tied these two women together. That oak table that had come to the farm as a donation the winter of 1871-72, so it seemed like the only appropriate place to review the box's contents. We sat flipping the thin, ecru-stained pages from their home well into the deep-blue evening. Our dripping noses and puffed eyes the next morning were evidence of our evening research.

I don't remember exactly when I met Effie for the first time. She was the neighbor girl who was my age. She was fearless and usually the first to jump out of a barn loft or skim under a farm fence. Her family had lived through the fire, and she was born in a stranger's house in Ahnepee three weeks after the conflagration. In a way we had it easier. We didn't need to explain our unusual family structures to anyone in our immediate neighborhood. Occasionally there would be a newcomer who thought it was strange that there was an unusual number of burn-scarred bodies in the community. It wasn't unusual for a child to only have one parent or for their dead father's brother to now be their stepfather. These mixed households continued for so long that often even if the members had different last names, it was assumed they were blood related.

Our house was no different. Emmee and Magdaline were my mothers. Uncle Frank, Jacques, and Antoine were my fathers. Lenka, John, James Crow, and Leopold were my siblings. Hilda was my aunt. Hilda's children were my cousins and Tom, Magdaline's brother Leo, and Cédonie's husband Pierre Baudot were my uncles. My grandparents were dimly lit characters from a far-off land and there were two other siblings that I would never meet. In reality, Emmee, Antoine, and Leopold were my siblings, and Uncle Frank and John were the only other blood relatives in the group. The rest became family out of necessity.

Effie's family consisted of her mother who never fully recovered from what the doctor called "burned lungs", and a father who had lost several fingers from burns sustained in the fire. There was a woman she called her grandmother, or *Grand-mére* Joséphine, who wasn't related in any way other than she owned the neighboring farm which had been burned to cinders. The woman had been a widow before the fire and now needed a home. She was more than happy to care for Effie as her way of helping with the rebuilding. Effie was an only child and as I sit here now, I wonder if it was due to the damage to her parent's bodies from the smoke and fire.

My actual father died on Christmas eve 1871. He had let on to everyone that he was in better health than he was. Starting the beginning of December, he required constant care and had stopped eating about ten days before he passed. Emmee didn't have a lot to say about him or his passing. When I asked Magdaline, she would only tell me that he had been deeply hurt by the deaths of two wives and had suffered from the smoke after the fire. Magdaline had much more to say about my mother, even though she had only known her for a few short days versus the months she had spent with my father. It was Leopold who told me when we were both gray at the temples that my father had such a hard time with our mother's death that he denied that I was his and left me to Emmee's care. As a father and grandfather, myself, I cannot imagine what would turn me away from one of my children or any child that needed me. I guess it was a different time.

Sitting here thinking about my family I could almost feel Magdaline's puffy soft, always warm, short fingers sliding my fringe to the side so she could see my eyes, Emmee standing at the basin looking out the window. Emmee often stood at the window, minutes too long. My mothers.

We were incredibly fortunate that Uncle Frank had taken out an insurance policy on his property in 1865. That money along with the earnings from the mill allowed us to be some of the first people to rebuild an actual house in the neighborhood. John would often sit in one of the mismatched wooden spindle chairs in the big house kitchen and talk about having to purchase logs and wood to build a house when just months before the trees were considered a nuisance. He would slap his dusty knee and say, "It's the craziest thing to have to buy trees to build a house when once I nearly cursed them all."

The house came about when a group of three men from the city came through in the early spring of 1872. Magdaline remembers it as Milwaukee, but Leopold would swear that it was Manitowoc. They carried with them sketches of a simple, sensible, not-quite square, house that had two floors and an attic. They could help build the house with local labor and would help source the materials for windows and doors.

The house was a rectangular box roughly thirty by twenty-five feet and built of logs that were easily twelve inches deep. They were so deep they created cavernous window ledges where Hilda always placed the starter garden seedlings each spring. The ground floor had always been three rooms. One with the kitchen, dining and sitting area and then two small rooms that were first used as bedrooms. The second floor had three rooms with a small hallway and a pull rope that drops open the hatch to the attic. Facing another winter in the barn, the group agreed to move into the house before it was finished. The floors were rough lumber, and the walls inside and out were exposed logs. Bricks were on order and being made at Macco Brickworks in neighboring Red River. The bricks after being fired came out a color that was neither red nor brown, but something in between. The settlers from Europe would have known the benefits of stone and brick buildings from their homelands. After the fire most felt that even if they had to replace the items in a house due to a fire, having a shell to restart was better than nothing.

Many of the houses built after the fire were clad in these raw umber colored bricks made locally. There were a few of these new homes clad in the ashy local field stones and some had what was later referred to as "Cream City Bricks" which were light in color and came from Milwaukee. The Gaspard house didn't get its brick until spring of 1873. The interior walls were covered with plaster in 1874. I heard John say one time that maybe if all the old cabin's interiors had been completely coated with the white plaster his mother and grandmother would have had an easier time in the Wisconsin woods. This was the only time I had ever heard him reference his mother's health struggles. It certainly wasn't a story that was spoken about often. I remember very clearly the first time I heard about how Aunt Odile dropped her basket during the fire. I was maybe ten at the time and the story was floating through the floorboards in the deepest of night after the day of *Kermiss* activities. I lay as still as I could. I was curious about the story but unsure if I wanted to remember the unknown aunt in this way. I didn't sleep the rest of the night. Instead, I imagined Aunt Odile surrounded by children I never knew in the woods.

Neither they nor Aunt Odile ever saw this house or the crowd that inhabited it after the fire. Looking around today I cannot believe how many people lived in this house that first year. Granted the men left for the lumber camps and some of the younger girls worked outside of the farm, but there were still nineteen to twenty people at any given time. In normal years October would have been the end of harvest, butchering season and the time to get traps ready for winter. October 1871 was a fight to survive in a different way. Often there weren't even the needed supplies if someone wanted to build a shelter.

Before the house was built, it was understood that if someone needed shelter, they could come to the Gaspard farm. We were so lucky to still have the barn when so many were facing living in a canvas tent for the winter. When we moved into the house, Magdaline, Emmee and I shared the smallest of the bedroom's downstairs. Marie Louise before she passed, slept on a cot by the stove to keep her warm through the night. An elderly couple called Delbressene moved into the second small bedroom on the ground floor. They had been in Ahnepee, when the fire broke out and when they finally returned to their farm there was nothing left. They paid our family to live in this room for several years, hoping to rebuild their own home and farm buildings. Mrs. Delbressene somehow obtained a spinning wheel from one of the donation wagons and it still sits in the corner of the cramped room today. Unfortunately, Mr. Delbressene passed away leaving Mrs. Delbressene to sell the land and move to Ohio where she could live with a nephew. Emmee remembered Mrs. Delbressene left for Ohio in 1874.

The large bedroom upstairs housed Hilda Schoen, her two daughters and Lenka. Hilda's husband and son had found them in our barnyard after the fire for a happy reunion. They started working to rebuild their own farm while using the barnyard as a home base. Her husband and older son went to work in the mills to earn money to rebuild, but one week Mr. Schoen didn't return. Eldest son Klaus explained that he had fallen dead, clutching his chest the day before at the mill. Hilda gave the farm to Klaus but stayed with us since they hadn't built a replacement house. Ultimately, she never left. Her eldest daughter Regina and John married in 1873. I had a teacher in elementary school that said that it was completely unusual that a German and Belgian would marry. But to us the Shoens had become family before the marriage. The teacher hadn't been here for the fire and held no sympathy for children who were orphaned, given to other family members to raise or had parents who had remarried into other families. I loved Regina Shoen. She was always the first to start humming a song and was always willing to jump in and play a bit with us children.

The smallest bedroom was Uncle Frank's. It was only wide enough for a single bed with a chair at the foot. I could picture him with his wool-stocking-clad feet hanging over the side of the bed, arm holding his head up while he read from a book. It was his one luxury to spend a short while reading on a Sunday this way.

Antoine, Jacques, Pierre Baudot, and Tom shared the third room with various others as it was needed. The attic was where Magdaline and Emmee's "boys" lived. John, Leopold, James Crow, Peter, and Klaus Schoen would race up the ladder to the room under the eaves each night. They didn't care that they were sleeping on mats on the floor, they were "the boys". On both ends of the slanted roof attic room were half-circle windows that gave the space some light. I've heard some say that these windows were so they could see another fire coming, but I'm not sure about that. These windows appear at the top of barns built at the same time, so I think it was just the style.

One of those "boys", James Crow was a double survivor. The tale goes that James Crow got his appendix operation in Ahnepee after the fire by the town barber. Whenever children would ask him about it, he would get a twinkle in his ebony eyes. It was more likely that he was cared for in the apartment above the barber shop after an actual doctor performed the life-saving treatment. It was the following spring when Jacques saw him carrying a crate into that barber shop. Jacques said he ran across the street and was nearly run over by a wagon when he saw the boy. Everyone in the barnyard had assumed the worst, that an Indian boy would not have been given the surgery or care needed to survive and had likely died. Jacques held a good amount of superstition, and he needed to pinch James Crow's arm to make sure the boy wasn't an omen that day.

According to Jacques, the barber's wife had been raised in Massachusetts and been told family lore about two young brothers who were her distant uncles who had been kidnapped by the Iroquois Indians. The story goes that the boys were so well cared for by their captors that the eldest uncle did not want to leave the Indian band when they were discovered. He argued that they had become his family. The barber's wife felt that she was repaying the kindness that was offered to her uncles by caring for the orphaned Indian boy.

She cried fiercely when James Crow decided to go back to the Gaspard farm and leave Ahnepee. James Crow never forgot their kindness and visited them as often as he could. The barber and his wife left all of their worldly goods and savings to their adopted son James Crow. The childless couple left me in charge of their estate when they passed away several years later. They worried that because James Crow was an Indian, that the government would try and take it away from him. So, I was tasked with ensuring that their legacy went to James Crow in a way that he could safely utilize. He chose to rent out the building for many years.

James Crow lived with us on the farm until he turned sixteen. He then somehow managed to secure a position on a Great Lakes ship. The barber's wife would meet him at the docks any time she thought his ship would come in. After thirty years on ships, he returned to the farm and helped streamline getting our milk to market. After Emmee passed he and Lenka moved to the single-story brick house that was built across the road in keeping with Antoine's plan.

God bless Lenka. These past few years, her eyesight had been failing. Over the years Emmee and Magdaline took her to doctors as far south as Milwaukee. We never learned why she was deaf. Effie and I worry about her fleeting sight. It seems so unfair that someone who was orphaned so young and fought to contribute to society should now have to lose another sense. The entire family worked for years to try and find information on her family or even relations that came to the area after the fire. Emmee told me that it was three full years before Lenka wrote out what had happened the night of the fire. With the help of Tom, they worked out which school yard she was near when he picked her up and ran. Unfortunately, she was part of the Bohemian settlement who had nine of their ten families completely erased by the fire. When they took her to the spot where Tom thought they had first met, she stood for a minute with her nose to the air taking in the smells and then turned around slowly. It was

Tom again that picked up the now nine-year-old when she started silently sobbing and slipping to her knees. She had explained to me later that in her childish mind she thought that she was meant to help us in the barnyard and that her mother and father would be so proud of her for doing so, and then they would all be reunited and happy. At that moment the reality hit that she was an orphan, and we were her new family.

Being nearly guileless, she decided that she wanted to be a teacher like the one who had opened the world for her with her slate and chalk. Lenka became a teacher to other deaf children. For many years one or two of these children would be sent to us by their families to learn from Lenka. She would help break the sound barrier and meet them at their abilities. She very often would get students to exceed all expectations. While they were with us, they would complete chores and learn how to care for themselves. During Easter, Thanksgiving, and Christmas these thankful families would send beautiful baskets of food, colorful cards, beautiful yarn, fabric, and one even sent Lenka a gold bird on a chain that she still wears today. Lenka had been a favorite of every child born in our family and had been my best friend since I could remember.

Lenka was also part of the reason why Leopold decided to become a doctor. John told me that after the fire the local doctor stopped by the barnyard to administer however he could. Leopold would stand beside the doctor as he visited with each person enthralled by the process. My friend Julius also became a doctor. He once told me that in our township at least six men had become doctors after the fire. Before Julius passed away, too young, he left his stamp on hospitals in Green Bay.

Leopold came back after attending medical school in Milwaukee and living with Uncle Leo to base his practice in Bottkolville—sorry Euren. You would think after all these years I would remember to call it by its new name. Leopold spoke French, Walloon, English, German, Czech, and Latin with his patients. If there was a patient he couldn't speak to, he would summon Magdaline to use her skill with languages to the patient. They would joke that between the two of them they could communicate with a horse if required. Leopold told me that he felt called to be a doctor after the fire, because he never wanted to feel hopeless when people were in need. I knew there have been a few times that he had spoken with Emmee when a patient's case seemed helpless. They would discuss what natural herbs and simples she might have to ease suffering. If the weather was fair, I would see Leopold nearly every day.

Calling Leopold to Magdaline's bedside on her last day on earth nearly killed me. Leopold and Magdaline had formed an unbreakable bond the day of the fire.

On October 8th, they had been sent mid-morning to collect more water for the barrels. Because the streams and wells were nearly dry, they would need to drive the horse and wagon further and further each day to find enough. That day they had gathered the water and, on the way, back noticed a young girl trying to lead a cow, horse, and some hens back to a lane through the woods. The girl explained that their fence line had burned out the week before and these animals were overly skittish for some reason. They took the time in the haze of smoke to help the young girl get her menagerie back to the clearing. When they got there a man with wild hair, a dirty shirt and no leg below the knee on his right side stepped out of the door on crutches. The girl told them that he was her father and had lost his leg in the Civil War. He had seemed angry with them, so Magdaline and Leopold turned to leave. The girl followed them to the edge of the woods and thanked them for the help. Neither Leopold or Magdaline ever saw the girl nor her father again and no one knows if they escaped the fire.

Their goodwill toward the young girl had taken more time than they expected, and it was close to 6:30 p.m. when they reached the bottom of the giant hill to the farm. With the extra weight of the water, they needed to stop and let the horse rest more than usual and the thick smoke made the mare irritable. People tried various ways of tying blinders on horses, mules and donkeys to get them to perform during the fires. Leopold that day had tied a long piece of fabric in a series of weaves around the horse's head in the hopes of keeping it calm. When they reached the first crest, it became clear that something was dangerously wrong. Animals were running in circles, and the wind was twisting and keening. The mare started making snorting noises and was throwing her head violently. By the time they unhitched the horse, Magdaline said she could barely stand due to the wind. Out of nowhere two figures huddled together appeared and urged them to run. About one hundred paces from where they let the horse go was a ledge of rock on the backside of that first hill crest. Within the ledge were shallow cave-like openings and that was where the quartet pointed their fumbling run. Leopold said he fell part of the way down the ledge, which was how he had scraped his leg. The group scrambled on the uneven surface that kept moving and felt along the side for an opening. The first one they found Magdaline started shoving people into it. It was extremely tight, and she scraped her forehead on the rock overhang. She was the last to enter the crevice when the first wave of tornado fire came over the ridge. Shocked by the heat and sound she brought her hands up to her face, which was how she burned her forearms and singed her hair. They pushed even tighter into the nook hoping to get away from the heat and flames.

When the rain started, Leopold told me that Magdaline let out a screech of shock and pain that he dreamt about for years. They weren't sure if it was safe to come out of the den, so they stood there listening in the dark. When it felt safe, they uncurled themselves and sat on the rocks. It was James Crowe and his grandmother who had stumbled upon them at the crest. For years there was a group of Indians who lived on that crest. There was no real record of how many of these native people died in the fires on either side of the bay that fall.

One of the real heroes of this story was Madgaline's brother Leo. As he told the story, he was in his Milwaukee store when he found out that the night before a massive fire had burned the state north of him and the city of Chicago south of him. Churches and other organizations in Milwaukee started calling for aid to send to Chicago and Leo was happy to send them some, but he was more concerned about his sister north of Green Bay. It was several days later that he read in a newspaper that indeed the area that Magdaline was residing had been hit by the fire, but the details were thin. At that point he decided that he needed to put together aid for his sister and the family she lived with and if they didn't need it, he would give it to people who did.

It took him almost two weeks to secure the items and get them on a ship headed to Kewaunee County. When he got off the boat, he saw a town trying its best to cope with a dramatic change in the weather as well as a community disaster. By some sort of magic, Leo ran into Jacques, who was in Ahnepee collecting any supplies he could for the encampment. Magdaline had sent him a letter in August that described each of the characters in her neighborhood and when Leo saw the wild-haired *Métis* with a belt that was a red woven scarf, he walked straight to him and asked in French if he knew his Magdaline. He and Jacques picked their way back to GrandLez and the barnyard in a borrowed wagon. Leo always said the landscape looked like what he imagined were the end times in the Bible.

Leo's shrewd thinking brought a wagonload of items that were necessary for survival through the winter. He brought mittens, scarves, woolen coats, boots, and fabrics to make items using a sewing machine tucked in the bottom of the wagon. There were wool blankets and linens. Cooking utensils and coffee, salt, sugar, and flour. He had even tucked in what was called a stein with a pewter hinged lid that belonged to Leo and Magdaline's father. He thought it might bring comfort to his sister. The stein still sits on top of the fireplace mantle in what was Magdaline's house.

Emmee said that as Leo walked around the barn that first visit, he would stop and pull out a leather-bound notepad that was no larger than two inches, and he would scribble in it frantically. He was making a list of items to bring back on his next trip. I knew he had asked Emmee and Magdaline to bring Leopold, Marie Louise, Lenka, and I with him to Milwaukee at least through the winter, but Magdaline insisted that they were needed here.

Leo came back often and brought items from his Milwaukee store and had even helped *Madam* Waulet get her GrandLez general store stocked. I knew Uncle Frank and Antoine tried to pay Leo back over the years. Once they even offered to buy a neighboring piece of property so he could open a store here. But Leo stayed in Milwaukee, which afforded us another luxury that not many in my day had on offer. Twice a year, sometimes more, we would board the train and go to Milwaukee to visit Leo and experience the city. We saw orchestras and museums, a giant library and learned more about the world. I could still picture Leo standing behind the giant copper cash register in his store. Barrel chested balancing on a pair of pin straight extra-long legs, glossy black hair slicked to his head and so much kindness in his eyes that it lit the entire room. Leo the Great.

There were still items around these farms from Leo's generosity. When Antoine and Uncle Frank started planning out the future farms, they decided that they would keep the houses and barns grouped together at the corners of the plots. That way, if another disaster were to happen, they could easily get to the people in the buildings. The hand water pump, nearly all the furniture in the big house and so many tools were all from Uncle Leo. Antoine was forever thanking him and kept all these items in like-new condition.

Emmee reminded me many times throughout my life that our brother Antoine was not the same man after the fire. He had lost everything but a patch of land. Sometimes you could feel the sadness radiating off him from three feet away. I often struggled to get him to communicate with me in something other than a handful of words and his silent retreats seemed overly dramatic to my young self. Antoine refused to speak about the fires. If it was brought up during a *Kermiss* or during a visit with neighbors, he would silently get up and leave the room. Antoine didn't sleep much and if he did, we were usually awakened to screaming and thrashing. I learned later that most households who had survived the fire suffered from the lack of fully quiet nights. Sometimes Emmee would need to get up and shake him away from his nightmares. He would then join us the next morning at breakfast hollow eyed and miserable. Emmee said he was embarrassed by the nightmares, Leopold told me that it was likely like what soldiers in the Great War were calling shell shock. He explained that it was when someone lives through something so stressful their mind had problems reckoning with and they couldn't control their reaction. Antoine was the only one who knew exactly where Sophie, Cédonie and the children were buried. He had dug the graves and lived with the ghosts.

When I was about eleven, I became fixed on why we had family who were not buried under stones in the churchyard like other people. We weren't really the only family who had deceased members who weren't in the churchyard, but it felt that way to my young mind. Today I think back and feel ashamed of the pain I was inflicting on all my elders by forcing the conversation. Emmee and Magdaline tried to ease my mind. Uncle Frank tried to explain how urgent it was to get the bodies buried after the fire so the rest of us could remain healthy. My friend's father explained that some people were able to place a plain stone or wooden cross on the location of the grave, but there was no money in those early years after the fire to move bodies nor was their money for engraved markers. It was Jacques who put my mind as close to ease as it could be in this matter. He explained that on his mother's side the Indians didn't have engraved headstones, rather they had sacred areas where their dead had left their bodies for the next world. The headstones were not necessary for us to remember the family we had lost. They were in the air and the ground and in the trees all around us. Jacques pointed to the tree line and said that the secret was in the woods.

Neither Antoine nor Pierre Baudot ever remarried. Pierre rebuilt his house roughly an eighth of a mile down the road from our farm and had a widow named Mary Smith and two young boys move in with him. They weren't married, slept in separate bedrooms and when Pierre passed away, he left his farm and belongings to the boys. Chris the older told me that Mary Smith was not their mother but had taken them in shortly after the fire. They had been living with their elderly grandfather who wasn't able to run to the creek bed when the fire came. They had no idea where he had died and when they went back to their farm there were trees that had been lifted out of the ground, not just burned. Mary Smith was their only option. Mary Smith died in 1875. It was the first funeral I remember attending as a child. Chris and his brother Jonathan both live in Green Bay and were successful business owners.

Pierre Baudot and Antoine never seemed to get past the loss of their family in the fire. As a father, I'm not sure I would get past it either. Pierre threw himself into his farm and made it successful. There was always speculation about his relationship with Mary Smith, but I think it was a mutually beneficial arrangement more so than romantic. He needed someone to see to the house and more traditional feminine roles on the farm, she needed a home, both people felt haunted to me. Antoine and Emmee shared a house until he passed at the age of sixty-two. Magdaline found him slumped next to a fence pole in the field. She always said she thought it was near the spot he had buried his family, but I don't know for sure.

There were several marriages in October 1871. Some had been planned previously and the couples moved forward; others were completely convenience based. Lost spouses and families to support were far more pressing than love. One of my school chums was from a family of twenty-four children. His father had six surviving children from two previous wives. One wife died in the fire. My friend's mother had eight surviving children from the husband she lost in the fire, and they went on to have seven more children together.

Magdaline and Uncle Frank married in 1874 and built a single-story version of the big house. It was also clad in local brick and included a porch the length of its front that became a gathering spot after chores and on Sunday afternoons. Magdaline gave birth to two girls but neither lived. It was a topic that I never dared to mention. I remember my small boy's heart breaking at the sadness in my mother's eyes when each small coffin was interred. The one time I remember it being discussed Emmee excused herself from the room with tears in her eyes and Magdaline sat stone-still like a pillar of cement.

There were other children who came along and brought new life to the farm. John and Regina built a home across the road from the big house which was called a Queen Anne style house built of modern lumber and not logs. The T-shaped two-story house had little porches at the corners, pretty spindles, and bits of wooden trim. Emmee once said she was so glad they built across from her so she could admire this pretty house every time she looked out the window. The interior was equally modern with a front parlor room that was wallpapered and had a giant carpet rug. Regina gradually brought those touches to every room when she had spare time and egg and cream money to spend. Their five children continue to come back to the house to visit their brother who took over running the farms after John and Regina passed away.

There was a lightness to the children who hadn't been born when the fire changed everything. While their parents struggled to deal with grief and often physical pain, this next generation had been born into literally a new world. I knew several local children couldn't understand why their parents reacted to things the way they did. One of my schoolmates who was two or three grade levels behind me, was born to a mother who was so afraid of another fire that she insisted they all sleep in full clothing, just in case they had to flee. She despised being cold and would be seen splitting huge quantities of wood to keep the cabin uncomfortably warm year-round. She remembered the days after the fire and the bone-chilling cold. Already chilled from spending the night in a creek bed her clothing was in tatters and singed from the flames. She never wanted to be that cold again. My schoolmate accepted that his mother had to do these things to keep moving during the day. His older brother rebelled. Starting with little things like letting the fire go out, hiding the axe and eventually he ran away at fifteen. Some thought he had joined the circus; some thought he had gone west to make money in mining. She missed him dearly, but his exit didn't deter her from doing what kept her sane.

Probably the strictest contrast was in families where the older children had known their parents before the fire, had helped try to save their farm from flames and then had to help rebuild in the new charred world versus siblings born after the fire. The elders were often wary and almost looked hollow when contrasted with the vibrance of these new children. The younger children lived nearly two lives. They were extremely subdued when in the presence of their parents and elder siblings, they knew early on that horrible things had changed these family members. They learned to regulate how they were in the world, how to interact with these family members to avoid causing any additional pain. Depending on the living conditions after the fire, many families picked up the habit of saving everything and even burying things that were most precious to them. When the stock market crashed, and the banks started closing in the late 1920s, you could bet there were many new freshly dug mounds in yards containing savings in tin cans. All the children had seen their parents struggle to rebuild and did whatever they could to protect themselves from the demons that chased their parents, often to the grave.

When I look over the records that Uncle Frank kept for the farm starting spring of 1872, I could feel the frustration, despair, hope and fears in each line of his faint pencil scrawl. Even though the trees were no longer the main obstacle to farming in Kewaunee County, there was severe damage to the soil, stumps that had been partially burned, lingering moisture issues, lack of money for seed, lack of feed for any of the livestock. Nearly every able-bodied man was working outside of the farm in mills, the elderly and women and girls were putting back together the homes and nearly everyone was trying to make shingles to gain the cash needed to build back to where they were before October 1871. I've heard the comment that the fire was a blessing. It cleared the trees and made way for farming to begin. Anyone who lived in the shadow of the people who had died or were forever injured physically or mentally from the fire would never have referred to it as a blessing. The work to make the land tillable changed, it wasn't easier, physically or mentally.

There were of course good years. The last house to be built was a *Sears, Roebuck and Company* kit home that arrived by railroad all ready for assembly. Sears had packaged everything, even the knobs for the doors. I still have the paperwork from 1908. It was model No. 113 with a Dutch gambrel roof and cost $1,062. This was the first building we were able to run electricity to when it found its way to this area of Kewaunee County. It was painted white and stood fresh like a wood floor trillium against the coneflower-blue Wisconsin summer skies.

We had made the shift to dairy farming along with nearly all our neighbors. Larger barns were raised, and silos were built for feed. Standing at the top of the hill you could look down into the town of Lincoln and see flickering orange light in the windows of those barns before the birds even started their calls.

Everyone on the Gaspard farm somewhat specialized in various aspects of the farm. John was gifted with understanding the cattle and growing the herds. Leopold could nurse a sick or injured animal back to life, Lenka had a gift for making cheese and Emmee was our fowl wrangler. She often said that she didn't even like the stupid birds, but always had a gander named that would follow her around the barnyards without coaxing. Her chickens helped the grandkids win ribbons for FFA and 4-H. When Emmee passed we talked about only keeping the fowl that we would use, since none of us could ever match her skills. The day we left the house to see Emmee buried, her stupid gander, called Gerry followed us all the way down the hill, honking and screeching.

I confess I hardly remember getting my daily chores done today with all this reminiscing. Picking up the papers we had set aside the night before, the first thing I read was in Edna Mae's hand. In the margins were beautiful and very precise drawings of flowers and animals, even a landscape on the back of one page. It was several pages into the leather book, before I realized that this was Edna Mae's diary. I wondered how much she had shared with Emmee of her fascinating life. Newspaperwoman, writer, artist, mother, widow, and survivor. She was never allowed to see her children after their father had them adopted by two different couples. She watched the man she described as the love of her life drown and she died waiting for her only living relative to come to Dunseith for her last breath. I had always been fascinated by Edna Mae. The last time she visited us on the farm my wife commented on how brave Edna Mae was. Edna Mae looked at her startled and said, "Brave was moving to North Dakota and homesteading as an unmarried woman. I'm just doing my best to make it through life." Edna Mae—an inspiration.

My thoughts were interrupted by my wife's sharp intake of breath. The paper waved in her hand to get my attention. "Did you know that Emmee didn't want to come to America?"

"What do you mean?"

"In this stack of notes for the article Emmee says several times while talking about her journey to Wisconsin that she didn't want to come here."

This was completely new to me. I didn't know anyone who had immigrated to America that didn't want to be here. I scanned through the papers and very clearly written in Edna Mae's hand it said she had tried to get out of coming to America.

"I guess no one ever asked her if she was happy to be in Wisconsin."

My wife gave an almost inaudible humph telling me how she felt about how women's voices were treated throughout the years. It made me smile. As much as she wanted to appear to be a traditional woman compared to Edna Mae, she had a healthy pinch of progressiveness.

Settling into this new information, I reread through all the papers over the next few weeks. I was so lucky that Emmee was forced to come to America with my mother. If she had passed alone on the ship, the Lord knows what would have happened to me, especially based on the reaction of my father when Emmee delivered me and the news in Wisconsin.

During my rereading the thought of Emmee wanting to stay in Belgium dimmed into the background as I focused on the strange skills my family seemed to possess. No one spoke about it during my entire lifetime. My grandmother's visceral reaction to the fire without having any way of knowing it had happened was unbelievable. The ability to quickly find wells for neighbors was something I thought was a trained skill. I didn't know that Leopold consulting Emmee on her "simples" when he no longer had an answer in traditional medicine for a patient was only natural.

I became a little fixated on it, wondering if I had missed seeing a gift like this in one of my children. My wife told me I was being foolish. I did have a special gift, she said. I had survived birth at sea, a trip halfway across the United States and a fire that had murdered many.

My Thoughts on the Fire

My first introduction to the fires of 1871 was in grade school in North Dakota. The fire was discussed in history class in conjunction with the Great Chicago Fire and was mainly spoken about as the Peshtigo Fire. When I moved to Wisconsin in 1997, my friend Cynthia and her daughter Maggie introduced me to the book *My Sister's Keeper* by Beverly Butler, which was a young adult novel about the Peshtigo Fire. From there, my friend Karen and I made a day trip to the Peshtigo Museum and memorial. In the years that followed, whenever anniversaries of the fire would be announced, I would read the newspaper articles and follow any media coverage. I knew there had been a fire that same night on the east side of the Bay of Green Bay thanks to the Tornado Park Memorial between Brussels and Sturgeon Bay marking the deaths at Williamsonville.

Williamsonville was what we would refer to as a company town. Employees of the Williamsonville Mill lived and worked in the community. It's estimated that there were at least 77 people living there at the time including the extended families of the town's founders and namesake Fred and Tom. In December of 1871 Tom Williamson's account of survival along with his mother appeared in newsprint. The terror still lingered, and depression was clearly setting in for the survivors. A few years later Tom was said to have regretted sharing his account with the media. I am thankful he did but understand how difficult it must have been to navigate through the loss of your family, business and your employees while those who had read the saga knew details you may have wanted to forget.

Williamsonville, now Tornado Park is the largest physical public reminder of the fire from the east side of the Bay with a large monument, peaceful wooded park and well marker. The Belgian Heritage Museum in Namur also commemorates the fire each year with programing that helps visitors understand how the weather played a vile role in the destruction and how the residents rebuilt. Hugging the Brown and Kewaunee County line, the Shrine of Our Lady of Champion holds an all-night adoration and holy rosary procession on October 8th in remembrance of the Miracle of the Fire. That night as the fire approached residents from the neighboring farms came to the chapel that Adele Brise built and walked and prayed throughout the night for survival. It is said that nothing burned inside the fence. Everything around them was destroyed and the fire left char marks on the outside of the fence. October 9th is also commemorated as the day Adele first saw the Virgin Mary in 1859.

These are all wonderful tributes to those who died and lived to rebuild after the fire. But I wanted more information. What about Kewaunee County? The maps showed it as part of the path of devastation, but how bad was it? How many people died? How did it shape the future for this area? Was there a memorial or a list? These questions drove me online, into historical societies, museums, and online archives. With each visit it became clearer that there wasn't a list. People knew about the fire. Some knew that they had family that had survived but it had happened too long ago to be top of mind. At that point, I heard about a local author's book *When the Night Rained Fire: October 8, 1871, Kewaunee County and the Great Fire by Virginia Feld Johnson*. It came out the year of the 150th anniversary of the fire. Virginia's work used tools I was familiar with for my amateur genealogy hobby. Newspaper archives, census info and family histories were things I used as I tried to reach the holy grail of ancestry the coveted Mayflower ancestor.

I started with newspaper archives and the first human story I read was about two neighbor women. I don't know if they still have family in the area, so I will not use their names. This is the composite of what was written in the newspapers. There were six children between two families who lived close to each other. All six children were at one of the farms in the evening of October 8th, 1871. The neighbor mother ran to retrieve her children, but somehow both the mothers and all six children died in the fire. The fathers survived along with a few others on these farms. There were a lot of things that ran through my mind while reading the details, including how I hoped they were friends and that there had been the tiniest bit of comfort in being together in those last moments. These names were how the idea to create a list of the missing and deceased for Kewaunee County started.

I combed newspapers and started a spreadsheet of the names I could find, but there weren't many. I needed more data, which was how I turned to the U.S. and Wisconsin Censuses. I started comparing the 1870 census against the 1880 census and then cross-checking it with the 1875 Wisconsin census. I was able to narrow down the lists and found that the list of missing from the 1880 census was much larger than the 150 that was quoted as deaths in newspapers. It was also clear that the path of that October fire was close to that drawn on early maps.

While combing through the data one of the items jumped out. In the 1870 U.S. Census there were just a few women listed as widows in all of Kewaunee County. In the 1875 W.I. census there were fifty-nine women listed as widows for Kewaunee County. You could easily conclude that potentially forty or more of these women were widows because of the fire just four years before the state census. This number didn't align with the 1872 local newspaper reporting of there being nine deceased in the town of Lincoln—mostly women and children.

Comparing the lists takes time and patience. I honestly don't think there is a name spelled the same way on either the 1870 or 1880 U.S. Census. One year the Belgian names are all spelled incorrectly and then next it's the Czech names. At the time of printing for this book I am about 85% done with Kewaunee County, but it will be an ongoing project. Families may recognize an unusual spelling and be able to shed light on what happened to a person listed as missing. Updates to the lists will be made on the website 1871FireProject.com as they are completed.

On the site there are people listed as missing or deceased. If the name is on the deceased list, then it was found on more than one source that that person had died during or after the fire and they do not appear in the 1875 W.I. Census or the 1880 U.S. Census. It is documented that after the fire Kewaunee County was hit with a series of outbreaks of Typhoid, Cholera, dysentery, and respiratory infections likely due to the compromised immune systems of people who were injured in the fire, poor sanitation, and lack of proper shelter and food. For all these reasons I include individuals who died in the burned areas anytime from September 23-June 30, 1872.

If a person is missing it could be due to several things. They may have moved out of the U.S., remarried with a different last name, been adopted into a different family and some may have lived long healthy lives, but the census taker spelled their name so terribly that no one could connect them to another record. I often thought about the story of a trainload of passengers who arrived in Peshtigo the morning of the fire and may or may not have died in the fire, but we would never know for sure. Wisconsin was expanding through immigration and there could be similar stories from the east side of the bay that were like the unfortunate train passengers on October 8th in Peshtigo.

Ultimately, I don't have an exact number of people who died in the fire. When this book was printed there were more than seven hundred missing from the 1880 census who were reported in the 1870 census in Kewaunee County and more than 600 deceased between Door and Kewaunee Counties.

Possible reasons they were missing:

- They moved and didn't get counted in the 1880 census
- They went back to their home country
- They moved to Canada/Mexico
- They died from an epidemic like typhoid sometime before the 1880 census
- They missed being counted in the 1875 WI or 1880 census
- The name was misspelled to the point where it's impossible to find the correct person
- They died in the fire and there was no record
- They died after the fire and there was no record
- They lived but the family in Kewaunee County with the same surname wasn't aware of any tie
- They died but the family in Kewaunee County with the same surname wasn't aware of any tie
- They sold their land and wouldn't show up on the Atlas
- They were adopted into another family and there aren't records
- They were buried where they passed without marker
- After the fire was so chaotic for this area of the county that putting an accurate record of the dead or dying was moved further on the long list of survival needs

The biggest thing I learned through the research is that the fires had been serious and ongoing that entire fall. For some reason I had interpreted the events leading up to October 8th as being the equivalent of burning a small leaf pile. Instead, there had been large and small-scale fire fights from Manitowoc to Door County and Oconto or Marinette County as early or earlier than August of that year. It speaks to human nature. 1871 Wisconsinites worked hard every day to provide shelter and food for themselves and any livestock. The added toil of firefighting and prevention that autumn became part of their daily lives. The smoke was bad, but they had work that needed to be completed to live through the winter. As the days continued it was probably hard to tell if one was worse than the next. They couldn't or didn't want to go back to Europe, they had made it through building a shelter, dealing with the mosquitos, the lack of neighbors and I'm sure lack of food at times. Being in the thick of this, why would they have lifted their head and simply left for something easier? They wouldn't and they didn't.

I touch on the discouraging coverage of the fires in newspapers leading up to October 8th in the book. Post Civil War era newsprint is interesting. There was some evidence that newspapers of the time had been cautioned throughout the U.S. for being too dramatic and jumping to the sales catching headlines without the facts behind them.

I recently read a newspaper clipping about the Battle of Antietam during the American Civil War and the author states 'not to dramatize the number of dead.' Antietam was often called the bloodiest day in U.S. history with almost 13,000 casualties and 3,550 dead from both sides. If that wasn't drama, what on earth was their definition? A similar comment was found in an article the day after the Titanic sank. The comment essentially states that while the ship sank there were probably very few deaths, but they didn't want to overstate. Perhaps the papers sent to cover the burned area of the fire had been reprimanded for sensationalism in the past and didn't want to be in a similar position. Causing them to downplay the outbreaks before October 8th and then not fully report on the number of dead, injured or missing. Coverage of the story is much thinner than what we would expect today.

I had been told by more than one individual that the Belgians didn't speak English, so there would be no way for a newspaper reporter to get correct details after the fire. I do believe that the Belgians spoke Walloon to each other, just as I am sure the Germans spoke German to each other. Where this theory doesn't hold is in the fact that the Belgians moved to the area because there were more French speaking people. Second, Rosiere shop owner, postmaster and Belgian, Charles Rubens had spoken to several reporters and had shared the details of the terrifying night moving his family from one shelter to the next as they tried to outrun the fire.

I don't think additional newspaper coverage would have completely changed the way the fire is remembered in Kewaunee County, but it may have helped with the narrative. There was a University of Wisconsin-Green Bay oral history record that I listened to from an individual who claimed their family didn't have any damage from the fire, but based on my research, their ancestors had at least six neighbors die in the fire and very little property left standing where they could take shelter. To be fair, maybe their family just didn't talk about the fire and by the time of the interview it would have been three times, or greater grandparents who had been there for the fire.

There is a comment I have heard more than once that diminishes the hardship that the people from both sides of the Bay endured during the fires and rebuilding. "The fire was a blessing; it got rid of the trees so we could farm." This statement can be found as early as the 20th anniversary article in the *Kewaunee Star.* It should be very clear that in those early recovery years, it wasn't a blessing to be hungry, sleeping rough, ailing from burns internally or externally all while trying to rebuild your life, not to mention the grief over the loss of family and neighbors that continued for months after the fire.

It's as if they were saying that this area became successful in farming because those people died. We wouldn't say thank goodness Hurricane Katrina knocked out the levees so we could get new ones, even though people died.

I also encountered the comment it was the "good old days". This comment always reminds of a visit with my sister Michelle to the rebuilt cabin of the Charles Ingalls family in Pepin, Wisconsin. We had toured all the locations the Ingalls family had lived in the Upper Midwest while Charles tried to become successful at various jobs. I could safely say there were several locations that were less than charming. The Banks of Plum Creek in Minnesota felt downright oppressive and since the creek flooded, likely scary for the family or at least Caroline, who was tasked with the childcare. The current caretakers even have a sign on the gate stating, "Remember Laura Ingalls Wilder nearly drowned in the creek". Life in the 1870's was not *Little House on the Prairie*. Heck, *Little House on the Prairie* wasn't the "Little House on the Prairie" from television. Taming Wisconsin was dangerous, lonely, and a complete gamble, and the fire didn't make it easier.

The list below outlines where characters came from. Some were from just a few sentences in a newspaper; some stories were better documented.

- Emilie Gaspard was completely made up but based on many books I've read about young women crossing the ocean to come to America. There was a Gaspard family in Kewaunee County on the 1875 atlas, but they were not in the town of Lincoln where the fictional Gaspard family was located.

- I chose Emilie as a name for two reasons. First, Emily M. Dhuey nee Jeanquart. Her daughter Linda Opicka nee Dhuey lovingly conserved the cabin her ancestors built when they arrived in Wisconsin in the 1850's along with other artifacts and buildings. Their difficult ocean crossing and first winter spent in this tiny cabin helped add color to the book. Second, I have a niece named Emily. I did choose the French spelling to align with the year the character was born.

• Magdaline grew from a photo of my ancestors from Alsace Loraine/Odessa, and the giant head bows the women wore. To my knowledge none of the women from that family traveled on their own to the U.S., but there were several young men in my family tree who went to Odessa, which was Russia at the time or the U.S. and Canada.

• Magdalina was my great-grandmother's name, and I came across her name in several records spelled Magdaline, which was how the character in this book got her name. Her son Peter was my grandfather and nothing like the Peter in this book.

• *Grand-mére* Marie Thérèse Lateau was made up but her cousin Anne Louise Lateau with the stigmata was a real person.

• Leopold Gaspard was a nod to the franchise of doctors that came from Kewaunee County and reminds me of my godson Tucker.

• Julius, Atlantique's friend was a nod to Julius Bellin, which Bellin Hospital was named after in Green Bay. He was one of the six-plus doctors who came from the town of Lincoln after the fire.

• Odile Joséphine Meurice Gaspard was in honor of a very small snip I read in a newspaper about a woman who was driven mad after the fire and other stories of women who were homesteaders whose minds were injured by the elements they lived through.

- Sofie Gaspard and her friend Cédonie were a tribute to a well-documented newspaper statement about two women who died with their children in the fire in the township of Lincoln, Kewaunee County. They aren't the real women and children who perished in the fire, but the story touched me and needed to be told.

- All other Gaspard family members were made up.

- Lenka was based on two stories. One was that of a young girl who emerged three days after the fire from the ruined forest and the other was that of a deaf girl who survived the fire, who lived with her family through several generations and eventually lost her sight in old age.

- Doctor Antoine was based on a real doctor who did lose a child in the fire and then died himself shortly after. His wife died leaving their daughter in the care of the family all before 1874.

- Hedda Karlson was based on a story repeated in a couple of the 1871 newspapers about a young woman who arrived in Green Bay to meet her Norwegian fiancée only to find out that he had died in the fire. There was a chance that this was just a myth, but it was an 1871 "viral" myth in the newspapers.

- Edna Mae was loosely based on one of my ancestors who worked in newspapers from Michigan to Montana in the 1930-40's and died in The San Haven Sanatorium in Dunseith ND of TB. She traveled and did typesetting and some writing for newspapers but also won awards for her artwork.

- Edna Mae's mother was based on my two times great grandmother who did indeed homestead before she was married in Eddy County North Dakota.

- The sister at the chapel that didn't burn was a reference to Adele Brise and Our Lady of Champion.

- The character Leo was inspired by a photo I saw in a box at an antique store. It was a tall man standing in his shop. There was a stove in the middle with two other men lounging in mismatched wooden chairs. He had the kindest expression on his face and stick-pin legs. He was named after my great-uncle Leo.

- Mrs. Nancy Higgins was a real woman from Kewaunee County who was outspoken about women's rights as early as 1869. When I read a bit of her background, she seemed like the perfect person to come to the aid of those in the barnyard.

- Mary Smith was based on a few different stories of women who lost family in the fire, then took care of children who needed them, sometimes moving in with strangers, and unfortunately dying young.

None of the fire survivor stories were made up, they were stories found in the newspapers, including reports like that of the two brothers who had survived in the swamp hoping the trees didn't fall on them. There were people who found dead bodies they didn't know in their wells. There were people thrown together with a report of as many as fifty living in a partially burnt barn for over a year. And the list goes on. It was possible that the newspapers made the stories up, but many of these were short paragraphs with simple statements, not serial articles. These stories were also strictly from Kewaunee County or reported in the papers about Kewaunee County.

I did my best to use the names of the Kewaunee County communities as they were in the time of the voice in the writing.

GrandLez was now Lincoln

Bottkolville was now Euren

San Saveur was now only a small cemetery in a field

Ahnepee (before 1879) Ahnapee (1879-1897) and all its spellings was now Algoma (after 1897)

Thiry Daems still named this after Constant Thiry and Fr.

Edward Daems

New Frankin still named this

Champion was the closest community to Our Lady of Champion and the chapel that didn't burn

Misere was now just a blip with a beautiful schoolhouse, technically in Door County

Rosiere still named this

The First Nations People were referred to as Indians during this time, which was why they were called that in the writing. *Métis* were a real group that stretched from Montreal to central North Dakota. The fur trade moved people throughout the region more than seems possible considering the geographical elements, unknown international borders, feuding fur trading companies, indigenous residents and migrating First Nations People, not to mention wildlife and weather. There was no way to begin estimating how many First Nations People died in the fire or shortly after, but I will continue to seek the information.

Yes, there were repeated names of characters. As I worked through the census there were so many duplicate names and often across nationalities. Jean Baptiste, Mary, Joséphine, Theresa, Pierre were just a few that would show up so often just on one page of the census that it made sense to have repeating names with neighbors. There could be a Joseph listed as Bohemian, and a Joseph listed as Belgian on the same page. Plus, the repeat reinforces that people ended up blended after the disaster.

Why was he named Atlantique?

Ship-born children were sometimes named after the vessel or location of their birth. Here were a few that were notable:

- Atlanticus – found in 19th century emigrant registers for babies born mid-Atlantic.
- Oceanus Hopkins – an English baby born aboard the Mayflower in 1620.
- Arabella Morris – born aboard the immigrant ship Arabella en route to Australia.
- Pacifico – used in Portuguese and Spanish records for boys born on the Pacific crossing.

Where was Wallonia?

Wallonia was the southern part of Belgium and borders Luxemborg, France, and Germany. Wisconsin has the largest Walloon immigrant population, mostly congregated in Brown, Door, and Kewaunee Counties.

What was the Wallonian Language?

Unfortunately, it was endangered. It's a romance language drawing heavily from German and French. The Walloons would have had some knowledge of French and common Walloon words would have been close enough that a person who was good with languages, like Magdaline would be able to communicate.

Examples

English: Hello

French: Bonjour

Walloon: bondjoû

English: How are you?

French: Comment allez-vous?

Walloon: Comint vos dalez?

The Walloon language was phased out as you read to signify the shift to being in America. Many Belgians in Wisconsin gained citizenship, voted and served in the American Civil War after they immigrated. All these actions dispel the clannish myth of the Belgians.

Are there gravesites to visit in Kewaunee County?

Theories on why there were no markers for those that died in the fire. Based on how the fire behaved and some comments in print, the bodies in Peshtigo and a few scant notes for Kewaunee and Door County were reported in various states.

- Unrecognizable
- Shrunken
- Ashes with some identifier near the ashes
- Seemingly untouched but dead
- Partially burnt
- Possibly suffocated
- Possibly thrown by the tornado force winds
- Possible suicide by firearm or knife
- Died post fire of burn complications
- Died post fire of lung complications
- Died post fire from typhoid and other diseases
- Died post fire from exposure
- Died post fire from food insecurity

- Died post fire from mental insecurity
- Died post fire in childbirth
- Died post fire due to complications of old age

There were groups that came through the area to help bury the bodies of both humans and animals. Based on Peshtigo and a few lines for Kewaunee and Door County the bodies were handled in different ways.

- Buried where they fell
- Buried in the churchyards
- Buried in family graveyards
- Buried in wells
- Marked with uncarved stones or rough wood

crosses

- Unmarked

First Nations and groups like the *Métis*

There is mention that there were Native Americans who had perished on both sides of the bay, but there was no tribal affiliation mentioned in the newspapers. These people were not in the census.

In tandem with the book, I've created a website – www.1871fireproject.com – On the site is where the most up-to-date lists of the missing and deceased from Kewaunee County. A list from the Peshtigo fire museum and the start of a list from Door County are also located on the site. This is an ongoing project being updated as information was found.

Notes and Resources

Books

Ambrose, Stephen E. *A Wisconsin Boy in Dixie: Civil War Letters of James K. Newton*. North Coast Book, University of Wisconsin Press.

Ball, Jacqueline A. *Wildfire!: The 1871 Peshtigo Firestorm*. X-treme Disasters That Changed America, Capstone Press, 2007.

Bauer, George. *Peshtigo*. G. Bauer, [year unknown].

Brieno, Linda. *Colors of the Firestorm: The Great Peshtigo Fire*. Brieno Publishing, 2003.

Butler, Beverly. *My Sister's Keeper*. Whitman, 1961.

Charles River Editors. *Peshtigo Fire of 1871: 0The Story of the Deadliest Fire in American History*. Charles River Editors, 2014.

Davenport, Don, and Robert W. Wells. *Fire and Ice: Two Deadly Disasters (Fire at Peshtigo; Shipwreck on Lake Michigan)*. Willow Creek Press, 2002.

Egan, Timothy. *The Worst Hard Time: The Untold Story of Those Who Survived the Great American Dust Bowl*. 1st Mariner Books ed. Boston, Houghton Mifflin Co., 2006.

Ernst, Kathleen. *The Lace Maker's Secret*. Henschel HAUS Publishing, 2018.

Geiger, Corey A. *On a Wisconsin Family Farm: Historic Tales of Character, Community and Culture*. The History Press, 2021.

Gess, Denise, and William Lutz. *Firestorm at Peshtigo: A Town, Its People, and the Deadliest Fire in American History*. Henry Holt and Co., 2002.

Janus, Edward. *Creating Dairyland: How Caring for Cows Saved Our Soil, Created Our Landscape, Brought Prosperity to Our State, and Still Shapes Our Way of Life in Wisconsin*. Wisconsin Historical Society Press, 2011.

Kahlert, John, and Albert Quinlan. *Early Door County Buildings and the People Who Built Them, 1849–1910*. Peninsula Publishing, 2003.

Knickelbine, Scott. *The Great Peshtigo Fire: Stories and Science from America's Deadliest Firestorm*. Capstone Press, 2006.

Leschak, Peter M. *Ghosts of the Fireground: Echoes of the Great Peshtigo Fire and the Calling of a Wildland Firefighter*. HarperCollins, 2002.

Loew, Patty. *Indian Nations of Wisconsin: Histories of Endurance and Renewal*. Wisconsin Historical Society Press, 2001.

Looney, Edward. *Our Lady of Good Help: Mary's Message and Mission for Adele Brise and the World*. TAN Books, 2015.

Lempereur, Françoise, and Xavier Istasse. *Les Wallons du Wisconsin*. Racine: Les éditions Racine, 2011.

Martin, Xavier. *The Belgians of Northeast Wisconsin*. Wisconsin Belgian-American Research Collection, 1970.

Mercier, Charles. *Peshtigo 1871: Peter Pernin's Peshtigo Fire Memoir – The Finger of God was There!*. American Journal of french Studies, 2022.

Monson, Marianne. *Frontier Grit: The Unlikely True Stories of Daring Pioneer Women*. Shadow Mountain, 2016.

Pernin, Peter. *The Great Peshtigo Fire: An Eyewitness Account.* Wisconsin Historical Society Press, 1971.

Sangers, Fr. Willen, OSC. *Fr. Eduard Daems, OSC: Father of the Colonists in Wisconsin.* Norbertine Center for Spirituality, 2000.

Stevens, Michael E. *The Making of Pioneer Wisconsin: Voices of Early Settlers.* Wisconsin Historical Society Press, 2018.

Stone, Ted. *The Legend of Pierre Bottineau & the Red River Trail.* Pogo Press, 1997.

Tlachac, Math S. *The History of the Belgian Settlements in Door, Kewaunee and Brown Counties.* Badger Printing Co., 1970.

Waulet, Josie. *François.* Self-published, [date unknown].

Wells, Robert W. *Fire at Peshtigo.* Hill and Wang, 1968.

Wilder, Laura Ingalls. *Little House in the Big Woods.* Harper & Brothers, 1932.

Brink, Carol Ryrie. *Caddie Woodlawn.* Macmillan, 1935.

Drews, Lynda. *The Maid and the Socialite.* Door County Publishing, 2021.

Johnson, Virginia. *When the Night Rained Fire: October 8, 1871, Kewaunee County and the Great Fire.* 2015.

Steward, Elinore Pruitt. *Letters of a Woman Homesteader.* Houghton Mifflin, 1914.

Apps, Jerold W. *When the White Pine Was King: A History of Lumberjacks, Log Drives, and Sawdust Cities in Wisconsin.* Wisconsin Historical Society Press, 2020.

Baird, Elizabeth T. *O-de-ji-wa-win-ning or Contes du Temps Passé: The Memoirs of Elizabeth T. Baird.* State Historical Society of Wisconsin, 1947.

Larson, Ronald Paul. *Wisconsin and the Civil War.* Arcadia Publishing, 2017.

Defnet, Mary Ann. *From Grez-Doiceau*. Self-published, [year unknown].

Web and In Person Resources

"Peshtigo Fire Museum." *Peshtigo Fire Museum,* www.peshtigofiremuseum.com/. Accessed 29 Apr. 2025.

"Kewaunee County History Blog." *Blogger,* https://kewauneecountyhistory.blogspot.com/. Accessed 29 Apr. 2025.

"UW-Green Bay Archives and Area Research Center." *University of Wisconsin–Green Bay,* www.uwgb.edu/archives/. Accessed 29 Apr. 2025.

"Belgian Heritage Center." *Belgian Heritage Center,* https://www.belgianheritagecenter.org/en-us/default.aspx. Accessed 29 Apr. 2025.

"Heritage Hill State Park." *Heritage Hill State Park,* https://heritagehillgb.org/. Accessed 29 Apr. 2025.

"Kewaunee County Historical Society." *Kewaunee County Historical Society,* http://www.kewauneecountyhistory.com/. Accessed 29 Apr. 2025.

"Agricultural Heritage Center." *Wisconsin Harbor Towns Association,* https://wisconsinharbortowns.net/places/kewaunee/agricultural-heritage-center/. Accessed 29 Apr. 2025.

"Manitowoc County Historical Society." *Manitowoc County Historical Society,* https://www.manitowoccountyhistory.org/. Accessed 29 Apr. 2025.

"North Dakota State Archives – San Haven." *State Historical Society of North Dakota,* https://www.history.nd.gov/archives/stateagencies/sanhaven.html. Accessed 29 Apr. 2025.

"1876 Atlas of Kewaunee County, WI." *University of Wisconsin Libraries,* https://search.library.wisc.edu/digital/ATES47S7N4OINR8G. Accessed 29 Apr. 2025.

"An Interview with Prof. Charles E. Mercier." *American Journal of French Studies,* https://american-journal-of-french-studies.com/an-interview-with-prof-charles-e-mercier-about-his-new-book-peshtigo-1871. Accessed 29 Apr. 2025.

"Mystics of the Church." *Mystics of the Church,* https://www.mysticsofthechurch.com/2009/12/anne-louise-lateau.html. Accessed 29 Apr. 2025.

Ancestry.com. www.ancestry.com. Accessed 29 Apr. 2025.

Newspapers.com. www.newspapers.com. Accessed 29 Apr. 2025.

Find A Grave. www.findagrave.com. Accessed 29 Apr. 2025.

Door and Kewaunee County Online Newspaper Archives. Accessed 29 Apr. 2025.

Videos

Rebuilding Paradise. Directed by Ron Howard, performances by Steve McCarthy and others, Imagine Documentaries, National Geographic Documentary Films, 2020.

Humiston, Karen. *Stories from the Archives: The Great Peshtigo Fire*. Presented by Brown County Library, 2022. YouTube, https://www.youtube.com/watch?v=UquhunnM9Pg. Accessed 29 Apr. 2025.

The Great Peshtigo Fire. Featuring Scott Knickelbine, PBS Wisconsin, University Place Series, Wisconsin Public Television, 2021. PBS, https://www.pbs.org/video/university-place-great-peshtigo-fire/. Accessed 29 Apr. 2025.

Afterburn: The Creek Fire Documentary. PBS, 2021. TV Movie.

Maui Wildfires. NBC News Coverage, August 2023. NBC, www.nbcnews.com. Accessed 29 Apr. 2025.

Language Dictionary

Walloon Language

Mi – me

Mame informal for Mother

Grand-mére formal for Grandmother

Pére formal for Father

Popa informal for Father

Feume - wife

Fré - brother

Efant - infant, child

Efants - children

Cuzén - cousin

Fi - son

Feye - daughter

Mes fiz - my sons

Grand-pére formal for Grandfather

Nonke - uncle

Tante - aunt

Soû - sister

Fiyes - girls

Djouvas - boys

Leus pareints - their parents

Mes fréres - my brothers

Omes - Men

Femes - Women

Ene fiye - a girl

Gamin - boy

Ome - husband

Families - families

Family - family

Petits-efants - grandchildren

Bele-soû - sister-in-law

Mèrci - Thank you

Mèrci, ine camarådes - Thank you my friends

Malureu - sad

Å r'vèy - goodbye

Oyi - yes

Aler - go

M'lome - my name is

Speculoos - traditional Belgian spice cookies

Sabots - a wooden shoe worn in various European countries

Grez-Doiceau - is a municipality of Wallonia located in the Belgian province of Walloon Brabant

Bois-d'Haine - the name of a village in Wallonia, Belgium, specifically in the province of Hainaut.

Dutch Language

Kermiss – originates from the Middle Dutch word *kercmisse*, which is a combination of *kerc* ("church") and *misse* ("Mass"). It originally referred to a festival or fair held to commemorate the dedication of a church.

French Language

Maintenant nous marchons - Now we walk

Bouillabaisse - stew/soup

Chemise de nuit - nightdress

Parles-tu français - Do you speak French

Métis - a distinct Indigenous people in Canada, descendants of unions between European (mainly French) fur traders and Indigenous women (often Cree, Ojibwe, or Saulteaux)

Swedish Language

Mor - Mother

Far - Father

Morfar - Grandfather

Syster - Sister

Moster - Aunt

Farbror - Uncle

Bondkakor - Swedish farmer cookies

Rörstrand - Swedish porcelain manufacturer

Dalmålnings - also known as kurbits painting, is a distinctive style of Swedish folk art

Hemgifts - Swedish bridal dowry

Min dotter, försök att sluta gråta. Vi kommer att lösa det här problemet. - My daughter, try to stop crying. We will solve this issue.

Norwegian

Fortell henne hva du vet- Tell her what you know.

German Language

Drücken - push

Er ist hier - He's here

Jetzt gehen wir - New we go

Herr mein Gott - My God

Sprichst du Deutsch - Do you speak German

Ich heiße - name

Mutterkuchen – placenta

Knoephla - dumpling

Cree Language

noh-tâ-wi-nan ki-se-ma-ni-tonoh-tâ-wi-nan ki-se-ma-ni-to - Watch over us to help us

Czech/Slovak Language

The Lord's Prayer:

Otce nas, Jenz jsi na nebesich, posvet se jmeno tve prijo' kralov
    stvi tve.

Bud' vule tva jako v nebi, tak i na zemi.

Chlen nas vezdejsi dej nam dnes.

A odpust nam nase viny,jako i my odpustime nasim vinikum.

A neuved nas v pokuseni, ale zbav nas od zleho.

Zdrávas, Maria, milosti plná - Hail Mary, full of grace

Our Father, who art in heaven, hallowed be thy name.

Thy kingdom come.

They will be done, on earth as it is in heaven.

Give us this day our daily bread.

And forgive us our trespasses, as we forgive those who trespass
    against us.

And lead us not into temptation but deliver us from evil.

Zdrávas, Maria, milosti plná - Hail Mary, full of grace

Discussion Questions

1. Emilie doesn't want to leave her home, but due to her age must travel with her mother to the United States. How does the book change the generalized narrative about emigration from Europe in the 19th and 20th centuries?

2. Edna Mae surprises the Gaspards by being a female in a traditionally male career. What do you think in the family experience made them comfortable with having Edna Mae conduct the interviews?

3. Grand-mére seems to have some unusual gifts, at times she seems to be able to see into the future. Why do you think she didn't know that Emilie wasn't going to be able to stay with her in Wallonia?

4. In the middle of the ocean, Emilie becomes the sole caretaker of her premature brother. Why do you think she didn't question taking on the role, or reversing her journey and going home to Wallonia?

5. Pére Joseph Gaspard has no experience as a woodsman and very little practical knowledge of farming, instead he has trained as a shoemaker, which was not uncommon with immigrants during this period. How does the reality of farming in Kewaunee County Wisconsin in 1871 shape Pére's reactions?

6. Magdaline has skills, personality traits and experiences that Emilie doesn't. Do you consider Magdaline to be the deuteragonist or the guide character in this story?

7. There are several myths about immigration in the United States. One is that each group of immigrants stuck closely to the same cultural and language group and didn't mingle with others. Another is that it was a melting pot of languages and people had to help each other to survive. Where either of these myths proven or disproven in Secrets in the Woods?

8. Odile and her mother struggled with mental health issues, which ultimately ended in a mental health crisis for Odile. Why do you think the author felt it was important to show this aspect of immigration or homesteading? Why do you think popular culture has been slow to discuss the demands on mental health during this time period?

9. Post-Traumatic Stress Disorder (PTSD) was not a terminology that was used in either 1871 or 1931 but both Emilie and Edna Mae would have been familiar with terms like "Soldiers Heart" from the Civil War and "Shell Shock" from WWI. Which characters exhibited PTSD from events in their life?

10. Edna Mae states that she is confused about why she has allowed herself to become entangled in an abusive relationship after being raised in a household that was the exact opposite. How do you think she ended up in the relationship with Peter?

11. The Métis man Jacques acts as a reminder that there were people and commerce taking place in the center of North America long before 1871. What other things does this character try to impart as reminders throughout the story?

12. The stories woven together about the fire came from brief mentions in local newspapers, yet Edna Mae calls attention to the fact that the coverage before the October fire wasn't robust and the author notes that post fire coverage feels fragmented with few full accounts printed. Do you think that more news coverage would have

prevented deaths? Would it have helped or hindered the rebuilding of the region?

13. The Peshtigo Fire appeared recently in an episode of a popular television series, and The Great Chicago Fire had a documentary recently debunk the O'Leary cow legend. Has revisiting these fires taught us anything when dealing with fires like the more recent Paradise Fire or the Maui Fire?

14. Emilie and the author explore theories on why people didn't talk about their experiences before, during and after the fire. Which theory do you think is most likely?

15. There are parallels between Emilie and Edna Mae's life experiences that they discover through the interview process. How do you think society had changed from the 1870's to the 1930's with the parallels of abuse, witnessing tragedy, loss and female roles?

About the Author

Susan was born and raised as the fifth generation to live on the family land in Northeast North Dakota (nearly Canada). She moved to Wisconsin in 1997, living in Door and Manitowoc County and now resides in the pastoral Kewaunee County. Married to Quentin, they share their home with Olive and Penny, their silly Labrador retrievers, and Gil, their ever-lazy cat. As a devoted reader of historical fiction and nonfiction, she brings her passion for history and desire to educate readers into her work. With twenty-five years of experience in global advertising and marketing, she holds a master's degree in communications and currently contributes her expertise to the Green Bay Austin Straubel International Airport.

Visit her website at www.1871fireproject.com

or at www.historiumpress.com/susan-levitte

www.historiumpress.com